Liza's
Gift

Liza's Gift

NOVEL TWO
OF THE
STRIVE I
DUOLOGY

W. L. Lyons III

iUniverse®

LIZA'S GIFT
NOVEL TWO OF THE STRIVE I DUOLOGY

iUniverse books may be ordered through booksellers or by contacting:

iUniverse
1663 Liberty Drive
Bloomington, IN 47403
www.iuniverse.com
1-800-Authors (1-800-288-4677)

ISBN: 978-1-4917-4528-1 (sc)
ISBN: 978-1-4917-4527-4 (e)

Library of Congress Control Number: 2014917016

Printed in the United States of America.

iUniverse rev. date: 10/02/2014

Acknowledgements

I would like to thank my wife, Darleen, for her patience that allowed me to extoll the glories of science and reveal an engineer's agonies brought on by oppressive government regulators. Not only did she give valuable advice over our evening martinis, she critiqued and proofread the manuscript. Thank you Darlin' Dar. Or as an engineer would say, thanks D^2.

Because I'm an engineer struggling with the mysteries of the English language and novel writing, I relied on my Santa Clarita writers group whose foundation is Stephanie Weier and Toni Floyd. Thanks to you both for your thoughtful comments and encouragement.

Beta readers are a novel's first exposure to the real world and gratitude is due to: Barbara Cochran, a dear friend, Paul LeCoq, a fellow novelist and high school chum, Don Stout, a patent lawyer who saved the plot from legal blunders, Tom Tucker, a fellow member of my writers group and Debi Zolonski, a friend of my wife who likely has a masochistic bent.

As with my first novel, my son W. L. Lyons IV designed the cover. Needless to say, I'm a very proud father.

Chapter 1

Horrified, Lauren tried not to retch. Her husband's swollen eyelid, the color of a month old banana skin, bulged from his battered cheek and forehead. Her glance fell on his right arm, encased in a splint. In stark contrast to the mottled purple of his bludgeoned face, his pale fingers blended with the white sheets of the bed. She turned from the comatose figure to the emergency room nurse and stammered, "My God, what happened?"

"The police sergeant said he was mugged. If you ask me, it looks as if someone hit him with a baseball bat. But don't worry; your husband will be fine." The nurse, professional looking with a short hair-do and clear nail polish, tugged the privacy curtain, closing a small gap in the beige fabric. "Before you came, the cops hung around for a while hoping to question him, but left when Mr. Morgan didn't regain consciousness." She checked the I.V. drip and grunted. "Good. The doctor sedated him to reduce complications from a possible concussion." She smiled and patted Lauren's arm. "He'll sleep for a while. We'll move him upstairs to his own room shortly. If you need anything, just yell." Her blue tunic swished as she spun and bustled out the door.

"Thanks," Lauren whispered to the departing figure. She sat on the hard plastic chair alongside the bed and shuddered, recalling last night's debacle. *Why did I think a birthday party would get his mind off all our troubles?* Lauren cradled her head in her hands as she replayed the scene in her mind. Wyatt had drained the half-empty pint bottle of vodka left over from her Scrabble parties and lurched out the door for more. She'd been dumbfounded because he was always a one-glass-of-wine guy and never had been intoxicated, not even a little. When Lauren tried to stop him, he shouldered past her and drove off. Later, when a police officer called saying Wyatt was in emergency, she almost panicked. Although they had traced his car through the DMV, they needed confirmation on his identify. Terrified, Lauren called her neighbor, Sharon, asking her to babysit Timmie and raced to her husband's side.

The orderlies had wheeled Wyatt to his own private room where silence, in stark contrast to the cacophony in emergency, smothered Lauren. She swallowed, trying to settle her stomach. Her eyes wandered around the room, pausing on the monitor that flickered with the beat of Wyatt's heart. The room's chill penetrated Lauren's thin blouse and she crossed her arms trying to stop shaking. Despondent and overwhelmed, she began counting the floor tiles, a diversion from rancorous thoughts about Wyatt's injuries, the eviction notice, the recent death of her mother and failure of their company. But most troubling was Madison. Lauren lost count when the bland tiles disappeared under the bed, so she studied the second hand of the wall clock as it crept towards the future, to when Wyatt would awake.

Almost two hours passed and the bright California morning sun splashed though the window and cast a sunbeam across Wyatt's smashed face, causing him to stir. "What…"

Lauren leapt from her chair and cradled his bristly chin in her hands, avoiding the bruises and staples. "Honey? Can you hear me? Honey?"

"What happened?" Wyatt moaned. His good eye fluttered open and he turned his head from side to side. "Where am I?"

"In the hospital. You're going to be okay."

"Hummm." Wyatt closed his eyes and grimaced. "Feel awful."

"You were robbed. Beaten. But you'll be okay," Lauren repeated. She pressed the button to summon the nurse, held her husband's hand and impatiently tapped her foot. "What's taking her so long?"

Wyatt rubbed his temple and winced.

"Do you have a lot of pain?" Lauren asked.

He shook his head, "Aches."

Lauren, hoping to set her husband at ease, quipped, "You're just hung-over. That was quite a bender you went on last night."

"Don't remember."

"Count your blessings and try to relax."

"Do I know you?"

Stunned, Lauren grasped Wyatt's shoulders and looked him in the eye, her nose inches from his. "Yes! Lauren, your wife. Look at me!"

Wyatt's face scrunched up as if trying to concentrate. "Oh, yeah. Cute freckles. I remember."

Relieved, Lauren sat on the bed and caressed Wyatt's shoulder. "That's right."

The nurse swept in and seeing Wyatt awake, smiled. "Let's see now…" She studied Wyatt's face and glanced at the monitors to check his vital signs. After a moment, she patted his arm. "Lookin' good, Darlin'. Welcome back." She nodded to Lauren. "He seems stable. I'll see if the doctor is available to drop in and check your husband."

With a grateful nod, Lauren replied, "Thank you. If you have something for his pain, I'd be grateful."

With a bob of her head, the nurse said, "I'll check the doctor's orders," and left.

Lauren released her pent-up breath and turned to the hulking, bearish figure in the bed. "You rest now. I'm going to stay right here, but I need to go to the nurse's station and tell them I'm spending the night. Also, I'll call Sharon to see if she can stay with Timmie. Be right back."

As Lauren rose from the bed and started toward the hallway, Wyatt's blank stare dissolved into a frown. "Timmie?" he asked.

Lauren stopped and wheeled to her husband. "Timshel, your daughter," she screeched. "We call her Timmie, remember?"

It was mid-afternoon the next day and Lauren's scratchy

eyes bore witness to her wakeful night on the hospital day bed crammed in a corner of Wyatt's stark room. On his morning rounds, the doctor had said, "Mr. Morgan has a bad concussion. It appears he has trauma-induced amnesia. I expect he'll come around soon enough. Also, the swelling on his arm has to go down before we can apply a cast. We'll hold him another day or two, just to see how things progress."

Troubled by the grim diagnosis and the doctor's uncertainty, Lauren scowled, sipped water from a glass and resumed counting floor tiles. Her mind wandered, skittering over her troubles like a flat rock tossed across a pond, and finally settled on Madison. *Was it true she'd seduced Wyatt? Madison with her damned gorgeous green eyes and stunning figure? Was it a prolonged affair or a simple romp in bed? Is my marriage finished or teetering on the brink?*

Outside in the hall, two technicians chatted, but their medical lingo failed to attract Lauren's attention. Weary of worry, she stepped to the window and saw nothing but a grungy rooftop brooding under winter clouds that had sprung up, smothering the once cheerful sun. With a shrug, she returned to her chair and glanced again at her watch.

At last, Wyatt stirred from his sleep and looked at Lauren. "Hi, Dear." Unable to bend his right arm, he rubbed his forehead with his left. "Roaring headache. Got something to knock it out?"

Lauren picked up the button to summon the nurse. "I'll find out if they can bring you something. You have to be in top shape for your visitors this afternoon."

"Visitors?"

"Yes. Mike and Bernie."

"Mike? Bernie? People I know?"

"I'm sure you'll recognize them. They're your business partners who helped with Optimal."

Wyatt rubbed his temple. "Whatever."

A lump rose in Lauren's throat. Had the doctor told her the truth? Would Wyatt's mind come back? She tried to push the gnawing dread away, determined to heal Wyatt through dogged persistence.

Finally, the nurse breezed in, listened to Lauren's request for a painkiller and with a tilt of her head, hurried away.

For lunch, the orderly had cranked up the bed and positioned the utilitarian stainless steel tray table. The dark brown plastic tray of food, guaranteed bland, also had a small cup of Tylenol. As Wyatt took the pain pills, water dribbled down his chin and onto the blue gown. Then he struggled to eat his lunch and spilled a blob of Jell-O on his chest. "Why can't a grown man feed himself?" he complained. "Damn splint is impossible." At last, he gave up and allowed Lauren to help. She settled into the role of a soothing mother and grinned, recollecting the days she spooned pulverized peas into her infant daughter's mouth. Wyatt, mopping his chest with a napkin, grumbled, "You'd think I could work a fork with my left hand; it's like I'm a total spaz."

"Fuckin' right about that," Mike boomed as he strode into the room. "You prove that every time you try to run a lathe or mill."

Lauren leapt from her chair, ran to Mike and gave him a warm hug, his push-broom mustache tickling her cheek. "I'm so glad you made it." Turning to her husband, she said,

"Look, who's here, Honey." With no response from Wyatt, she whispered to Mike, "He's not himself. He has a terrible concussion and can't remember much."

In anguish, she slid her fingers through her hair. "Hospitals are so lonely. I…we…could use a little of your cheer."

Mike moved closer to Wyatt and studied his face. "Holy shit, my friend. Been through a meat grinder?"

Wyatt frowned and shrugged in apparent confusion, his good eye flickering from Lauren to his visitor and back.

"Honey, do you remember Mike? Your business partner?"

"Who?"

"Come on, man," Mike said, leaning on the bed rail. "I'm the guy with the machine shop. The guy you teamed with to start Optimal Aviation Systems and make the pressurization system."

Wyatt's jaw trembled and his gaze sought Lauren's face. "Don't remember…"

Lauren flicked a tiny strand of pixie-cut hair back from her face. "Don't worry. The doctor says your memory will come back. It simply takes a little time." She nodded to Mike and gave him a thin, tight-lipped smile. "It's only been a day and a half."

"Hell, knowing him…"

"Hi, everyone." Framed in the doorway stood a skinny older man, balding with soft gray eyes. "Holy cow!" he said as he approached the bed.

"Oh, Bernie, I'm so glad to see you," Lauren said, walking around the bed. She nestled in his sinewy arms, stifling back tears. Shaking her head, she said, "He's a bit addled right now. Concussion."

Bernie, a life-long bachelor, looked uncomfortable in Lauren's embrace and sidled next to Wyatt. "I can't figure who'd be nuts enough to take on dude as big as you, Wyatt. The other guy must be splattered over the landscape like a train wreck."

"It's Wyatt who looks like a fuckin' train wreck," Mike corrected.

Lauren flinched and hoped the jibe didn't penetrate Wyatt's soggy mind. Mike, she knew, wasn't being mean, but candid as always.

Bernie grinned. "It's only a small derailment, Mike, not a train wreck. Our guy's tough as tool steel, right?"

Wyatt's vague stare fell on Bernie for a moment and then his eye closed and he drifted off to sleep, overcome by the pain medicine.

It saddened Lauren to know Wyatt was unable to quip with his friends—unable to recognize them. She looked at him, his boundless energy and vitality crushed by an anonymous thug. Lauren wanted to protect him from the pitying stares of the two "strangers" and yearned to gather her husband up and spirit him home where she could nurse and heal him. She wanted him whole for their daughter, Timmie. *Damn that mugger.*

Mike stood on one foot, then the other and shrugged. "Our guy is fucking out of it. What do the doctors say, Lauren?"

"Come," she beckoned. They strolled down the hall, stepping aside for interns and a gurney until they came to the lounge. It was small, but bright light bathed the room and heavy carpet gave it a quiet, soft aura. Large windows looked out on the hectic activity in the hallway, reminding Lauren that this was a place of serious business.

"We can talk in here." They settled into overstuffed chairs and Lauren continued. "Wyatt's concussion is more severe than the doctor originally diagnosed, so they plan to keep him another night or two. Regardless, I plan to go home this evening and be with Timmie. Sharon, our neighbor, babysat last night and would appreciate a break, I'm sure."

Lauren rubbed her weary eyes and took a deep breath. "There's so much chaos. On top of the doctors and nurses, the police came again early this morning hoping for a statement. They asked if Wyatt had any enemies, or sold drugs, but gave up because Wyatt was too confused to remember anything. They said they'd check back in a week or so. The sergeant didn't seem optimistic they'd catch the assailant." She gulped. "It's all too much to handle."

"Count on us, Lauren," Bernie said, his slender body smothered in the hollow of the chair. "Don't worry about the business, just focus on getting Wyatt back on his feet. Mike and I will tidy up the loose ends at Optimal. Who knows, the inventory and engineering might be worth something."

Mike nodded and crossed his legs. Metal shavings from his shop floor sparkled on the soles of his shoes. "Right. I'll collect the castings, planning sheets, drawings and all that crap. You never know what might turn up." He winked at Bernie.

Bernie's head bobbed. "Go ahead, Mike. Tell her about that hard-nosed patent attorney of ours."

Mike's anthracite eyes seemed to dance in his head.

"Art's not saying much, says he needs more time to confirm a few suspicions. Been hinting he has something on an employee at the Patent Office in Washington. 'Not the time to quit,' Art said."

Lauren was astonished. "What are you saying? There's a chance Optimal will be okay? That we might get a patent after all?"

"Too soon to say for sure. Our bulldog lawyer is a tight-lipped old fucker. I can only say what he told Bernie and me, 'Don't abandon ship.'"

"So there's hope?"

Bernie nodded. "All we know for sure is a sleazy turkey back east ripped off our patent. Art has got ahold of a string and he's pullin' it. If we're lucky, there's a big fish on the end of it."

Lauren's thoughts flew back to when Wyatt, embroiled in the new company, basked in his design accomplishments and savored the challenges. She felt a broad grin tug at her cheeks, but then remembered. "We've no money, guys, not a single cent. We're so broke that Wyatt and I are being evicted from our home. Even if we get the patent, we're doomed."

Mike frowned. "I'm not so sure. I have my machine shop, Bernie still has a job at Wyatt's old firm and you're working, so among us there's still an income stream of sorts."

"You're delusional, Mike," Lauren moaned. "You're having difficulty meeting payroll and servicing the loan you took out to help fund Optimal. Even combined, our cash situation is pathetic." Once more, despair squeezed her, making her shoulders sag. "There's simply no way. Not in this economy."

Silence settled in the room like heavy snow. Mike uncrossed his legs and his chin sank to his chest while Bernie avoided Lauren's gaze and wiggled his foot. Through the windows, Lauren could see a portable x-ray machine, pushed by a green-clad technician, glide along the hall, perhaps to a rendezvous with a fracture. Smothered in debilitating anxiety about Wyatt, her mother's sudden death and the haunting specter of Madison, she fidgeted. "I can't sit here and sulk. That helps nobody. I'll take a peek at Wyatt and go home. I'm beat. I hope in a week or so you can visit Wyatt at the house and chat. He should be better by then."

As she stood, Bernie gave her a warm hug. "Get some rest. Call me if you need anything; I'll be here faster than a lightning bolt."

Lauren basked in Bernie's kindness and with misty eyes, squeezed his hand saying, "Thanks for being here…" She choked back a sob, waved at Mike, then turned and went to Wyatt.

Chapter 2

Lauren straightened the afghan covering Wyatt's legs and flashed an encouraging smile. "Here's yesterday's newspaper, Honey—they never deliver on Christmas. Besides, I don't think you've read this one yet."

He'd been home from the hospital a week, submitting to her fawning devotion with vehement protests. While his headaches had diminished, Wyatt's memory seemed to linger in a realm of confusion, which worried Lauren. She pressed her husband with, "Do you remember the time we had dinner at Sharon's?" or, "Remember when Mike ran the hot air test stand in the middle of the night?"

Wyatt always scowled and pressed his fingers to his temple, saying, "I guess," meaning he hadn't a clue. Still, there was progress. The gash on his head was healing nicely and they had a doctor's appointment between Christmas and New Year's Day to remove the staples. However, Wyatt's constant complaints about the cast on his arm irked Lauren. Trying to soothe him, she rubbed his fingers to restore circulation. "The doctor said you'll be in the cast until mid-February, remember?"

"Hell yes, I remember!" he snarled. "I don't have to like it, do I? And stop saying, 'Do you remember?'" Wyatt snatched the newspaper and slapped it on his lap. "Look at this mess!" He pointed to the headline:

Stocks Tumble Again

"When are those idiots in Washington going to learn?" Wyatt growled. Garfield, nestled on his lap, looked up and then resumed his slumber, the way cats do.

Lauren chuckled under her breath. *He's on his soapbox again. He's getting better.* She plopped in her new recliner alongside Wyatt. "I think when the cast comes off, you should run for president. You have *my* vote."

"Mine, too, Daddy." Timmie, still dressed in her jammies, inched her way toward her father, cradling a steaming mug. "Mommy says it's my job to make sure you have coffee. She says you're a real Navy man—no sugar or cream. That makes it easy."

Wyatt grinned at his daughter. "Thanks, Little One."

"I'm not little, Daddy. I'm nine and a half." She planted her feet, clad in tattered slippers, and put her fists on her hips, her round pudgy face looking very stern. "You have to stop treating me like a child."

Lauren snickered.

Having set her father straight, Timmie strolled to her room leaving her parents alone.

Until recently, Lauren considered Timmie to be a whiney, petulant child, but when she first saw her injured father, his face puffy, staples striding across his brow and an arm restrained in plaster, Timmie took a tentative step into adulthood by saying, "Sit down and rest, Daddy. I'll get the TV remote for you."

Lauren marveled at Timmie's metamorphosis and recalled her grandmother saying, "'Tis an ill wind that blows no good." That meant, of course, that good things usually accompany terrible events.

Once, while Wyatt slept, Timmie badgered Lauren, asking how she might help take care of "the patient." Together they agreed that coffee, house slippers and the lap robe were the purview of the fledgling nurse. They also decided Timmie would retrieve the newspaper and set out the cereal boxes with milk every morning. Lauren had looked fondly at her daughter and shook her head, amazed.

Lauren suspected Timmie was aware of the frantic financial crisis swirling in the Morgan household. The child's nascent transformation became very apparent when Lauren, in desperation, told her daughter she'd have to give up soccer because of "the situation" and fees. Timmie had crossed her arms and with a studied look that puffed out her freckled cheeks, said, "That's okay, Mommy. I understand." Lauren nearly wept, loving her daughter's newfound maturity, a development that dueled with her love for the little tyke who'd filled her life for nine years.

"Christmas tree is nice," Wyatt said, interrupting Lauren's ruminations.

Lauren nodded. "Timmie and I did our best. I had to stand on a chair to put on the treetop angel. I had visions of the hospital emergency room and a broken leg," she joked. Her grin twisted into a frown. "This year's gifts are really skimpy. I did my best for Timmie, but I didn't get anything for you."

"You gave me a great letter. That's the best gift a guy could get. I gave you bankruptcy. That's a lousy deal and I'm sorry. When I said 'I do,' I vowed to take care of you, but I've screwed up everything. I'm so helpless, I can barely brush my teeth."

"All I want is your health. We'll find a way to deal with the bills." Lauren knew her optimism about the finances was a lie. With no income, even the smallest expense drew her shoulders into knots. It was useless to explain to Wyatt how she juggled the household bills and struggled to placate the accounts receivable clerks from Optimal's vendors.

The only bit of good fortune was the fact it took at least six months to evict them from the house. Even the utility companies normally granted a grace period. "The situation" bewildered Lauren and she couldn't rely on Wyatt to help solve the immense problems, not yet. She knew she was a meticulous thinker and felt adrift without a concrete plan.

Wyatt punched the TV remote and searched for a football game. He stumbled on one, slurped his coffee and stared at the screen, looking disinterested.

Lauren's eyes wandered around the room where the fresh-looking easy chairs, last year's Christmas present to each other, contrasted with worn carpet and dingy paint. Her glance fell on the Christmas wreath above the fireplace, which reminded her of her mother's lavish holiday decorations. It had been only six weeks since Liza died and Lauren, her sadness exacerbated by the holidays, longed for the companionship afforded by her mother, even though they quarreled regularly. The Morgan's modest home was in stark contrast with Liza's posh mansion in Beverly Hills. Untroubled by the comparison, Lauren drew her slender legs under her and yielded to a warm surge of sparkling childhood memories.

"You want to watch something, Dear?" Wyatt asked, interrupting Lauren's indulgent melancholy. "This game is as boring as french fries without catsup."

"No. I'm sure there are other games to watch, if you want."

As he grabbed the remote, the doorbell rang. Lauren answered and found her cheerful neighbor on the porch with her daughter, Jenny. "Hi, Sharon!" Lauren said. "Come in. And a Merry Christmas to you both."

"And to you," Sharon chuckled, her bountiful waist straining against her blouse. "Here," she said, extending her plump hand that cradled a warm apple pie. "You can't have Christmas without one of my pies."

Lauren took the dish. "We *love* these. Last year I had to hide a couple of slices from Wyatt so Timmie and I could steal a taste." She strode across the room and showed Wyatt the treasure. "Look what Sharon brought us, Honey. It's still warm."

Wyatt's dull gaze fell on the crisscross crust oozing apple and cinnamon scents and he nodded. "Thanks."

Sharon giggled and once more shook with mirth. "I just can't let Christmas pass by without baking. Jenny always helps."

Jenny, half a year younger than Timmie, thrust out her chin, looking very important. Immense dimples punctuated her rosy cheeks as she said, "I stirred the filling and did the top too. Mommy wouldn't let me peel the apples though."

"We might reconsider next year, Jenny," Sharon said.

Embarrassed by her husband's obvious indifference, Lauren said, "Jenny, Timmie is in her room; want to go play?" As the child darted down the hall, Lauren pivoted toward the kitchen and beckoned Sharon with a tilt of her head. She set the pie on the tile counter and whispered, "Wyatt is coming around, bit by bit, day by day. His memory is improving, but he's very depressed. I'm worried."

"The holidays can be a drag," Sharon said, propping herself against the counter top. "As I've told you, I'm happy to help any way I can. I'm home all day and it's no problem to pop over and pitch in."

"But your new job? How would you find time?"

"It's just three hours early in the morning at Marcie's Donut Shop; mixin' dough, making frosting. I'm home by eight." Laughing, she patted her waist. "The big problem is I can't stay away from those yummy glazed goodies. I suspect they're not exactly featured on the NutriSystem diet plan."

Lauren smiled. "Donuts are tempting for sure. I hope this recession is temporary and the economy picks up so Jake can get his dispatch job back. Then you can go back to being a full-time mom."

"Come to find out, my husband prefers the shorter hours of drivin' the delivery truck. Jake used to complain about the crazy schedule and the stress of dispatchin'. Now, he comes home early, pops a beer and drops in front of the TV to watch football. I don't think he'd go back to his old position even though it pays more. Here it is, Christmas Day, and there was no way to get him over here to say hello." A sad look descended over her eyes and Sharon absently patted her short greying hair. "He ain't much, but then I ain't much."

"That's not true! You're a super mother with a fantastic daughter. If you ask me, Jake is a very lucky man."

"He doesn't think so; says I'm not the best tire on the truck. No matter. We're gettin' by. It's you I worry about, with you taking a leave from work to nurse Wyatt. Money gotta be tight with your business failing and all."

"Don't remind me," Lauren said, scowling. "I'm out of personal time and Wyatt doesn't get unemployment because he didn't pay himself wages—took a draw instead. Bills are like an avalanche, burying my desk and our lives. Health insurance from my work helps, but the deductibles are colossal. If that weren't enough, they're foreclosing on the house. Honestly, I don't know what to do."

A somber looking frown crept across Sharon's round face. She shifted her weight and crossed her plump arms as if to fill the awkward silence. She sighed and said, "You're the best friend I have and Jenny and Timmie are thick as thieves. I feel we've become part of the Morgan household." She paused and inspected her fingernails. "For me, Jake's disappeared. Gone away to Coors and sports. We hardly talk any more. You've told me how Wyatt sinks into his engineering fog—how he ignores everything that isn't science. In a way, we're in the same boat, aren't we?"

Sharon's observation jolted Lauren. She firmly rejected any comparison of the two men. Lauren worshiped Wyatt and his mind, thrilled to listen to his scientific ramblings and rejoiced in his engineering achievements. Wyatt was not a beer-bellied sot snared by TV. Her husband was a formidable, driven man, capable of great things. And she loved him. Lauren collected her thoughts, and taking care not to offend Sharon, said, "We enjoy your friendship and Timmie adores Jenny. It's just that Wyatt's not himself right now. His recovery will take a few weeks. We just have to hang on until he's well enough to get a job."

Sharon grunted. "Right now you could use a hand. Let me fix lunch for Wyatt or drive Timmie and Jenny to school so you could go back to work. Even watch Timmie in the afternoons. Let me help you out, 'kay?"

"Okay." A tiny smile caressed Lauren's lips and serene thoughts filled her, knowing that Sharon was there for her, a backstop. Lauren's fear of "one-against-the-world" diminished and the mellow tune, "Thank God I Found You" by Mariah Carey, wove its way through her thoughts.

"That's that," Sharon chuckled. "I'd better collect Jenny and get back to fix dinner for Jake. We'll talk tomorrow."

Later, the holiday ham was in the oven and Timmie had gone next door to ogle Jenny's Christmas loot. Lauren wrestled with the twist-top on a bottle of cheap Zinfandel and her mind drifted back to her mother. Although their relationship had been contentious, even combative, Lauren missed Liza. It felt odd to have no parents, no one to call her "daughter" and no one to sit alongside to thumb through family photo albums. She could visualize the opulent mansion where she was raised. Vivid images paraded through her consciousness: sunlight bursting through cut crystal goblets at lunchtime, stuffy looking paintings staring from the walls and an exquisite Ming Dynasty vase that stood aloof in the study.

A startling thought came to her. *So what if mom's house is upside-down? The paintings, the Bentley parked in the garage, her jewelry, crystal—they might be worth something.* Why hadn't she thought of it before? Lauren shook her head. She'd been dwelling on her father's demolished stock portfolio and the mortgaged mansion while ignoring the contents of the house. In her grief, the only thing she'd done about the estate was to engage a security company to watch the empty house. And that only because Wyatt had insisted.

Her mind's eye darted from room to room, cataloging valuables and her heart swelled with encouragement as the sum grew. Lauren was certain she was the sole heir, but depression about her mother's death sidetracked any thoughts about investigating. *I wonder if I could sell a few things. Mom's attorney called a while back and left a message. He wanted to talk about the estate. Maybe Lee Wong at the bank could help me.*

Then Lauren drew herself up short, remembering the last time she saw her mother alive, Liza was going through the Sotheby catalog, doing the same thing—hoping to sell. Ashamed for acting like a vulture hovering over her mother's grave, she shoved the thoughts of Liza's legacy aside.

Lauren set the opened wine bottle on a tray alongside two goblets and carried them to the small table between their easy chairs. Wyatt, in spite of the harsh flickering cast by the football game on television, had fallen asleep. "Wyatt, wake up." She shook his burly shoulders until he snorted and smacked his lips.

With a sheepish grin, he said, "Guess I nodded off. This game is no better than the first one. What time is it?"

"Sunset Ritual time, Honey," Lauren purred.

"Some sunset; it's as dark outside as Steven Hawking's black holes. Hate winter. We're in sunny Southern California, right? So where's the sun?" Awkwardly, he twisted in the chair, picked up the remote in his good hand and snapped off the TV.

When he turned and faced her, Lauren was still appalled by his ghoulish complexion and the red gash across his forehead. Diverting her eyes, she filled the glasses, handed one to Wyatt and raised her wine saying, "To your health. You're on the road back."

"I suppose. Still can't remember squat."

"You're improving every day. Remember what the doctor said? 'Takes time.' Be a little patient, that's all." Lauren settled back in her chair and let the raw bite of the cheap wine assault the inside of her cheeks.

Lauren feared Wyatt's improving memory might dredge up recollections of Madison and she debated broaching the subject. When Madison joined their company three years ago, Wyatt melded his profound mechanical engineering gift with her phenomenal electrical design and computer skills to launch Optimal. Mental sparks flew between them as they ironed out the design of the cabin pressurization system for executive jets.

From Lauren's viewpoint, it was the perfect combination of two incredible scientific minds illuminating the path to their company's success. Yet, when Lauren first saw Madison, she recognized potential trouble—trouble embodied in the woman's striking green eyes. Moreover, Madison was stunning: an hourglass figure, long shiny mahogany hair and an aura of pure sexiness.

As the busy months passed, Lauren hunted for signs of illicit romance, but found none. Wyatt, as usual, dwelt in his "engineering fog" and seemed oblivious to Madison's conspicuous charms. Then a few months ago, Lauren sensed a wraith in the air; something had changed between Wyatt and Madison. Her suspicions burst into reality that night when Wyatt got drunk and Madison came over to "help." When she learned that Wyatt had slept with Madison. Lauren battled with her thoughts about the unresolved calamity—she had to tell Wyatt she knew and, critically, she had to find out where he stood. The burden of the unknown was crushing. As Wyatt's injuries healed, the more she dwelt on his infidelity. Fatigue, resulting from sleepless nights, clouded her mind. She'd forgotten to take her grocery list and after shopping, she discovered three gallons of milk in the refrigerator, one spoiled. Usually a fastidious housekeeper, dirty dishes piled up on the counter. Just yesterday she'd snapped at Timmie for little reason.

Something had to change. Should she wait to confront her husband until he was better? No matter she suffered?

She cleared her throat. *No. Now is the time.* Lauren squared her shoulders and looked directly at her husband. "Wyatt, I want to tell you something."

Wyatt fiddled with his wine glass.

"Honey, this is important. Look at me."

Wyatt's gaze slowly focused on his wife.

"Do you remember the night of your birthday party? The night you got drunk?"

"Sorta."

"Do you remember Madison?"

"Yeah."

"Well, after you drove off looking for more vodka, she came over and we had a big fight." Lauren gulped, struggling to continue. "She said she loved you and that I was a terrible wife—that I never understood your passion for engineering. She boasted that you two were a perfect match and even said she'd slept with you." Lauren shuddered. *There, I actually said it.* "I lost my temper and threw her out; slapped her—hard. She's not coming back, ever." Lauren leaned forward, waiting for his comments. "Honey?"

"That's okay." Wyatt's bushy brows drew together as his lips pursed. His hazel eyes rose to meet hers. "Good. She's a big problem." Wyatt slowly rubbed his scalp, avoiding the staples. "Slept with her? Yeah, guess I did… just once though. She got me drunk on champagne. I think it was the day we got the purchase order. Don't remember for sure. She was after me. Wanted to get married—like I wasn't already. Madison's nothing to me except she's a damn fine engineer. Meant nothing. I was drunk." Wyatt trembled and took Lauren's hand. "I was going to tell you."

Lauren squeezed his hand. "I love you, Honey, but I've been going crazy about this and hoped you just stumbled into a huge mistake. What really scares me is that you had an ongoing relationship, a prolonged 'affair' with her. Did you?"

Wyatt stared at his lap. "No. As I said, I was drunk. Guess I lost my head when we got that purchase order. You know how hard we worked for it." He shuddered. "'Let's celebrate,' Madison said. Lost my head."

"Our business is gone and we've no need for her anymore," Lauren said. "Madison is out of our life for good and I want to move on."

Wyatt swallowed and a tear wet his cheek. "God-almighty, I love you so. I was stupid, but now she's gone and I promise..."

"I know. I know." Feeling relieved, she tossed off the rest of her wine "You rest a bit while I get dinner on the table."

She called Sharon and asked her to send Timmie home, removed the ham and slipped Sharon's pie onto the oven rack to warm. She was comforted with their conversation about Madison and harbored a thought the issue was resolved. But her smile faded as she thought, *I hope that's the end of it, but it's odd he remembers Madison and their fling, but not much else.*

Chapter 3

With his jaw clamped tight and the cords of his neck bulging, Wyatt flung a can of shoe polish across the room and chunks of brown paste spattered the wall.

Startled by the noise, Lauren ran from the kitchen. "What in the world are you doing?" she bellowed. "Look at that mess!"

"I'll tell you what I'm doing," he hissed. "I'm *not* shining my shoes, that's what."

Apparently hearing the ruckus, a wild-eyed Timmie crept down the hall and stood in her mother's shadow. "Mommy?"

"It's okay, Timmie. Daddy's just a little on edge." Lauren put her arm around her daughter and glared at Wyatt. "So? How do you expect to polish shoes with a broken arm? You need to give things a rest; we've enough problems. And now you've upset Timmie."

"If this is her biggest problem today," he yelled, "she'll have a great New Year's. Hell, I *always* shine shoes on New

Year's Day—ever since the Navy, but a loony idiot with a two-by-four teed off on me. It sucks!"

Wyatt's childish furor over silly trivia—shined shoes of all things—squelched Lauren's urge to shout back. Instead, she laughed and countered. "If grubby shoes are *your* biggest problem today…"

Wyatt glowered and sputtered. "Dammit." A loafer fell from his lap with a thump. He bent to retrieve it, paused, turned to his wife and he, too, laughed. "You're right. You're *always* right. I'm in a terrible mood. You know that every New Year's Day, I mull over the past year, analyze and dope out mid-course corrections. I watch football, scrub shoes and let my mind fly. Somehow, that whole process is greased by shoe polish." He rapped on his cast. "This crazy torture device has scuttled my routine. Terrible way to start the year."

He looked at Timmie, cowering behind Lauren, her pale eyes wide. "I'm sorry, Little One. I didn't mean to upset you. My temper just got away from me. I apologize."

With a hint of a smile, Timmie eased away from her mother. "Don't call me 'Little One.' I'm big now."

"Too big for a hug?"

"Will you be nice?"

"I promise."

"Okay." Timmie scampered to her dad, gave him a quick squeeze and bolted toward the kitchen.

Wyatt took a deep breath and said, "I wonder how you put up with me; I can be such a bum." With his good arm, he thrust himself from his chair. "I'll clean up the mess. It's halftime anyway."

*   *   *

Afternoon shadows sifted through the soft pink shears of the front window as Wyatt made a meager attempt to follow the second game of the day. Losing interest, he looked over at Lauren who was reading a well-used paperback Sharon had lent. She looked demure and serene, cradled in her fictitious world with her legs coiled under her slender body. Elf-like, she twisted a strand of her fine blond hair around a finger. Wyatt grinned. *I'm damn lucky to have her.* Fed up with football, he jabbed the remote and the screen turned black. "Darlin'?"

After a moment's delay, Lauren marked the place in the book with her finger and met his eyes. "Humm?"

"You've been saying my memory is getting better. Just now, I remembered last year's game: SC Trojans and Wisconsin. Close game, but the Trojans won, friggin' turkeys. I'll never understand why anyone would name a football team after a brand of condoms. Tells you what's on their mind," he grunted. "You know what us UCLA guys say about SC? 'Pay your fee and get your B.' While they're dinkin' around with tailbacks, Cal Berkeley raked in 28 Nobel prizes, 23 of them in the hard sciences. UCLA, the 'baby' campus, hauled in 15 of 'em."

"Good grief, Honey, where did you get all that? There's nothing wrong with *your* memory!"

"Well that's old stuff. I still have trouble with recent things."

"Even so," Lauren said. "it seems like you're coming along rapidly now."

Wyatt scowled. "Yeah, rapid like the line at the DMV."

Timmie, her round, freckled face beaming, trundled across the room carrying a large bowl of potato chips.

"Here, Daddy," she said. "I'll be right back with your hot coffee. Mommy made a fresh pot. She showed me how to do it, so from now on, I'm the official coffee-making girl."

Wyatt grinned. "You've taken care of my most serious drug habit. You're a doll, Timmie."

With eyes twinkling, Timmie turned away from Wyatt and said to her mother, "He's better today, huh? I'm a super good nurse, aren't I?"

"The best," Lauren grinned. "Your father has a way to go, but he's on the mend."

"I hate to be talked about in the third person." Wyatt complained.

"Third person?" Timmie said with a quizzical look on her face.

"Never mind, Darling. Go get your dad's coffee." Lauren set her book on the hand-me-down coffee table. "You *are* getting better. Just yesterday when we were discussing Optimal and the troubles with the patent, you remembered Eric Magana, the guy who stole your design. You even had a glimmer regarding Art, our patent attorney. Your memory *is* improving."

"I'll tell you what I remember. I remember we can't put our hands on a dime, much less a mortgage payment. I just don't recall all these people you talk about, not even this Mike guy or Bernie. Not much anyway."

Lauren shrugged. "You're right about the money, but I'll figure something out—I'm an accountant, you know. As for Mike and Bernie, I've invited them over for a nice visit and an early dinner next week. I'll bet you'll know them when they come. They're a big part of our life; great friends."

"We'll see."

A proud grin radiated from Timmie's face as she inched her way across the room cradling a steaming mug of coffee and handed it to her father. "Here you are. Strong, like Mommy says you like." Having discharged her duties as nurse and caregiver, she retreated to her room.

With a grimace, Wyatt shifted his cast-encased arm and sipped coffee using his left hand. "We haven't heard from the cops, have we? A thug beats me half to death with a fence post, takes my wallet and evaporates. The jerk even charged stuff on our credit cards before you closed the accounts. Why can't they arrest the ding-a-ling? Is it rocket science? It's simple—find him and cut his balls off. Police complain how over-worked they are and then hole up in a donut shop gossiping like post-menstrual old ladies. It's another simple case of government ineptitude. Makes me sick!"

"Watch your language or else Timmie will be swearing like a sailor. Besides, the police found you in the gutter and hauled you to the hospital, right? They're not so bad."

"Maybe sometimes." He stared at his scuffed shoes on the floor and shook his head. "FAA investigators, Patent Office clerks, Lawyers—they're all idiots," he murmured.

Chapter 4

In spite of "the situation," Lauren was excited about entertaining again and whirled from kitchen to dining area to living room as she fixed appetizers, smoothed a colorful tablecloth and cleaned while Wyatt brooded in his chair.

"Honey, Mike and Bernie are due in thirty minutes. Can you set the barbeque?"

Wyatt groaned. "I'm beat. Why don't you just fry the burgers?"

"Come on, now," Lauren said, a touch of anger in her voice. "We talked about this. Ground beef is much better cooked over charcoal. It won't take you five minutes. Okay?"

"Easy for you to say. You have two arms. How am I going to wrestle a bag of briquettes when I struggle to shave even though I use an electric razor."

"Wyatt, I need your help," Lauren snapped.

Like an arthritic old man, Wyatt rose from his chair and plodded toward the back door.

"Don't forget the mesquite wood chips," she called after him.

A disgusted scowl painted Wyatt's face as he waved his good hand in disdain and slammed the door behind him.

Lauren frowned. Wyatt's depression rankled her. Like Don Quixote tilting windmills, she felt powerless to help him. As she folded mayonnaise into her potato salad, Lauren tried to muster a little optimism, a sense of cheeriness. Since his homecoming from the hospital, she'd donned a bright façade, cooked his favorite dishes—even though there was little money for food—and complimented him on his improving memory. But she found herself exhausted and weary of doting on his needs.

Something completely alien to her nature had emerged; Lauren found herself grappling with a quick temper. Before Wyatt's mugging, she'd breeze through the days with a smile and serenade her family with laughter. But now, her husband's depression and the lingering hurt from Wyatt's fling with Madison invaded her easygoing disposition; even Timmie's antics grated on her nerves.

She hoped that a visit with Mike and Bernie would bring a bit of cheer to the house and help Wyatt, but Lauren recalled the disastrous birthday party she threw before Christmas to cheer him. The party where he got drunk, ran off in the night and a thug mugged him. *This afternoon will be different,* she assured herself. *His old friends will bolster him—I'll bet he'll recognize them right away.*

As Lauren escorted Mike and Bernie to the weathered picnic table in the back yard, she savored the sunny January afternoon. *Another typical California winter day—enough to make a Minnesotan cry.* Her guests had just settled when Timmie, carrying two dishes, promenaded across the grass like a strutting drum major. "Have some tortilla chips, Mr. Graham," she offered. "The salsa is Mommy's homemade recipe. You too, Mr. White."

Mike's huge grin blossomed and he rubbed his hands on his shirt, spotted with cutting oil from an early morning foray into his machine shop. Bernie bobbed his greying head, but Wyatt stared at the floor.

Mike gathered a massive handful of chips saying, "Aren't you the best waitress in the whole world?"

Obviously pleased, Timmie placed one foot on top of the other and stood like a stork. "I made coffee if you want some. I make Daddy's coffee all the time."

Both visitors nodded.

"Black? Daddy says real men drink their coffee black." Without waiting for their concurrence, she scampered into the kitchen.

Bernie studied Wyatt, slouching in a chair. "Got your staples out, I see. Seems to me you're doing great."

Mike laughed. "Hell, those red spots from the staples look like a zipper. You're gonna have one sexy scar, my friend."

Dismayed, Lauren said, "The scar will fade in time. I bought an ointment to help it disappear. Right, Honey?"

Wyatt shrugged.

Cringing at the awkward moment, Lauren diverted the conversation. "Bernie, why don't you bring Wyatt up to speed regarding Optimal? Tell him what's been happening these past few weeks."

"Not much to say. We're using the office to store leftover parts. Mike and I are working to document the inventory and engineering stuff. Our patent lawyer wants every detail lined up like rows in an Iowa cornfield."

Timmie came out and eased a tray of coffee mugs on the table, then ran back into the house.

"You might recall, Hon," Lauren continued. "that the lease on our office doesn't run out for a while, so it's very convenient."

Wyatt stirred. "Yes. I know the place. Not much use any more."

"Art is our patent lawyer," Bernie said. "Remember? He's still working on our patent application. He claims Dynamag stole ours—blatant theft. We're waiting to see if he comes up with anything."

"Art?" Wyatt frowned, his brow wrinkling. "He the guy in that funny downtown L.A. office?"

"That's him," Lauren bubbled; pleased her husband was able to exhume the memory of Art's old art deco building.

Mike grabbed another handful of chips saying, "He's on a mission for sure. I'm not clear what good it will do. King Aviation and AirEnvironment are both retrenching because general aviation orders are shitty."

Wyatt's vague stare wandered off into the distance.

"Recall the two companies that were getting serious about buying our pressurization system?" Mike asked. "The one for executive jets?"

"Now that you mention it." Wyatt picked at a piece of lint on his tan Dockers.

"Well," Mike said. "King has decided that the general aviation sector is drying up—owning a private jet isn't politically correct anymore. They canned two-thirds of their employees and are relocating to Vancouver. When the buyer called to cancel one of my orders, he told me King plans to become a supplier to Boeing Everett. Says the Canadian regulatory situation is much more favorable than in the States. That's another fucking blow to my machine shop business."

Wyatt pursed his lips and said, "Everything's hopeless."

Not liking the tone of the conversation, Lauren interjected, "The economy has to improve sometime. It always has. There's talk that Washington plans to expand government programs for the infrastructure and the military. That could help things."

Bernie nodded, the fine wrinkles of his neck deepening. "The TV news said the Senate just passed a bill for more than 200 billion dollars for roads and bridge repair. Caterpillar stock jumped big-time. Congress is working on a plan to buy a bunch of new military aircraft. I hear that the Defense Department is negotiating with Maddox Aviation to modify a line of their executive jets into surveillance planes. That could put a lot of people to work, including us."

"Bullshit," Mike growled. "The only reason for this crap is to buy votes from the construction lobby. Surveillance aircraft? What are they gonna see? Arabs in a dark bar figuring out their next terrorist bombing? It's nothing but make-work. Put the money in the hands of industrialists and you'd get something."

"You're right," Wyatt murmured. "The government is already broke, so why do they run up more debt? Kids like Timmie will be holding the bag. It's immoral. Ought to be illegal."

Lauren watched her husband's eyes glaze over and knew his mind was shutting down, pressed flat by Mike's bleak picture. She struggled to find reassuring words, but found none. As an accountant, Lauren figured Mike's assessment was probably true and that Washington's reckless spending was a recipe for economic disintegration. Her throat tightened in forlorn resignation. Bernie's bravado felt hollow.

"Maybe you're right, Mike. Maybe not," Bernie said. "We don't run Washington but we can get prepared for whatever happens. We have a big stake in Optimal, so let's tidy up the loose ends just in case Art pulls off a miracle."

With a forced smile, Lauren said, "Makes sense. We should pull together. After all, Optimal has assets…worth something. Perhaps we can help Mike and his company pull in business." She looked at her hands for a moment. "Say, I'll bet the barbeque is ready. Anyone up to a burger or two?"

Bernie's "You bet," was closely followed by Mike's "Fuckin' A."

Thankful Timmie was not there to hear Mike's florid vocabulary, she said, "Wyatt, are you doing the honors?"

As Wyatt slowly turned his head, Bernie offered, "I'm a top notch burger man. I'd be happy to help out." He stood and tugged at his belt that drew his pants into folds like a drawstring bag.

"That would be nice," Lauren said. *He knows Wyatt isn't*

up to this. "I'll fetch Timmie. She would hate to miss any of the festivities."

The afternoon shadows crept across the small patio and the air became chilly, yielding to the waning sun. The tall pepper tree whispered in the light breeze while the scent of grilled beef lingered, lurking among the dishes smeared with catsup and potato salad. On the chaise lounge, Timmie played games on Wyatt's old laptop computer while Garfield, her cat, snoozed alongside. Bernie and Mike chatted about the economy, 3-D machine tool developments in Germany and the new Corvette. Wyatt sat alone with his eyes half closed, cradling the cast on his arm.

Lauren, shivering with the sudden chill, scavenged plates, glasses and a mustard jar, and hustled into the house. She took a deep breath. The mid-afternoon meal had gone well and she enjoyed the banter of her two guests. Although not frivolous or lighthearted, the conversation was a diversion from Wyatt's nagging complaints. As she hurried outside for another load of dishes, Bernie's soothing soft gray eyes fell on her and he rose to help. "You're a dream, Bernie," she said. "It's getting cool. We should all go back into the house."

"Good idea."

Inside, as Lauren spooned leftover potato salad into a Tupperware container, Bernie set dishes on the counter with a clatter. "Great day, Lauren. I appreciate the chance to visit and check up on Wyatt." He busied himself, dumping scraps into the trash. "He's not himself, is he?"

Lauren shook her head.

"He'll come back. He took one hell of a beating and has a lot on his plate with the collapse of Optimal and the whole patent disaster."

Bernie rinsed the dishes and stacked them neatly. "You look tired, Lauren. Be sure to take care of yourself. Get some rest. They've cut my hours at work, so I have plenty of time to come over while you catch a movie or do a little shopping. Just let me know."

"As if I could afford a movie," Lauren sighed. "You're right, though. I'm frazzled beyond words." Lauren closed the refrigerator door and turned. Bernie was at the sink, his back to her. His bald spot reflected the glare of the overhead light and his skinny frame looked frail, even considering his sixty plus years. A surge of affection blossomed in her. "Bernie?"

"Yeah?"

"I can't thank you enough. You're an anchor… I really need an anchor."

Bernie reached out and touched Lauren's arm. "Mike and I will help Wyatt through this. He's an inspiration and we owe him big time. You can count on us."

"You're the best," she said, smiling. "Let's collect everybody before they freeze."

Stepping into the bracing air, Lauren called, "Inside everyone. I don't need to add frostbite to my list of problems. Timmie, bring Garfield." She beckoned to Wyatt. "Ready to go in, Dear?"

With a slow nod, Wyatt struggled to his feet.

"I'm fucking ready," Mike said. Then he noticed Timmie nearby. His black eyes sparking, he shrugged at the child. "Sorry, Timmie. Bad word."

"Not so bad. Kids at school use that word all the time."

"No matter…bad word."

Everyone trooped into the warmth, Timmie juggling the computer and dangling Garfield while Wyatt shuffled along, massaging his hand.

Laden with the remaining dishes and leftovers, Lauren and her guests went into the kitchen while Wyatt sought his chair in the living room.

"Well," Mike said, "Bernie and I ought to get going. We don't want to overstay our welcome." Slipping into his jacket, he took Lauren aside. "I've been talking with Wyatt. I can see he's remembering more and more, but there are still gears clashing in his head. Seriously bummed out, I'm thinking." Mike crossed his arms. "I know what he needs. He needs something for his mind to tackle, a dose of hard-nosed engineering. He's not ready yet, but I'll find a place for him at Precision Tool working with me. A job. I can't afford to pay much, but it'll help pull his head out of his ass. What do you think?"

"How can you do that, Mike? I thought you are laying off people."

"I am. Fuckin' little prospects for the future, either, but now we're talkin' Wyatt. He's The Man, The Force and The Honcho. I'll do whatever it takes to bring him back. Besides, he might come up with an invention that would bring my company back from the brink." With a wink, Mike said, "He does things like that."

"Oh, Mike."

"You tell him…when you think he's ready to break out. Okay?"

Lauren choked back tears. "You have a deal."

Chapter 5

Lauren gritted her teeth as she jockeyed the car through heavy traffic.

"Where *is* this restaurant, anyway?" Wyatt complained. "Montana?"

"It's just a few blocks from here, Honey," Lauren said, irritated by his sullen attitude. "Try to chill, okay?"

"What's the point? This guy is just another thieving lawyer bilking clients $400 an hour. Let's do an about-face."

Lauren eased to a stop at a red light. "Don't be like that. You know he isn't charging us a dime. Now that your memory is pushing one hundred percent, he wants to go over the recent developments. He said it was important. Art had another appointment in the area this morning, so we decided to meet for lunch."

Wyatt took out his mechanical pencil from his shirt pocket, slid it under his cast and scratched. "Regardless, it's a waste of time. Even if we get the patent back, we haven't any money to crank up Optimal."

"It doesn't hurt to try, Hon. You're the one who always

said you love problems. How many times have you claimed a tough predicament stretches the mind? You're the most tenacious man there is; that's why I married you."

The light turned green and Lauren crept around a crew that was taking down Christmas decorations from the streetlight poles. "All I know is Art sounded enthusiastic," she continued. "We should give him the courtesy of our attention." As Lauren turned the car into a mini-mall, she said, "Here it is, Satoru's Sushi."

"Sushi? The old guy likes sushi? Well, at least the meal should be good."

Lauren grinned as she parked. Because she'd talked with Art on the phone several times since Wyatt's mugging, she was intrigued to learn the lawyer had started legal action concerning their patent application. He didn't want to get into details until he could meet with Wyatt, Madison and herself. When Lauren explained that Madison was no longer part of Optimal, Art seemed mystified, but agreed to get together anyway.

There was a spring in her step as Lauren bounced up the sidewalk to the restaurant door. Inexplicably, she felt like her usual bubbly self and hummed a tune under her breath. She was anxious to finally meet Art in person and her smile broadened. Pausing at the door to wait for Wyatt to shuffle up, she looked up at the sparkling sky and the nearby Verdugo Mountains that seemed to hang over her like a verdant breaking wave. *California is so beautiful. It will be a fine lunch.*

As they entered, the sushi chef flung a boisterous greeting from behind a spotless counter. Art was already in a roomy booth sipping hot green tea. Wyatt and Lauren joined him, slipping across the vinyl seat.

"Good to see you, Wyatt. Mrs. Morgan, I presume," Art said, reaching across the table to shake hands.

Lauren was enraptured by his cherubic round face, the fuzzy fringe of pure white hair hovering above his ears and the Santa Claus reading glasses perched on the end of his pudgy nose. His striking blue eyes glittered as he surveyed Wyatt. "How are you doing? Your wife says you're back on track."

"Okay, I guess. Memory's a lot better but this cast is driving me nuts. Although I've learned to use a fork left-handed, you can forget chopsticks."

"Chopsticks? House rules allow forks and even fingers. Not an issue." Art pulled out his cell phone and turned it off. "There's a lot to go over, but let's order first. Sushi list?"

Both Wyatt and Lauren nodded and seeing Art had already marked his choices, took the list and checked off their own selections.

When the waitress came, she asked, "Beer? Saki?"

Wyatt winced. "No way! Green tea and a side of steamed rice."

Lauren gave the list to the waitress. "Just tea for me."

Art's crystal eyes swept Wyatt's patchy red face. "How did you merit such a thrashing? Lauren briefed me, but fill me in on the details."

Wyatt shrugged. "What can I say? I've been friggin' depressed. Lost the patent, Optimal going under, eviction notice, and all that crud. So to cheer me up, Lauren threw a birthday party for me and I got drunk. Super blasted. Should know better; I'm under the table if I drink more than one glass of wine. Ran out of booze; went for more. The next thing I remember, I woke up in the hospital."

Art cast a quizzical looking gaze at Lauren. "Some party."

"That's the way it happened," Lauren said. "Both of us have been under tremendous strain."

"I can imagine," Art said as the waitress set several plates of sushi and a steaming pot of tea on their table.

They fell silent as they mixed wasabi into their soy sauce and poured tea. Lauren welcomed the pause. Embarrassed at having revealed their shortcomings to an outsider, her upbeat mood faded.

"Okay, here's the deal," Art begun, mumbling around a piece of sushi. "Several months back, I became suspicious about the delays back east—Alexandria where the Patent Office is, to be exact. I did a little digging—I have a good friend there—and turned up a strange coincidence. You remember Dynamag? The firm owned by Eric Magana? There's evidence showing he beat you to the punch with a patent application for a pressurization system nearly identical to yours. Even though I filed your request earlier than his, patent management sandbagged it. Somehow, they approved the Dynamag submittal first."

"That's right," Lauren said. "They kept demanding we clarify all sorts of details. They claimed our application was incomplete; told us to resubmit."

"Yeah," Wyatt said, taking a bite of his rice.

"Do you remember talking to Julie Ann Kelly in the Patent Office?" Art asked.

"Sorta," Wyatt said.

"I discovered that Magana and Kelly are an item. About the time they connected and started traveling around the world together, the Patent Office kicked Optimal's application up the chain of command for special reviews. Curious, don't you think?"

"Peculiar," Lauren nodded.

"Well, I had enough evidence to consider issuing a subpoena for Kelly to appear at a deposition; but first, I'd have to file a lawsuit. My argument was a bit thin, so I vacillated and said nothing to you."

"And then?" Lauren asked.

"The same day that Wyatt got mugged, I uncovered some key documentation and decided to file suit against Kelly. Later, I traced Magana and Kelly to a restaurant in Beverly Hills and had her served. They flew to the East Coast the next morning."

Excited, Lauren leaned forward, elbows on the table. "Does that mean the patent is ours?"

"No, not yet. This is just a deposition. Kelly will have to answer questions concerning her involvement in processing Wyatt's application. The suit may or may not go forward; it depends on the testimony."

Turning to her husband, Lauren said, "Do you hear that? Sounds like Art is on to something."

Wyatt stirred in his chair. "Isn't a deposition just a few questions? It's not an actual trial, right?"

Art finished his last piece of sushi and balanced his chopsticks across the edge of his dish. "Right. But under some circumstances, the transcript can be admitted as evidence in a court proceeding. That's why it's done under oath. I want to question Kelly to see if there was any funny business or if others might be involved. In my gut, I think we can nail this woman."

"Maybe so, but she's not the problem," Wyatt grumbled.

"It's that damn Magana. He's the one who stole my design. I can't emphasize enough how it burns me up to see a slug like Magana steal my creation. It isn't just a patent; it's my inspiration, my mind. Imagine someone stealing the Statue of Liberty. From my standpoint, it's not just a crime, it's a cardinal sin!"

"I understand," Art nodded, "but Kelly could be a direct pipeline into Magana's operation. We'll follow the leads as they develop."

Lauren clapped her hands. "Honey, that's marvelous! It sounds like Art has a chance to save Optimal. You'll have to tell Mike and Bernie right away."

Shrugging, Wyatt said, "Guess so. Nothing's concrete, though."

"Time will tell," Art said, flashing a scowl at Wyatt. "You have to show a little patience, Wyatt. Legal protocol takes time."

"We've nothing to lose, Honey," Lauren said.

"One last thing that concerns me is Madison," Art resumed. "As I recall, the LLC operating agreement made her a full partner. If Optimal comes back to life like I hope, we'll have to deal with that issue."

A clammy shudder shook Lauren at the mention of Madison's name. "She's no longer associated with us. She's out of the picture. Why worry about her?"

"From a legal standpoint, she's still a partner unless you have a signed modification to the LLC. Another complication—she contributed funds to the company."

With a dark looking scowl bathing his face, Wyatt clamped his arms across his chest and stared out the window.

"I'll study the LLC Articles of Organization to see *exactly* what Madison's role in Optimal is," Lauren said, gritting her teeth. *I'm guessing Art is right.* Lauren felt her shoulders knot with the prospect of dealing once more with "that woman." *I hope I don't see her face to face—I'd make another scene for sure.*

Lauren steered their ten-year-old Toyota through creeping traffic toward home while her mind raced through Art's revelations. The possibilities seemed stunning, and hope subdued her anxiety about Madison. Keeping her eyes on traffic, she said to Wyatt, "Isn't this exciting? Art thinks he can 'nail' Kelly. His word, not mine. I bet the trial will lead to Magana and we could be back in business."

"All this talk is just lawyer guff. How are we going to take on the Department of Justice? Sue the United States Patent Office? Float a huge loan from the SBA? We're whistling in the wind."

Frustration with her husband boiled over. "Stop grumbling," Lauren growled. "You fought the Planning Department over permits for the office. You got the permits. You argued with the Patent Office and got the provisional. You went to Oklahoma for flight tests and proved you had the best pressurization system ever. You won. It can happen again."

Lauren pulled into their driveway, switched off the engine and turned to Wyatt. "Remember Art saying that a provisional patent is just an application and that it's merely a placeholder in line? So why did they keep kicking our formal application back? It doesn't make sense. You always insisted there was something fishy about Magana and the patent. Suppose you're right?"

"So what? There's no money. The way things are going, we'll be lucky to have a roof over our heads in six months."

As she walked toward the house, Lauren struggled to contain her anger. Wyatt seemed like a stranger bound up in a web of pessimism and resignation. When he'd returned from the trip to Oklahoma after flight-testing the system, he'd been buoyant, determined and passionate, yearning for the future. That was the man she married, the man she loved, the man she yearned to return to her. Lauren clenched her jaw and resolved to restore the "old Wyatt."

Late that night, Lauren pondered his words, "No money." Wyatt's improvement and Sharon's help had allowed her to return to work which provided a steady, if modest income. While the hemorrhaging had stopped, Optimal's creditors and the incessant parade of bills besieged their finances.

Another worry—layoffs at her work had taken their toll. *They can't fire me, the only bookkeeper, right?* She sat at the computer, entered four more bills into the spreadsheet and blanched at the total. The checking account was nearly depleted and the Visa card was at its limit. Soon, she'd struggle to buy groceries. She had to do something. Fast.

Although it had been only two months since her mother died, Lauren pressed her lips together in determination, twitched the computer mouse and opened a new document.

There's no other way. Methodically, she began a list of things in her mother's house that might be valuable:

Dali (original?)

Bentley

Ming vase

Jewelry (diamond bracelet?)

Crystal...

Chapter 6

Sharon staggered through the Morgan's front door clutching two large grocery bags against her bountiful bosom. Panting, she trudged to the kitchen and plopped the sacks on the counter. As she turned to retrieve another load, Wyatt appeared from the back room.

"Hi, Sharon. More in the car?"

"Yup. Don't worry yourself; I'll get 'em."

Wyatt tapped the cast with his knuckle. "I'm worse than a bum, not helping."

With a dismissive wave of her hand, Sharon went back to her car.

Wyatt sat in his easy chair and sighed, fatigue racking him. Although he slept ten or twelve hours a day, he never felt rested. He knew why; he'd read articles on symptoms of depression and chronic tiredness was at the top of the list. It was as if a foreigner had taken over his body and ravaged his thoughts. He struggled to recognize himself and dark visions crept through his mind like rats in the bilge of a ship. Lauren had encouraged him to call the doctor and get a prescription for anti-depressants, but the thought appalled him. He could manage his own mind, dammit—hippie drugs were out of the question.

Why is my neighbor babysitting me? He was thirty-six years old with a physique of a football lineman, fully able to fend for himself. Ever since he launched the model rocket with his dad at age six, he knew his destiny in the world. Nothing had ever impeded his progress, but now, resignation overwhelmed him and he collapsed under sudden ineptitude. The old Wyatt would have fought back like the aircraft carriers at the Battle of Midway. But today, he'd succumbed to the ministrations of a nursery maid. His chin sank to his chest and he closed his eyes. *Crap.*

Sharon lurched in with another load. "Say, Wyatt, can you help put this stuff away, or tell me where things go? I have to hustle. Gotta pick up the kids at school."

Lurching up from the chair, Wyatt went into the kitchen. "I really appreciate your help, Sharon." He took a can of peas from one of the bags and set it in the pantry. "Veggies go in here." One by one, he stowed the canned goods.

"Because Lauren is back at work," he said, "we have a little money coming in. That, plus the cash we save by stopping after-school care will help dodge a disaster, but the bills seem to get bigger every day. No matter, we'll make it up to you somehow."

Sharon smiled. "When things get better, you can treat me to a big dinner at a fancy restaurant, 'kay? Gotta run. The kids will be waiting. I'll be back in twenty."

Wyatt gave Sharon a big one-armed hug. It seemed odd to reach around her generous girth, accustomed as he was to Lauren's lithe figure. He shrugged off the peculiar feeling.

Wyatt collapsed in his chair, turned on the TV and stared at a moronic game show without seeing it.

He'd almost dozed off when Timmie bounded through the door, yelling "Daddy! Look!" Flourishing a smudged piece of paper, she bubbled, "A perfect spelling test! Same as Jenny."

"Show me, Timmie. Come sit on my lap."

Timmie clamored into Wyatt's arms and jarred the cast. "Ouch, that's hard," she complained. "Look. Look. An 'A!'"

Wyatt gave his daughter a big squeeze. "That's wonderful, Honey. I'm very proud." Looking up, he saw Sharon staring at them with a forlorn smile.

"It's nice you and Timmie get along," she said. "Jake doesn't have much time for Jenny."

Flustered, Wyatt couldn't remember how long it had been since he'd hugged Timmie and now the gesture seemed awkward, yet touching. Once again, he sensed an intruder had possessed him. Ignoring Sharon's jab at Jake, he looked at Jenny. "Can I check out your paper too?"

Jenny scurried over and thrust out her sheet with a bold red "A" dashed at the top, same as Timmie's.

"You both are Einsteins," Wyatt joked. "I'll bet you can spell better than I can." He picked up his coffee mug and finding it empty, braced his good arm on the chair and strained to get up.

"No, Daddy. Sit down," Timmie commanded, snatching the mug. "It's my job to get coffee."

"I'll help," Jenny laughed and they scampered to the kitchen.

Sharon beamed. "You're gettin' spoiled, Wyatt. Now you have two nurses."

"My cast comes off in about three weeks. Can't wait. Still, it's nice to have a couple of devoted helpers like Jenny and Timmie."

Timmie inched across the room with the mug. "Filled it too much," she said with a wry grin. Jenny trailed behind holding a sack of potato chips. As if choreographed, the two girls presented their offerings to Wyatt.

"Thanks, kids," Wyatt said. "I'm set."

"Daddy, Jenny wants to hear a few of your Navy stories. I told her about the weird things you did on the boat."

"Not a boat. A ship. A destroyer. Yes, I had gobs of fun and saw lots of places around the world."

"Tell us the french-fry story," Timmie cried, clapping her hands. "It's the best."

"I'm not sure I want to bore Sharon and Jenny with a silly tale about potatoes."

"Pleeese," Jenny said. "Timmie says it's super funny."

Sharon settled into Lauren's chair. "Why not, Wyatt. *I'm* interested in your adventures."

"Well, I've nothing else to do." He leaned back in his chair, took a sip of coffee and closed his eyes. "I guess it was out of Guam...no, Yokosuka I think. Yeah, Yokosuka. It's near Tokyo, Japan. We'd been doing drills, firing the five-inchers. An old-salt machinist mate stole a casing from a spent round and hid it in the engine room. It was a big brass tube, closed at one end. Well, he cut it off so it was a foot long, cleaned out the burnt powder and stuffed a coil of copper tubing inside. I commandeered a mess of cooking grease and a bucket of spuds from the galley. Halfway through the mid-watch, we connected the copper coil to a steam line and turned the shell casing into a deep-fat fryer. Ate so many french-fries, we had to let out our belts three notches. Why we weren't caught I'll never know, because the smell of those fries seeped into every compartment on the ship, even officer's country. Now *that's* what I call defending our country."

Jenny looked mesmerized. "I love french-fries! That's better than camping in the back yard and roasting marshmallows."

"Tell us about the time the officer got mad when you asked to go downstairs to the bathroom," Timmie said, squirming in obvious anticipation.

Wyatt chuckled. "On a Navy ship, tradition is everything. They don't have stairs, only ladders, even if they look like stairs. No bathrooms either, just heads. So when I asked for permission to go downstairs to the bathroom, the officer puffed up like an indignant bulldog and yelled, 'It's permission to go below to the heads, sailor!' Yep, the brass can really get tight-jawed."

Both Jenny and Timmie nodded in unison, looking as if the most profound secrets of the universe had been revealed to them. "Gee, that's too cool," Jenny confided to Timmie. "My Dad was never in the Navy. You're lucky."

"He has a lot more of those stories," Timmie bragged. "Tell us about the beer and cigarettes, Daddy."

"No, I'll save those tales for another time."

Abruptly, Sharon lurched to her feet. "Now Jenny, if it weren't for your father, you wouldn't be here." Turning to Wyatt, she said, "Everything is under control, right? Lauren will be home soon and I need to start my laundry." She grabbed her daughter's hand saying, "Come along. You can help."

Wyatt touched his forehead in a left-handed mock salute. "Thanks for everything. I'd be dead in the water without your help."

*   *   *

Lauren trudged up the steps to her house, weary from a stressful day of work. She paused with her hand on the doorknob, worried that Wyatt would be in one of his foul moods. She dreaded facing his gloom that sapped her energy and left her despondent. With a sigh, Lauren opened the door and saw Wyatt asleep in his chair. She stole down the hall and peeked into the bedroom where she found Timmie watching television. Without disturbing either of them, she dashed off a quick note: "Next door at Sharon's" and retreated on tiptoe, welcoming the respite. *Dinner might be a little late tonight.*

The dark winter chill made Lauren shiver as she rang Sharon's doorbell. She clutched her sweater around her neck and bounced up and down on the balls of her feet, fighting the dank night. The porch light snapped on and Sharon's silhouette filled the doorway. "Lauren! What a nice surprise. Come in and get warm."

"I hope I'm not interrupting anything. I thought I'd take a peek at your latest needlepoint."

"Sure thing. I've just started a new one. A pride of lions. I love animals, you know." Sharon waddled to her easy chair where a warm pool of light from the floor lamp bathed a canvas panel, stretched across a wooden frame. "It'll be a pillow when I'm done," she beamed, handing it to Lauren.

"It's lovely. Must be a ton of work. I don't have patience for this sort of thing." Lauren cradled the piece and tried to appear fascinated, but had to admit she had little interest in needlepoint. She'd scurried across the lawn, her breath steaming in the chill, because she needed company. Lauren longed for a friendly, non-combative voice, a taste of laughter and a broad smile. Sharon could be counted on to provide all three. Handing the needlework back, she said, "Are you in the middle of dinner or anything?"

"No problem. Jake's watching a basketball game in the family room and doesn't want dinner until halftime. Jenny is doin' homework—I hope—or talkin' on the phone. So, sit and bring me up to speed on the Morgan household."

Lauren wiggled her shoulders as her tension ebbed. She walked across the variegated hook rug, settled on the worn sofa and crossed her ankles. "Things are doing better. It's great to be back at work—just to get out of the house. My husband can be a real trial, sometimes," she said with a tight grin. "One thing for sure, I appreciate the help you've been by taking the kids to school, looking after Wyatt and all that."

Sharon tilted her head. "Not a problem."

"My paycheck gives us a tiny bit of breathing room," Lauren continued. "Although we're still desperately behind on the Visa bill, I found a way to make a partial payment on the mortgage, so the bank has backed off for a while."

Sharon grinned. "I just *knew* you'd pull a rabbit out of

the hat. You have a way of taking charge; you'll be out of hock in no time."

"It's not so simple, at least until Wyatt finds work. For now, I'm working on an alternative plan that concerns my mother's estate. Her death, combined with the holidays, has been disheartening—hard to get up steam, as Wyatt would say. But it's mid-January already and I have to do *something*."

"I remember you saying your dad gambled and blew his investments."

Lauren nodded. "Yeah, he did. The stock portfolio is worthless and the housing bubble has driven down prices— actually, the house is upside down. I wasn't very excited when mother's attorney left a message to call. At last I connected with him and confirmed I'm the sole heir. He suggested I look into the contents of the house. I'll have to work on title transfers on the cars, things like that, but I'm free to sell anything I wish.

"I decided to talk with my banker who introduced me to Emile Beaulieu, an art dealer who handles estate sales. Emile and I did a walk-around and he thought a few personal items in the house might be very valuable, so I made a list. It seems there may be some big numbers. Wyatt thinks I'm crazy."

"Hmmm," Sharon breathed. "Maybe things are rosier than you think."

"Emile got a quick appraisal on a small diamond ring and sold it for several hundred dollars. It was so easy. He plans to list several pieces of crystal and perhaps the Ming vase next. He's contacting his established clients to see if they're interested in the smaller items. Emile plans to engage a local auction house to sell the more expensive things. Wyatt could use a little good news, although the sale of the ring didn't impress him. 'Drop in the bucket,' he said."

"Forget Wyatt! You can start your own business and make a fortune."

Lauren laughed. "Fortune? I doubt it. There *is* a Dali painting that could be very valuable, but Emile said the art world is full of forgeries. Right now, we're going to focus on other things that will bring in quick cash."

Lauren shuddered with guilt, ashamed to be plundering her mother's belongings. She draped her arm over the sofa back. Rationalizing, she visualized a path back to her normal life: soccer for Timmie, exciting work for her husband and restarting her monthly Scrabble party— shelved because of "the situation." A few days ago, she'd even discussed the matter with Sharon, who'd substitute for Liza. Although Lauren knew that Sharon's idea of a rollicking good time wasn't crossword puzzles, a feeling of gratitude and genuine affection for her neighbor prodded her to explore the idea. In the easy silence, she deliberated once more, but a bitter, sour boding swept over her. The loss of her mother, a regular at the Scrabble parties, squelched any desire to resume. "Sharon, about that Scrabble party thing, I don't think…."

Chapter 7

While Lauren dwelt in California's balmy weather, it was another blustery, cold winter day in New Jersey. Eric Magana crept in the Trenton traffic, wipers of his new Porsche Turbo Cayenne slapping wet snowflakes. The red glow of brake lights and slush thrown from passing cars did not deflect his thoughts. He turned up the heater and reviewed his plans for this morning's meeting with Dynamag's management staff.

He was in trouble. As the automotive business retracted, Dynamag began losing money. Eric needed options and decided that diversification was the only plausible solution. He could not rely on car parts to support his lavish lifestyle.

Unexpectedly, his new girl friend provided the answer. A stunning looker, Julie Ann made heads spin like gears in a transmission. Eric loved the envious stares of men whenever she walked alongside him; arm candy in the extreme. It was she who mentioned the provisional patent for an airplane cabin pressurization system and how it amazed everyone in the Patent Office where she worked.

Always interested in an angle, Eric investigated. Julie Ann's prowess in bed dissolved any doubts of getting into the aviation business. So he'd rationalized: *Hell, airplanes are the same as cars—machines that haul people place to place.*

It had been a simple matter to manipulate her into handing over detailed information, but Eric needed time to submit his own patent application. He pressured Julie Ann to use her "charms" to delay the formal patent application from that naive engineer in California.

Eric smiled as thoughts of her raced through his head: long blond hair, a willowy figure and a rhythm in her walk that always gave him an erection. Images of her naked skin in Paris, New Delhi and Bogotá danced in his mind. He was reminiscing about a certain erotic encounter in the back of his jet when his grin turned into a scowl: *Now she's tangled up with a damned lawyer in L.A.*

Preoccupied, Eric allowed his car to skitter sideways before settling in behind a mud-caked sedan.

But now he had to focus and pull the project together fast—to be ready when Washington announced the new military aircraft. Eric had committed everything to this new project. He must man-up and take charge. There would be no backing down.

As he squinted through the streaked windshield, a familiar apparition startled Eric: his father's face scowling back at him. It had happened several times. Sometimes as he shaved, the stern glare of his father would appear in the steamy mirror, or perhaps when he switched off the lights at bedtime, the man's image lingered behind his eyelids. "You're a loser," his father always said. "You're not fit to haul chips in my shop. What's this schmoozing with clients crap, taking politicians to dinner? Be smart and get your ass out on the floor; crank handles."

Eric sneered at the ghostly face on the windshield. *I've tripled the size of Dynamag since you died. Maybe you founded the company, but I put it on the map. How? Connections, you bag of bile. Screw your engineers and machinists.*

A large box van swerved in front of the Porsche, spattered the windshield and obliterated the ghostly, age-lined countenance. Eric shook his head to clear it. *Damn, why did my father locate in this New Jersey hellhole?*

His stomach still churning, Eric tried to think about business. He expected the usual lip from his Operations Manager, Rubin Berkowitz, but he'd worked too hard to reel in this project to have that stuffy old-timer sidetrack things. He had to get his managers in an arm-lock and train two new-hires on the pressurization. Their job would be to convert the Optimal drawings to the Dynamag format, design a few missing parts, write a procedure or two and get the valves into production…fast.

It was almost nine in the morning when Eric slid into his reserved parking spot at the factory. He snatched his Bally attaché case from the passenger seat and bolted through the numbing flurries into the foyer still cluttered with boxes of Christmas decorations awaiting storage. *I ought to get maintenance to haul that crap off and burn it.* With a scowl, he hurried to his plush office.

Eric settled behind his huge mahogany desk and glanced at his watch. *Damn traffic. Late again.* With a snap, he opened his briefcase, drew out a thick bundle of papers and a laptop. He jabbed the intercom button. "Judy, let's get that meeting going. Did you distribute the agenda?"

"Yes, Mr. Magana. Everyone has copies."

"Okay. Jump on it. Get everyone together in five minutes."

"Yes, sir."

Eric strode into the glass-walled conference room and sat at the head of a long carved teak table where his management staff perched uneasily on elegant leather chairs. He dropped his papers and laptop on the table and surveyed their attentive faces. Judy, his secretary, peering over wide-rimmed glasses, sat at the far end and opened a note pad. Adverse to modern recorders, she would summarize the proceedings and email a comprehensive set of minutes to everyone an hour after the meeting concluded. After he'd blessed the draft, of course.

Eric rubbed his tanned jaw. "I'm certain you've heard the rumors," he began, "that Dynamag has acquired a new product line: cabin pressurization systems for executive jets. You'd have to be comatose not to know the shrinking automotive market has hammered our company. So diversifying into the aerospace sector will create a fresh source of revenue." Magana turned to his fresh-faced Engineering Manager. "Ryan, this project has lots of unfinished work. First thing, you'll need to train these two new people fast. We got to get the show on the road faster than a dragster."

With a wave of his hand, Ryan pointed to the newcomers. "This is Chris Needham, an aerospace engineer and our new drafter, Taylor Teague."

The new engineer nodded. In his mid-thirties, Chris had longish dishwater hair, thin eyelashes and a pale complexion, giving him a mousy appearance, almost seedy.

Taylor, on the other hand, looked to be twenty and was plain looking. She wore no makeup and her brown hair was disheveled. But her sleek slacks and fitted blouse accented her athletic figure. Taylor acknowledged Ryan's introduction with a blush.

Feeling expansive, Eric rose and leaned on the table, his eyes flicking from face to face. "It will be a madhouse for a while, but from an engineering standpoint, it's a cake walk. The basic design is complete. All we have to do is take the patent disclosure plus the key blueprints and fill in the gaps. In a few weeks, valves will be streaming from our production line like water from a fire hose." He slid the bundle of papers down the table to Ryan. "I'll leave it to you to brief Chris and Taylor on this material."

"Wow!" Ryan exclaimed as he spread out one of the drawings. "This is dynamite. Every dimension, tolerances, material list—everything. How did you get hold of these?"

"You know me—connections. I have an 'in' with Nick Nolan, a buyer at AirEnvironment, a big airplane system supplier and our future customer. He's promised to place an order with us as soon as we pass the quality surveys." Eric smirked. "While we were talking, a CD or two somehow appeared in my pocket."

Eric chuckled to himself. *With a little persuasion on my part, Nick found a way to 'acquire' drawings from that two-bit company. The owner was an idiot— had no business sense. He thought he could engineer his way into a fortune. My "connections" and savvy put an end to his fantasies.*

The Sales Manager, a wiry young man with a heavy five-o'clock shadow, cleared his throat. "What's with the market? Why would AirEnvironment buy these? What quantities?"

Eric sat and rocked back in his chair. "Well, Skip, the overall airplane business is in the tub just like cars. The good news—I possess some very reliable information—is the military will order a bunch of surveillance planes based on an executive jet made by Maddox Aircraft." Eric crossed his arms in satisfaction. "AirEnvironment supplies Maddox; that's our market. Not only that, but I snatched pricing info as well. We're wired."

Skip nodded. "I read an article in the Wall Street Journal regarding that order. Washington is trying to pump up the economy. The announcement could come any day."

"Count on it," Eric confirmed with an exaggerated wink. "I'll set you up with the important government people and I'm working on getting into Maddox, too. You won't have to break a sweat."

"Not to pour cold water on this deal," the Quality Assurance Manager said, "but I expect big problems in getting certification to manufacture airplane parts. Not only will the FAA stir our soup on general aviation hardware, but the Defense Contract Management Agency, DCMA, oversees any military orders."

"Russ is right," Rubin Berkowitz agreed, scratching his nose. "I've dug into the aircraft industry's standards and figure it would be easier for a beagle to give birth to a camel than for Dynamag to expand into either commercial or military aviation. I think we should stay in automotive; it's the only thing we know." Rubin crossed his legs and frowned. "Sometimes I wonder if you have two brain cells to rub together, Eric."

Although he'd anticipated the old geezer's resistance, Eric was outraged that Rubin criticized him in front of everybody. "You're getting too cautious in your old age, Rubin. You know damn well that Ford is contemplating bankruptcy because they can't compete. Same with the Koreans and Japanese. Hell, Chrysler has been bought up by Italy and even Jaguar sold out to India. The business is coming unraveled, and you want to hang tough. You need to shit or get off the pot."

Rubin hated vulgarity and winced, his lined face wrinkling. He'd joined Dynamag thirty-five years ago as a young assembler from the Jewish area of Brooklyn helping Eric's father. He'd scrambled up the ranks by working sixty-hour weeks and studying engineering at the New Jersey Institute of Technology. Now, as Director of Operations, he ran the day-to-day activities of the company.

"You're asking a plumber to do brain surgery—ain't gonna happen." Rubin ran his stubby fingers through a curly mass of salt-and-pepper hair. "We've put together a great machine shop, but it's geared to automotive processes, not aviation. That's a huge difference." He gestured toward the two new faces at the table. "Engineering may say they'll get along okay, but Needham and Teague will be inundated by the weight/strength trade-offs, failure analysis and the myriad studies and documentation the aircraft people demand. We are a VW Beetle, not a NASCAR machine."

With a withering glare, Eric hissed, "The decision is final—we're in the cabin pressurization business. It took me a hell of a lot of work to snag this opportunity. Let me say it again: we have drawings, the patent, cost breakdowns and even qualification test data. My source assures me we'll get a big purchase order as soon as we pass muster. Everyone, and I mean *everyone,* better get behind this and make it happen." Eric stared at Rubin. "If you don't like it, you can pack up and find work somewhere else. Same for the rest of you. Got it?"

Two weeks had passed and Eric was frantic when he learned of the increasing complexity of the new program. Frustration knotting his stomach, he barged into the engineering offices and found Needham in Taylor's cubicle, staring at her computer monitor. Eric set a large accordion folder on the desk. "There's only two more days before the DCMA survey, Chris. We're going to need these procedures updated right away."

Chris mopped his brow as he leaned over Taylor's desk. "I'll take a look as soon as Taylor and I sort out a couple of things on this aneroid capsule. Trouble is, Dynamag's drawings and procedures always refer to industrial specifications. We have to convert everything over to aerospace standards."

Exasperated, Eric growled, "What's this crap about updating documents? It's as simple as washing a car. This is becoming a royal pain. Do I need to kick a little ass?"

Taylor blanched. "There are only a dozen or so Optimal drawings and we're nearly done with those, Mr. Magana," she murmured, peeking over her eyeglasses. "But there's a hundred more to generate on our own."

"True," Chris confirmed. "Maybe a couple of your other drafters can help."

"A hundred?" Eric was astonished. "Hell, there's just

two or three valves in the whole system." Disgusted, he growled, "Whatever it takes. But get on the procedures first. That fool government auditing team is coming in— DCMA, remember? Chris, I want you to oversee their survey. I want to review everything with you tomorrow night. Make sure we're ready."

"It's not just DCMA for the military stuff," Chris said. "For the commercial certification, the FAA gets involved. Actually, an organization called MIDO will conduct the survey next week."

"MIDO? Never heard of them."

"They're part of the FAA and the ones that certify the facility and manufacturing processes," Chris explained.

Perplexed, Eric sputtered. "Dynamag has dealt with the government regulatory maze for years. We have an extensive operating procedure called a 'Production Part Approval Process.' It covers everything. Just hand it to this DCMA guy and the FAA. Tell them it's our plan."

Chris shook his head. "It won't fly. These guys are very rigid and a plan governing the manufacturing of automotive rear-view mirrors and dash escutcheons will get us nothing but laughs. I'm working on the key sections of a new quality manual, but it's impossible to be ready day after tomorrow. We scheduled DCMA in too soon. The only good news is we have another week before the FAA is due."

His face red with anger, Eric rapped his knuckles on the desk. "Every friggin' engineer is the same—tweak, ponder and futz forever. We're not in business to bow to pompous inspectors. I have big expenses to cover. Your job, Chris—and Taylor—is to shine like a headlight reflector when those survey teams show up. I can't put up with any more delays. Understand?"

Eric jabbed the accordion file. "Just worry about Engineering and these procedures," he snarled. "I'll take care of the rest." He shoved the folder on top of Taylor's keyboard. "Get on this. Now." He spun and strode out of the room.

Taylor's soft brown eyes grew as big as dinner plates. "Goodness!" The young college student tugged at her ragged looking ponytail and shivered. "I guess I have a lot to learn about industry."

Chris smiled. "Relax. Eric is like a rooster that wandered from the barnyard. He doesn't realize it'll take a lot of time to get on track. The DCMA survey is just the beginning. Eventually, Engineering can manage the drawings and procedures, but wait until Dynamag has to build a bunch of specialized test equipment. Worse, the factory floor has to update tooling for things such as 'J' threads. Engineering is just one piece of the puzzle. When he says he'll take care of everything else, he'd better get Rubin involved."

Chris picked up Eric's folder and spilled its contents on the desk. Taylor's and Chris' eyes fell on the pile and they sighed in unison.

The last day of January ended with a blinding blizzard and temperatures in the teens. While Trenton shivered, Eric quaked in a livid rage. The DCMA team had just left, leaving behind a vast wreckage of rejected procedures, disapproved drawings and long lists of unqualified tooling. He glowered at the end of the conference table and contemplated firing his entire staff. The thought pandered to his virile self-image, but pragmatism, bred of thousands of fierce industrial skirmishes, yanked the reins of his thoughts. Simmering, he rose from his chair, paced to the window and back. He balled his fists and leaned on the table, a heavy gold chain swinging beneath his neck. "Okay, troops, what the hell do we do now?"

Rubin cleared his throat. "This airplane business is like rain at a picnic. You're asking us to learn a foreign language and gave us too little time."

"I agree," Chris said. "With more help, maybe we could be ready in two or three months."

"You're out of your mind," Eric roared. "You've been working on this for a month and all we have for our trouble is a calamity. Did you see the inspectors? They looked as if they were dealing with children, snickering and winking. The only thing they liked was the coffee."

Rubin leaned back in his chair and put his hands behind his head. "You'll have to admit the job is bigger than you expected. Chris and Taylor are burning hours like cordwood, but they're still buried. We're gaining on the mechanical design side, but electronics and software are way beyond anything we've ever done. I've been working weekends to help out, but it's not enough."

Russ, the Quality Assurance Manager, cowered to one side muttering, "Big job."

"I don't need a list of where you guys fell on your butts," Eric stormed. "I'm working on hiring a good electrical engineer, someone who knows the meaning of 'action.' I'll take care of the damn electronics; you stick with the mechanical stuff." He stared at his Quality Manager, cringing in his chair. "Russ, convert our Production Part Approval Process into something the government likes. Keep it simple."

"If you do that, they won't come to the dance," Rubin interjected.

"What are you saying?" Eric said. "I can't take a shit without a goddamn government inspector's blessing?"

The question dangled in the air like the tail of a kite on a breezy day. Eric stood, stared menacingly at the assemblage and thundered from the room to his office. *I'm surrounded by idiots. I can't rely on them to do anything. It's time to flex major muscle and telephone my guy inside the FAA. I'll find a way to weasel inside DCMA, too. Connections rule.*

As he sat at his desk, his glance fell on a note from Judy, his secretary. "Call Julie Ann Kelly re: subpoena." Eric rested his head on his hands, feeling mauled by petty problems and inept people. *That's her goddamn problem, not mine.*

Chapter 8

An early morning sunbeam peeked through the bedroom drapes heralding Valentine's Day. Wyatt stirred and gathered Lauren next to him, her head resting on his shoulder. They cuddled beneath the toasty flannel sheets for twenty minutes before their daughter's rustlings announced the household business had begun.

Lauren hummed as she made breakfast. Timmie, chatting with a girlfriend from school, juggled the phone while sipping milk, painting her upper lip white. Their lazy breakfast of oatmeal and grapefruit brought Wyatt a sense of coziness and filled him with strange sentiments. He gazed fondly at his daughter and a lump grew in his throat. *There it is again...the stranger in my head. Why am I getting choked up?*

Starting in early January Wyatt had searched for an inexpensive Valentine's Day trinket to honor his love for Lauren, but struck out. One day as he puttered in Optimal's shop, he had an inspiration, and commandeered a small casting from the pressurization system, zipped over to

Mike's, machined it into a shiny paperweight and had a gooey inscription engraved on it. Although it was nothing but a small chunk of an airplane, it was his personal chunk, created in his mind. Symbolically, he would perch on Lauren's desk at work and keep an eye on her. Wyatt snickered with pleasure when Mike accused him of being "a sentimental old fucker."

As he knew she would, Lauren cooed over the gift and kissed him heartily, her fine hair tickling his nose.

That night the Morgan trio went to a fancy dinner where Wyatt, contrary to his normal social estrangement, enjoyed the festive holiday crowds. After a brief pause in the teaming waiting area, they were seated at a linen-draped table garnished with polished wine glasses, faux candlelight and a small placard reading "reserved." The dark dining room, hushed by thick carpet, pleased Wyatt, weary from months of parsimonious living. He and Lauren set aside their financial distress and ordered steaks and a nice bottle of Zinfandel while Timmie indulged in mac and cheese. Wyatt even let Timmie have a sip of wine, drawing a sputter and scowl from the child's puckered face.

At first disdainful of Lauren's attempts to sell Liza's things to raise money, he was happy she had been successful enough to cover the cost of the wine.

After the main course, Wyatt and Lauren conspired against Timmie by introducing her to crème brûlée instead of her usual ice cream. After hearing Timmie's enthusiastic praise, Wyatt joked, "I'm afraid this little culinary adventure will cost her thousands of bucks over her lifetime."

Reluctant to end the evening, the adults savored a cordial of port and Timmie munched on peppermints that the thoughtful waiter conjured from his apron. They squirmed through the crowds waiting in the foyer and darted across the parking lot, evading the evening chill. Imbued with the evening's camaraderie, they sang "Row, Row, Row Your Boat" all the way home, filling the car with laughter and joy.

Prompted by a wink of the late night moonrise, Wyatt made love to Lauren for the first time in almost two months. He was bewildered when she sobbed afterwards, stroking his chest and kissing him. Wyatt hugged her slender body so hard, she gasped for breath. He caressed the small of her back and nipped her neck, small delicate nips, and was content.

It felt odd to be free of the cast. Wyatt's arm had atrophied and was the color of an arctic glacier except where he'd scrubbed off yellowed dead skin, leaving a baby-fresh pink hue. He gave his limb little thought as he drove toward the IHOP restaurant for lunch with Bernie. His mood hadn't been this good since before Christmas and a broad smile lifted his boyish cheeks.

Wyatt walked into the restaurant and saw Bernie sitting in a corner booth reading a newspaper. Wyatt dodged a platter-bearing waitress, slid across the vinyl seat and shook Bernie's hand. After ordering coffee, Wyatt asked, "How are you doing, you old geezer?"

"Okay, I guess. Well, maybe not so okay."

Concerned, Wyatt tilted his head and said, "Not okay? What's going on?"

"Things at work are grinding to a halt. They've cut

both my pay rate and hours. I've lost my medical insurance and won't be eligible for Medicare for another two years. That's big trouble for a sixty-three year old guy with a bad back from bending over lathes and mills all his life." With a quick, nervous motion, he tossed the newspaper to one side. "Plus, I've had to lay off all but two of my guys, which means I'm cranking machines most of the time and downing Tylenol like it was popcorn."

"Heck, Bernie, if I were you, I'd grab Brian by the throat and remind him that you've worked at Simmons for years. He owes you some consideration."

A frown deepened the wrinkles on Bernie's face, aging him. "I tried that. Your old boss says orders for airplane components have dried up. He even blamed you for his problems because you quit the company—what, two years ago? He grumbled that it's been all downhill since then."

"That's crazy."

"At least I have a job as long as the company survives," Bernie said, rubbing his bald spot. "But there's no guarantee unless the economy turns around."

Wyatt shook his head. "Well, you're doing better than I am. We're broke and I'm petrified about job hunting. The last time I looked for work, the airplane folks clamored for engineers. This economy has hammered everyone and it's getting worse. It's like I'm walking straight into a forest fire."

"Gotcha," Bernie muttered.

"Here's your coffee, gents. Ready to order?" The waitress, a middle age Latina with blue-black hair pulled into a tight bun, drew her pen from a starched apron and flashed a perfunctory smile.

Welcoming the diversion, Wyatt selected his usual burger and fries. Bernie stayed with breakfast ordering an omelet and English muffin.

As the waitress bustled away, Wyatt said, "At least I have health insurance through Lauren's work." Suddenly, he bit his lip, realizing he'd pointed out his good fortune after Bernie's sad news. Trying to lighten up the somber moment, he continued, "You have a job and I have insurance. I think we should combine forces."

A tight smile creased Bernie's face. "We tried that already. It was called Optimal. Didn't work out."

Bernie's blunt statement was like a kick in the gut. Wyatt slurped his coffee. *Right. Bernie put several thousand dollars into Optimal. Bet he could use that money now.* Wyatt brooded, knowing his business ineptitude had cost Bernie and Mike big time. Even his own family was buried in money problems. He coughed, trying to clear the anguish from his throat. The morning's lightheartedness deserted him and he retreated to awkward chatter about the weather.

After what seemed to be hours, the waitress served them. Wyatt stared at his plate a moment. He reached for the saltshaker and realized the burger looked nauseating. His usual robust appetite fled before the onslaught of remorse, for his failure to bring Optimal to fruition.

Bernie spattered his omelet with Cholula and took a bite. "You're right; things are getting worse. Look at this." He handed the newspaper to Wyatt.

The front page was dominated by the headline:

Detroit Closes More Plants

After a quick glance, Wyatt dropped the paper on the seat beside him. "Yeah. This was on last night's news. Europe is in worse shape. Germany has slipped into a recession and there are riots in France over cuts in government subsidies. Our fearless leaders in D.C. are printing more money: Q.E. six they call it; maybe it's seven or 413…hell, I don't know. All this when inflation has topped eight percent."

"We can't blame Washington; they're catering to the voters who want freebies," Bernie grunted. "Tax the rich and the corporations. That's what gets politicians elected. The public is the problem. Nobody wants to work for their own ski boats, health care or retirement."

Wyatt nodded in agreement and then frowned. "Have you heard about that Bellington guy?"

"Who?"

"E.J. Bellington. He's a Libertarian candidate running for president. He likes to be called Frank because he says that's what he is…frank."

Bernie shook his head. "Nope. Never heard of him. It doesn't matter because Libertarians never get elected anyway."

"You're right, but I'm going to watch him anyway," Wyatt said. "What are the alternatives? More Democrat and Republican smoke-clouds? It's time for Washington to get out of the way."

"You're preaching to the choir, my friend. You and I want everyone to pull their own weight, but 300 million Americans want a free ride. What politician can get elected on a platform of 'earn your own way' in today's moral muddle?"

"Well, I can't vote for the monster that has its hand around my wallet. I'll check out Bellington for sure."

They ate in silence for a while. Wyatt just nibbled, their conversation casting a despondent pall over his already sour mood.

"I do have some interesting news," Bernie said.

"Not more depressing economic stuff, I hope."

"Nope. This concerns your good friend Madison."

"Madison? She's no friend of mine."

"Maybe so, but she thinks she is. I get a call from her every so often. She's worried about your mugging and health, plans for Optimal….stuff like that."

Uneasy talking about Madison, Wyatt asked, "Why would she be interested in my plans? I don't have any."

"I don't know, but she gets really pushy; pumps me for scuttlebutt."

"Well, I hope you didn't tell her anything," Wyatt hissed. "It's none of her dang business."

Bernie looked surprised with Wyatt's vehemence. "What was I going to do? I had to be polite. I mentioned your cuts and broken arm. Mentioned that your memory was coming around. That's all."

"I don't want you talking with her anymore," Wyatt growled. "I'm done with her. Optimal is kaput and I have no need for that woman. She's out of my life for good."

"Madison can be stubborn. She pointed out she's still a partner in Optimal. I'm certain I'll hear from her again."

"You have caller ID. Don't answer."

An awkward silence followed the terse exchange. Wyatt tried to quell his anger at Madison, knowing his blunt words had rankled his friend. He pressed his lips together in a thin line while Bernie spread jam on a piece of toast.

Wyatt pushed his plate aside and slurped coffee. Madison was a real witch. He'd allowed her to invade his family and his integrity. Yet contradictory memories of their inspirational evenings troubled him. He remembered when they tackled tough design problems and rejoiced in their synergistic mind-melds. They'd shared flashes of insight and exalted over mutual achievement. Then she'd changed—morphed into a predatory stalker, a malevolent home wrecker. He shook his head as his thoughts congealed. There was no forgiveness in his heart; he was determined to nurture his hate for her.

Clearing his head, Wyatt gazed at Bernie. "I apologize for being short with you about Madison. It's too bad things didn't work out when you and I worked together at SAC. We had a great time late at night, knocking heads about tolerances, tooling points and all that. Like mushrooms, I guess—as soon as the factory grew dark, we'd poke our heads through the manure. We made great music together."

Bernie smiled. "Sure did. It's a pity that Brian didn't go for your pressurization ideas. You'd still be working there had he jumped at it." Bernie set his elbows on the table and propped his chin on his bony fists. "I sure enjoyed working with you. The shop floor is lonely now that you're gone."

Wyatt blushed. "Yeah. Too bad Brian is scared of innovation."

Once again, there was silence, but it was an easy quiet, not as tense as before. Bernie picked up the check. "It's on me."

They strolled out toward their cars and shared an awkward hug and a firm handshake. Wyatt was turning to his car when Bernie said, "One other thing about Madison. She wants to see you."

Chapter 9

On Valentine's Day, just two days ago, Wyatt's house had been full of happiness and laughter. He'd exchanged greeting cards, hugs and friendly quips with Lauren and Timmie. Even Garfield had a Valentine for him, signed with a paw print. Gratified by the congenial sense of family, Wyatt embraced the festivities with fervor.

Then "The Alien" returned.

Yesterday, after collecting the mail, his euphoria was flung against the shoals of poverty. While Lauren was at work, he'd thumbed through the envelopes and flyers, setting the bills aside. On opening them, he was stunned by the large sums they owed. Not only were the continuing invoices from Optimal's vendors numbing, but the utilities and credit card charges were astonishing. He looked for the checkbook and discovered Lauren had made a rare partial payment to the mortgage company, leaving the bank balance near zero. There was no money. Frantically, he searched his mind for solutions.

He knew Lauren continued to sell Liza's belongings,

bringing in a sporadic infusion of cash, but the meager funds evaporated the moment insistent demands of the creditors struck. Besides, her liaison with Emile rankled him. It wasn't Emile's job to support the family; it was *his*. Every check Lauren brought home reminded him of his failure as a provider. Morose, he stared at the pile of bills, dwelling on his inadequacies.

"The Alien" was back.

Wyatt stood in front of his small workbench in the garage and tried to remember why he was there. His eyes wandered from tool to tool, all arranged in precise groups on the pegboard: wrenches for the car on the left, woodworking stuff in the center, nippers and a soldering iron for electrical work on the right. He couldn't think why he'd come and turned to leave when: *Ah, screwdriver...bad light switch.* He snatched a small blade screwdriver and, apathetic about the task ahead, snapped off a circuit breaker and headed to a rendezvous with the bathroom switch.

The repair completed, Wyatt sank into his chair and lamented over his botched partnerships with Bernie and Mike and the terrifying prospect of encountering Madison again. Even though he'd recovered from his injuries and his memory had returned, he dwelt in the house of misery.

That evening, Lauren came in carrying her briefcase and an empty lunch sack. "Hi, Honey; have a good day?"

"Good day? How in the hell can I have a good day?" Flinging his hand toward the stack of bills, he growled sarcastically, "There's a heap of good news. Bills by the ton. Isn't that fun?"

"It's not so bad," Lauren countered. "Emile sold more of Mother's crystal today. Around $150. That will help."

Wyatt gritted his teeth.

"By the way, where's Timmie?" Lauren asked.

"Next door with Jenny. Guess I'm not good company."

With a soft grunt, Lauren murmured, "I can imagine."

Agitated, Wyatt folded his arms. *Another gloomy night with my supposedly supportive wife.*

As a scowl clouded her husband's face, Lauren said, "Look, I've a piece of nice Swiss cheese and a bottle of 'Two-Buck Chuck.' Let's have our Sunset Ritual and relax, okay?"

"Thought it was up to $2.50. Can we afford it?"

"Come on, Wyatt. Can't you lighten up a bit?"

"What is there to lighten up about? The collapse of Optimal? The patent fiasco? Scars smeared across my face? How about the $200 electric bill?"

"Dammit!" Lauren screamed. "I'll give you some 'How-a-bouts.' How about tackling the problems rather than sniveling?" Her small hands clenched into fists. "How about showing a little understanding for your family? How about bringing back the man that lit up my life?"

Wyatt cowered before his wife's onslaught. He had never seen her so infuriated. His mind scrambled from dismay to shouting back and from confusion to self-righteousness. Unable to comprehend the fury enveloping him, Wyatt crossed his arms and stared into space.

"Have you nothing to say?" Lauren demanded, her blue eyes glittering in anger.

Wyatt shrugged and looked up. "I'm…It's…It's all too much for me. I just can't deal…"

Lauren glared at him and snarled, "You're too much for *me* and I can't deal with your helplessness. You have to get hold of yourself and stop your chronic bellyaching. I don't know why you're so adamant against taking an antidepressant drug, if only for a few weeks."

Wyatt shook his head. "I hate pills. I just need a little more time."

"If that's the case," Lauren stormed, "there's only one cure for your depression and that's a job. Get off your duff and look for work. Now!"

Wyatt flinched as her words struck the mark. Like always, Lauren was right; he had to find a job. He knew work would solve three big issues: assuage his shame for failing in business, bring in money and rekindle his passion for engineering. It seemed simple enough, but the chaos in the aircraft industry was daunting. Yet there wasn't any alternative. He tried to imagine cold-calling possible employers, enduring stressful interviews, and explaining the collapse of his company. The visions appalled him because he never had to beg for a position; he had no experience bragging about his skills to strange executives. But then again, he was one of the best damn engineers ever.

He nodded at Lauren and gave her a peck on her freckled cheek. "Okay."

*   *   *

Her outburst perplexed Lauren. It wasn't that she was ashamed to confront her husband, but the fact that she was capable of such a display surprised her. In a way, it felt liberating, the proverbial load off her chest. But it was more than shedding anxiety, more than venting pent-up frustrations; she had taken charge. If Wyatt chose to wallow in wretched misfortune, she would step up. She would not allow the family to falter. Resolute, Lauren squared her shoulders and went to the kitchen to begin dinner.

"You look tired, Daddy," Timmie said as she settled onto her dining room chair. "Did you take a nap while I was at school?"

"Sorta. I dozed in my chair," Wyatt replied with a wan smile.

"You were sleeping when Sharon dropped me off. Maybe you need a little exercise. My teacher says it's good for you."

"Guess I could walk around the block every so often, now that the cast is off."

"That's a good idea," Lauren said. "It gets nice and warm in the afternoon and the weather man doesn't expect rain this week." Amused to hear Timmie prodding her father, Lauren guessed that Wyatt felt under siege by both his women. After all, he was probably still reeling from her earlier tirade.

Timmie, spooning a wad of Beef Stroganoff into her mouth, paused and studied her father. "Your scars have almost gone away and your arm works fine. It looks like my nursing worked; you're almost good as new."

Wyatt grinned. "You *are* a great nurse. Your coffee is even better than mine and I appreciate you getting the newspaper and answering the phone. It was tough to do much with only one arm."

Timmie nodded and with a serious look on her round face, said, "Now that I'm nine-and-a-half, I have to think about my future. I bet I'd make a super good nurse."

Lauren stifled a giggle. She still struggled to accept her daughter's sudden maturity and savored the recent memories of a spunky, if dyspeptic kid. Timmie's solemn pronouncement concerning her pending career defied Lauren's stereotype of a nine-year-old. A sense of pride warmed her, and she took pleasure with the revelation that she might be a capable mom, after all. Half serious and half in jest, Lauren said, "Being a nurse is a great choice, but you might also give thought to becoming a doctor. That way you can take care of both of us when we're old."

Timmie's face scrunched up, squeezing her tiny freckles together. "Takes a lot of college, doesn't it?"

"About eight years plus another as an intern," Lauren advised.

"Mmmm. Maybe I'll be a nurse first." Then Timmie dove into the last of her Stroganoff.

Encouraged by her bold encounter with her husband and newfound rapport with Timmie, Lauren decided to press the job issue with Wyatt. "I've been thinking, Hon, that you can have a résumé put together by tomorrow and then start making calls and checking employment websites right away."

Wyatt grimaced. "I know I should, but it's only been a couple of months and my arm hasn't regained its strength. It still aches at night and I'm always tired—has me in dry dock half the time."

"I didn't realize your arm still bothered you."

"Yeah, it does. I hate to complain, so I didn't say anything."

Hate to complain? Yeah. Right. "Don't forget what we talked about before dinner," Lauren said. "You *must* find work—the sooner the better. You simply have to get going."

"I know, I know. But right now it seems…" His voice trailed off leaving a stark silence in the room.

Lauren was certain his problems weren't physical; it was depression. She could feel anger gripping her once more and grappled with surging exasperation. Her hand shook as she forked a few noodles into her mouth. "Look, you gain nothing by delays. First thing in the morning, sit down in front of the computer and knock out a résumé. I'll help edit it tomorrow night and then you're off to the races."

Staring at his empty plate, Wyatt said, "Well, I'm not sure."

"Wyatt! You promised!" Lauren shouted, slamming her fork on the table.

Timmie jumped and glanced first at Wyatt and then her mother. "Mommy, he's tired. Look at him. Give Daddy more time to get his energy back."

"You don't understand what's going on, Timmie," Lauren snapped. *Our little nurse is in over her head.* "He's much better and we need help with our finances."

Lauren drew herself up short, ashamed to have worried Timmie about money. Occasional sales of Liza's belongings helped fend off the bill-collector maelstrom, but the mortgage and credit cards remained extremely delinquent. Emile, the antique dealer, was starting to sell the larger, more valuable items and was working on the Ming vase. They might be able to hold off another week or two, but Wyatt could languish in his despondency forever if she didn't take action.

"Daddy is ready right now, Timmie. Trust me."

Timmie thrust out her chin, looking defiant. "You're wrong." With that, she went to Wyatt, patted his hand and stalked to her room.

Lauren was dismayed by her daughter's overt confrontation and wondered what Wyatt thought. Expressionless, he rose from the table, shuffled back to his chair and picked up the newspaper.

Weary of the day's disruptive episodes, Lauren began clearing the dinnerware. As she set the dishes in the sink, her glance fell on two Valentine cards still on the counter. Seeing they were for Wyatt, she picked them up and idly began re-reading them. Timmie's was an elaborate handmade one, covered with ruby crayon hearts and delicate Cupids. There was a frilly paper border surrounding the card, looking like a virginal halo. Timmie had signed it, "Your loving daughter, Timshel." Lauren's store-bought card looked tacky in comparison. The trite sentiments were shallow and maudlin in a commercial way. Dejected, Lauren tossed both into the trash.

Chapter 10

The late February air was brisk as Lauren walked into the bank. It had been over two months since she had seen Lee Wong and now she had a good reason to consult with him. She found him seated at his tidy desk, working at his computer. Before Lauren could put down her briefcase, Wong bounced from his chair, his eyes pushed to mere slits by a wide smile. He clasped her hand with both of his, saying, "How nice to see you again, Mrs. Morgan."

"Come on, Lee. We're on a first name basis. Remember? It's Lauren."

"Yes, of course." He straightened his french cuffs and buttoned his coat. "Please, take a seat."

She sat, plopped her briefcase on the floor and opened it.

As she gathered a few documents, Lee unbuttoned his coat and settled into his chair, lacing his fingers together. "When you called, you said there was good news. I'm anxious to hear because I know things have been difficult."

"Difficult is a euphemism, Lee. It has been a disaster.

But as I mentioned, things are showing signs of turning around."

"Excellent."

"Over the past few weeks, I've been working with Emile Beaulieu, the dealer you introduced to me. He's been selling a few items from my mother's estate."

"Yes. I was sorry to hear about your mother."

Lauren nodded, "Thanks. Perhaps you'll think it odd, but I feel awkward about pillaging my mother's things. I guess there's no alternative because there's so little money that I struggle to pay a few utility bills and fend off the mortgage people. About a month ago, I met Emile at my mother's house and he began cataloging some of the more important items. He seemed pleased and suggested a few might be valuable."

Lee picked up his fountain pen and tapped it lightly on the desk. "I've worked with him many times and he's certainly knowledgeable about estate sales. Antiques can be mystifying. It takes an expert."

"My mother's lawyer says Emile has an impeccable reputation. Judging from his commission, he must be stellar," Lauren joked.

"Knowing you, there was no stone unturned before engaging him. Due diligence and all that."

Grateful for Lee's compliment, Lauren bobbed her head. This was typical; he always had friendly words and encouragement.

Lauren's thoughts returned to business. "Emile," she said, "contacted a few of his regular collectors and within a week had sold an 18th century gate leg table and a nice vintage French Jean Lurcat tapestry. Better yet, he also sold a rare Ming vase. My net," she said waving a check, "exceeds two thousand dollars."

"Wonderful," Lee said. "That will be a big help." He rubbed his delicate hands together and beamed.

"I hope more is coming because we're still way behind with our mortgage," Lauren said. "Emile has begun inquiries about a Dali painting—could be very valuable, but there's a good chance it's forged. He said authentication could get very complex and time consuming."

She shrugged. "For now, I think it would be a good idea to open a separate checking account to track receipts from the estate. There may be unforeseen tax ramifications."

"Very wise. I'll take care of it right now. Will you be depositing the entire check or do you want some cash back?"

"I'd better deposit the whole thing. There are a lot of bills to pay."

With a casual wave, reminiscent of the Queen Mother's, Lee summoned a clerk. "Prepare the paperwork for a new checking account, please. Mrs. Morgan's particulars are in the system; no need to bother her."

"Yes, Mr. Wong."

"It will take only a few moments," he said, setting his pen down. "How is Mr. Morgan? I was hoping to see him."

"He just wasn't up to coming today."

Lauren didn't want to talk about it. Wyatt's lingering depression gnawed at her, eroding her usual confidence, leaving jitters and a quick temper in its place. It was all the more maddening because physically he had regained his normal robust appearance, which clashed with his childish whimpering and grumbling.

"He's not back on his feet yet?" Lee nudged his pen a

few inches across the leather trimmed desk blotter. "Are the doctors optimistic?"

Lauren wanted to dismiss further talk on the matter, but Lee's soft eyes exuded kindness and genuine concern. Drawn into his silent invitation to confide, Lauren felt her rigid façade dissolve. "It's not that. He's struggling with our financial situation and the collapse of Optimal. Wyatt is so depressed he can't muster the energy to cope with even the simplest things."

Lee propped his chin on one hand. "I see." He prodded the pen another inch. "These things take time. Your husband has gone through traumas that would destroy most men. However, I imagine he's encouraged with your success in selling things from the estate."

"He doesn't seem to be."

"That's odd. Why?"

"This is only a guess, but Wyatt's very traditional and takes pride in caring for his family. The idea that I'm the breadwinner crushes him. I have a job; he doesn't. I inherited some money; He hung a massive mortgage on our house and then lost everything. He also agonizes over the fact that he squandered the investments of two good friends because of his perceived stupidity."

Lee took a deep breath. "I can understand."

"There's more to it than money. Wyatt isn't just another engineer; he is passionately immersed in his craft. I have seen his ecstasy as he designs aircraft parts and the excitement when he 'conjures'—his word—new concepts. Can you imagine what he thought when his technical acumen failed to bring Optimal success? It's as if his heart had been torn out."

"Perhaps he'll come to realize today's business environment made the creation of a new endeavor nearly impossible. It wasn't so much his shortcomings as ghastly restrictive Federal regulations that caused Optimal's failure. Almost daily, our bank receives new directives to set aside additional funds so we can make risky mortgages to unqualified homebuyers. The increasing default rate prompts the government to mandate bigger reserves, which freezes out businesses like Optimal. Banks are chasing their own tails. It wasn't Wyatt's fault; it's Big Brother. Your husband is a talented man, so remind him that I'm confident things will work out for the best."

"I'll do that," Lauren replied. She eased back in the chair and closed her eyes for a moment. Comforted, she breathed deeply, immersed in Lee's assurances.

"Here are the papers, Mr. Wong," said the clerk, laying a small bundle of papers on the desk.

As Lee perused the forms, Lauren reflected on his comments and took solace in his sympathy. The banker, she decided, had a knack for shining a light into the dark corners of the Morgan dilemma. The tenseness in her shoulders diminished and a warm sensation filled her. Lee knew Wyatt would be all right and his affirmation bolstered her own optimism. *Lee is a nice man. I think I'm actually quite fond of him.*

"Everything is in order. Sign here and here," Lee said, indicating with his pen. "Here is a book of temporary checks to use until we print the official ones."

Lee smiled as he gathered the papers and verified Lauren's endorsement. "That's that," he said, sliding the bundle into a folder. "The funds will be available by morning...I'll see to it."

"I can't thank you enough, Lee, not only for your financial support, but also for listening. I'm a bit sheepish about burdening you with my troubles."

"My honor. Maybe next time, if we have a moment, we can have tea together. There's a quaint spot right across the street. I think you'd like it there."

Chapter 11

Wyatt had thrashed through another sleepless night, his skittering mind dueling with visions that bounced from imaginary job interviews to self-flagellation about his lethargy. Finally, at five in the morning, he crept from bed, donned his sweats and retrieved the newspaper from the driveway. After making a pot of coffee, Wyatt hunkered in his chair where the light of the floor lamp battled the Sunday pre-dawn gloom.

He sighed, breathing in the velvet silence of the house, disturbed only by the soft rumbling of a distant truck working its way through its gears. He flipped open the paper and saw the headline:

Inflation Roars

He clenched his jaw. Every day brought more news of a collapsing economy. The constant deluge of bad tidings did little to bring the comfort of callousness, but aggravated his nagging skepticism.

Desperate, he turned to the help-wanted ads. As usual,

the Sunday classifieds were sparse and he scanned the page: Elder-Care Attendant—$9.50 per hour; City Bus Drivers—excellent insurance and pension; Government Auditors—overtime guaranteed; Telemarketers—no selling required. Wyatt expected more, but when he turned the page, there were only used car ads. *That's it? No engineers? No machinists? Has the country's industrial might deteriorated into auditors and telemarketers? What the hell is going on?*

He tossed the paper aside, picked up his mug and tiptoed down the hall, pausing to peek at a slumbering Timmie. In his backroom office, he switched on the computer and clicked on email, hoping to see a reply or two from the headhunters he'd contacted. Then he checked Monster, CareerBuilder and Craigslist where he had responded to a few relevant ads, but there were no replies. He felt stymied.

Wyatt had submitted the résumés a week ago after he and Lauren had the big fight about job-hunting—more specifically—no job-hunting. The disastrous scene had left him shaken and ashamed. He had tried to explain his dread of the search and interviews, but decided he didn't understand anything himself. Although weary of blaming "The Alien," he'd continued to languish in apathy. But Lauren's verbal assault, on par with a destroyer's five-inch salvo, jarred him into action. She had stood over his shoulder as he updated his résumé and, after a series of revisions, told him to post it on the web. Humbled, Wyatt sent it out that very night.

He shook his head at the memory and squirmed in his living room chair. Outside the window, the ink of night had begun to fade and chirping birds sang in harmony with the humming refrigerator. The coffee, now tepid, soothed Wyatt's throat as he took a sip. He rocked back in his recliner and began to think.

I've got to get in gear.

Wyatt figured he was like a heroin addict going through withdrawal...except it wasn't heroin, it was calculus. He chuckled silently at the comparison: calculus and smack, but it was true. The words to an old song came to him, something about "the wind beneath your wings," and he realized that engineering kept him aloft, nurtured him and brought meaning to his life. Without his craft, he was naked and helpless. The events of the past months had blown him like a brittle leaf across the days of winter leaving him broken and lost in the gutter. Wyatt remembered when a challenging design problem captured his mind and fresh ideas thundered through his fingers into the computer. He transformed rudimentary concepts into elegant hardware that kept aircraft flying at 31,000 feet where the sky was deep blue and clouds, far below, shown puffy white. Images of days filled with excitement, joy and achievement danced in his head. He hungered to return to those times.

I've got to get in gear.

A touch of old-time eagerness nudged him and he cast about, seeking a plan, needing concrete action. He glanced at his watch: 6:15. The first sunbeams lanced through the window, making the lamplight look anemic. Suddenly, he felt a broad grin, fostered by a bold idea, tug at his cheek.

It's nine-fifteen in Massachusetts. I have to have a job, even if it's on the other side of the country.

He lurched from his chair, grabbed his mug and scurried down the hall to his office, taking care not to awaken Lauren or Timmie. He thumbed through his old business card file until he found: "Eduardo Morales, Lead Engineer, AirEnvironment Systems." Wyatt eased the office door shut and dialed.

Morales picked up on the second ring and said, "Hello; Ed here."

"Good morning, Ed. It's Wyatt Morgan. Hope I didn't wake you."

"Wyatt! Mi amigo! It's great to hear from you. What's up?"

Wyatt didn't know where to begin. Should he just blurt out, "I need a job" or bore his friend with a litany of troubles? Small talk to grease the skids? He decided on the last.

"It's been a while, hasn't it?" Wyatt said. "Guess it was last September when we did the flight tests on the pressurization system at Maddox Aircraft."

"Right. I think we talked on the phone after that, though."

Wyatt remembered the call. Ed had phoned to say a Maddox 750 had caught fire, and the FAA had grounded all planes of that model, including their test plane. That had been the torpedo that sank their ship—when Optimal slipped beneath the waves.

"Yeah, you're right." Wyatt shifted his weight and took a quick sip of coffee. "How are things with you? AirEnvironment hangin' tough?"

"Are you nuts?" Ed exclaimed with an incredulous tone in his voice. "You read the papers. Business is on the skids. Cessna, Maddox, Raytheon are all cutting way back. We've had our share of layoffs—maybe twenty percent of the overhead people like accounting and sales. We've had plenty of cuts in Engineering, too."

"I might have guessed."

"What have you been doing, Wyatt? We haven't been in touch since the fire, so I figured Optimal is still on its knees. Any news?"

Wyatt closed his eyes and tried to control his breathing. "Nothing good. Some fool car accessory company stole my patent. Dynamag it's called." He took another quick swallow of coffee. "Oh, we have a lawyer with a hyper-thyroid digging into the mess; says he's uncovered irregularities. I'm not holding my breath, though. Looks like I'm stranded on a reef. It's simple. Optimal is a one-horse company. If this Dynamag hangs on to my patent, I lose pressurization. The company is gone. I've no resources to develop other products—there's no way to start over."

"Things could get grim for sure," Ed said. "My company knows about Dynamag. They've assigned the project to me and I've been into their factory to investigate their pressurization system—it's a dead ringer for yours. The company doesn't seem credible, being an automotive firm, but they have very low prices...tempting. Our management is in serious negotiations with them. Odd you mentioned a patent lawyer...Dynamag was bragging on their patent. Is that the one you say they stole?"

"You got it. And no wonder their prices are low, I've done all the engineering for them! Damn thieves."

"Yeah, you and Madison did a bunch of fine design work. By the way, how is Madison?"

Wyatt gulped. "We're no longer associated with her. I don't know what she's doing now-a-days."

Ed laughed. "Too bad. She's drop-dead gorgeous. Smart, too."

Wyatt tried to conjure a snappy comeback, but the words clogged his mouth.

"Hello? You there?"

"I'm here." Anxiety prodded Wyatt; he had to get a job. Clearing his throat, he said, "I'm in big financial trouble, Ed. If I don't find a position soon I could lose my house. The real reason I'm calling is to see if there are any openings at AirEnvironment. I'll take anything: engineer, draftsman, even Q.C."

Silence hung like fog over the Golden Gate Bridge. "As I said," Ed finally murmured, "we're laying off. I'll be lucky to keep *my* job. You're the best engineer I know, but there are no opportunities at all. Sorry."

"Figured."

"But there may be a glimmer of hope," Ed continued. "Gossip has it that Washington may release a big contract to Maddox for a surveillance version of one of their executive jets. I'm also hearing rumblings of possible civilian orders coming out of China and India. If they materialize, we'll get busy; it's possible I'd need a good pressurization man to oversee Dynamag's qualification tests and production."

Wyatt gritted his teeth. "I'm plenty intimate with Dynamag's design." His eyes welled up thinking of the humiliation of working with Ed on Optimal's system and sending profits to that thug in New Jersey.

"Do me a favor," Ed said, "and keep in touch. Let me know if anything significant develops regarding your patent guy. That could impact our decision-making here."

"Will do. Thanks."

Wyatt slowly lowered the phone into its cradle and

stared at the wall. Through the door, he heard a toilet flush. *Sums up THAT conversation.*

At breakfast, he told Lauren about the phone call with Ed. He'd come away dejected, but Lauren, pleased he'd tried, gave him a warm squeeze and a lingering kiss. She also pointed out that something might develop with the pending government contract.

Lauren began clearing the table. "Why not touch base with Brian Simmons at SAC?" she suggested. "He loved your work."

"That was two years ago," Wyatt countered.

"So?"

Wyatt had no answer to that, so he finished his cereal and retreated to his office to think it over. Perched on the uncomfortable folding chair, he crossed his arms.

I've got to get in gear.

He pondered for a while, sorting through options, then decided.

Wyatt found his wife in the kitchen, where he said with a crooked grin, "Okay, I'll call Brian right away." She rewarded him with another hug.

The next afternoon, Wyatt jiggled his foot as he waited in the sparse lobby of Simmons Aviation Components, his old employer. The receptionist's desk, once the domain of Jennifer, a young woman with a ready smile, was vacant and a fine sheen of dust coated the desk pad and telephone. The carpet needed vacuuming and dated magazines were scatted haphazardly across a low table.

A dower expression distorted Brian Simmons' face as he trudged across the room. Wyatt's old boss looked haggard and wan as he offered a limp hand. "Been a while."

They walked down an echoing aisle alongside rows of empty cubicles into Brian's office. His desk was layered with musty looking stacks of paper and an empty Coke can lurked on a corner. As Wyatt took his seat, he noticed the upholstery was stained and a seam had come unraveled.

Brian plopped into his chair, his unruly hair looking like a dandelion blossom. "Bernie's kept me posted on your pressurization business, Wyatt. I knew all along it would never work out. You should have listened to me."

This was not the way Wyatt wanted to start the conversation. He had come to SAC, hat in hand, to beg for his old position, not to listen to a lecture about his failed company. He stifled an urge to stalk out and shrugged. "You're right, of course, but I had to give it a try."

Brian squinted, his puffy eyes nearly disappearing. "I suppose you're here to get your job back, right?"

"I was hoping."

"You saw the office. Just three people left. I'm sure Bernie told you the shop is down to just two guys. The place is so empty that if we all died, a vulture would starve. I spend all my time scratching for business, but it's all gone to China." Spittle collected at the corners of his mouth as he rambled on in an agitated voice. "I've given up my salary… been living off savings, just trying to meet payroll." Brian lifted a sheet of paper from his desk and waved it under Wyatt's nose. "If the backlog continues to shrink, I'll be out of business by yearend." Brian flung the sheet onto his desk. "Wouldn't that be a nice Christmas present for everyone?"

"I didn't realize," Wyatt whispered.

Bernie had told him that SAC was cutting back, but hadn't painted such a bleak picture. But now, having already taken a pay cut and had his medical insurance canceled, Bernie could be on the streets in a few months. What will happen, Wyatt wondered, to a sixty-something manufacturing guy in a world of nail salons and burger joints? Wyatt's own situation by comparison, wasn't so dire, but the realization wasn't comforting.

"SAC missed a big opportunity," Brian grumbled, his eyes narrowing. "A few months after you bailed out, we snagged a big Request for Proposal on a complex actuator system for the landing gear doors on a new Raytheon jet. Trouble was, there wasn't anyone left in Engineering that could handle the work. We had to no-bid a multi-million dollar job. There's no doubt you would have come up with a winning design, but you had to chase a crappy pressurization system. We'd be doing okay if we had that contract."

Wyatt crossed his arms and tried to shut out the thoughts swirling in his mind. What Brian said might be true. Although Wyatt wasn't familiar with the details of the R.F.P., he was a masterful actuator designer. He knew gear-door geometry could get complex, but he'd proven his skills on a half-dozen earlier projects. For him, complexity was fun, not an obstacle. The fact was, he might have bagged the job and today SAC would be in a stronger position. He thought of Bernie and guilt reignited his depression.

"So there you are, Mr. Morgan," Brian fumed. "You got a bug up your ass and abandoned your department, me and everyone else."

Wyatt's eyes dropped to his hands clasped on his lap. "Sorry." He rose, tipped his head to his old boss and left the office. *Thank God Bernie's furloughed today; I don't think I could talk to him right now.*

Chapter 12

There's his car. Madison parked her Miata next to a tired looking Ford with license plates reading "STRIVE1." She glanced around looking for Wyatt, and not seeing him, twisted the rearview mirror to inspect her reflection. Peeking out every few seconds, she freshened her lipstick and ran fingers through her hair, making sure a strand fell across one eye, giving her a sultry look.

She'd known the location of SAC and driving there was the simple part. What worried Madison was the timing—she had to arrive when Wyatt was inside the building. If she were early, Wyatt would see her when he arrived and flee. If late…well, she'd miss him altogether. Either way, she'd lose her last chance to connect with him.

Over the past couple of months, Madison had called Bernie from time to time to inquire about Wyatt. Always reluctant to engage in casual chatter, Bernie was nevertheless polite. Yesterday, when Madison was fishing for information, Bernie had mentioned that Wyatt was going to SAC to look for work the next morning and when she prodded him, he said, "Around nine." Apparently realizing he'd said too much, he clammed up, but that was all Madison needed.

With the Miata's top down, Madison lounged in the early March sunlight. Warm in the crisp morning air, she recalled her sleepless night filled with excitement of seeing Wyatt once more. The scene she'd mentally rehearsed promised a chummy—but not too chummy—greeting followed by small talk about Wyatt's attempts to find work and the state of the economy. Then she'd move on to fond remembrances of their "mind-melds" while designing the pressurization system, the thrill of discovery and the complimentary nature of their technical skills. In this way, she planned to renew their unique bond forged in the sciences, thus denigrating Lauren.

Lauren—what a bitch. Madison clenched her jaw recalling their explosive fight and Lauren's stinging slap.

It had been just before Christmas when Madison had gone to Wyatt's place the night he'd disappeared. She'd told Lauren about the blossoming relationship she had with Wyatt and took pleasure to see Lauren's anguished face when she bragged that she'd slept with her husband. Maybe it had only been once, but Madison foresaw many, many more nights of passion. Lauren would be reduced to sterile spinsterhood while Wyatt would embrace a new life with the only woman who could understand him.

Madison's thoughts broke off when she saw Wyatt plodding toward his car, his head sunken between his shoulders and gaze on the ground. She snatched a last quick glance at her reflection in the rearview mirror and stepped from her car. "Hi, Wyatt; it's nice to see you again."

Wyatt froze, his head jerking erect. "Madison! What the hell?"

"That's no way to greet a friend and lover." She took a step closer to him. "How about a little hug?"

Wyatt recoiled and thrust out his hand like a halfback's stiff-arm. "What are you doing here? How did you know where to find me?"

"Why, I came to see you. Bernie and I were talking yesterday and he mentioned you'd be here trying to get your old job back. Did you?"

"Bernie told you?" Wyatt grimaced, a cloud settling over his face. "Damn."

Wyatt's surely attitude intimidated Madison and she bristled. Anxiously, she summoned her confidence and said, "Any luck at SAC?"

"No."

Madison shook her head, her mahogany hair settling over one eye. *He looks like he's talking to a scorpion.* With a sultry movement, she struck a sexy pose, imitating a typical TV starlet. "Too bad. Jobs are impossible to come by. I've been looking all over, but there's nothing. We're a pair for sure."

"No, we're not."

"We don't have to stand in the parking lot to catch up on the news. There's a nice coffee shop in the next block. Let's get you a caffeine fix."

"You have to understand, Madison, we're done with all this. I'm not having coffee with you or anything else. Now if you'll excuse me…"

Frantic, Madison scrambled for words. Just seeing Wyatt buoyed her love and she felt her face flush. Impassioned, she stammered, "No! No." Her mind flailed around, trying to grasp ways to hang on to him. "If nothing else," she blurted, "we have a business matter to settle. Our business agreement says I'm a partner in Optimal and that includes disposal of all assets. I'm entitled to my share."

"I haven't given it any thought." Wyatt glared at Madison and clamped his arms across his chest. "Optimal is going nowhere and has nothing of value. No need to worry about that."

Madison shrugged. "Who knows what the future will bring? Neither of us does. By the way, I lied about job hunting. I have a prospect, a good one working for an outfit called Dynamag, but it's in New Jersey. But I can't work all the way across the country—I belong at your side."

Wyatt's face turned red with rage. "No way. That's the idiot who stole my patent! He's a vulture feeding on my ideas and my work. I can't believe you're talking with that scum."

Desperate words rushed from Madison's mouth. "You may be right, of course, but we don't have any *real* proof he stole our patent. It's possible his engineers independently developed a system like ours—we just don't know for sure." She took another small step toward him. "Listen, I have an idea. Forget New Jersey; let's set up a small consulting company to work with aerospace manufacturers. Just you and me. We wouldn't need patents or bags of money; just hang out a shingle. We have a fantastic reputation in the industry; I bet it would be easy to find work. I've thought this over and it could be successful; I know it."

"Are you nuts? It's insane to think I'd consider reconnecting with you to start another company."

"But Wyatt, think of what we did. Together we invented the best pressurization system going. That means something."

"I'll admit that when it comes to engineering, we accomplished some incredible things."

"Exactly!"

Wyatt wagged his finger. "Hold on. Now I'm talking family. These last two months have opened doors for me. Since I was a kid, I had a fire in my gut about engineering and it devoured my life. Now, I've begun to understand my fanaticism for science ruled out important parts of living. I'm seeing new things, profound things, and those revolve around Lauren and Timmie. There was a time when you were an important part of my life, but when your zeal for science turned into lust for me—when you seduced me— any possible relationship between us vanished. There will be no negotiation on this."

Grasping the door handle on his car, Wyatt began to open it, but paused and turned. "I don't want to see you again. I'm going home to Lauren where I belong."

Furious, blind anger conquered any pretense of Madison's civility. "Lauren?" she shrieked. "That lump of Pablum doesn't know the slightest thing about you. *I'm* the one who understands your passions. *I'm* the one who can help fulfill your dreams." She gestured wildly. "Lauren is a loser, lost in her world of mediocrity. Do you know what she did the night you got drunk and disappeared? She slapped me and threw me out. I was there to help find you, to bring you back home. A lot of good Lauren did! See what happened to you?"

"Madison, that's enough."

Madison's feral outburst abruptly collapsed. She felt weak and hung her head, a tear trickling down a cheek. "I'm sorry. It's just that I love you so much. I need to be near you, to talk with you. I hated pestering Bernie, but I had to get closer to you, somehow. Don't blame him for helping me; I was the one who badgered him. Okay?"

As if he didn't hear, Wyatt yanked his car door open and stepped inside. The engine rumbled to life and Wyatt put the car in gear.

No. No. No. He can't. Not like this. Madison sobbed as she watched the car approach the corner, the turn signal blurred by cascading tears that wetted her lips and chin. The last she saw was Wyatt's license plate: STRIVE1.

Chapter 13

Wyatt was surprised when Lauren told him that Mike had a job waiting for him, now that he'd recovered. All last week she'd hounded him to join Mike and work at Precision Tool, even part time. So yesterday, in the interest of family harmony, Wyatt finally capitulated and phoned. It felt good when Mike boomed, "Want to work? Hell, yes! Get your ass over here."

The abrupt change in his mind-set startled Wyatt. He didn't have to grovel before a cynical Human Resource lady; he didn't have to explain Optimal's demise; he didn't have to brag about his skills and how they'd fit into a strange company. "Hell, yes," Mike had bellowed. He'd be working again.

Wyatt strode into the lobby of Precision, bubbling with the enthusiasm of a teenager. Like a starving bum gobbling a savory steak, Wyatt hoped his hunger for engineering would be slaked by day's end. He set down his briefcase and looked for the receptionist, but the forlorn desk was deserted. Instead, he found a buzzer, which he pressed.

While waiting for someone to show up, Wyatt wondered what he'd be doing. He knew Mike didn't have any proprietary products and no plans to come up with any, so product development was out. Perhaps he could design tooling, analyze machine sequences or review inspection techniques. It really didn't matter; he'd crank handles on lathes or mills if that's what Mike needed.

"Look at this," Mike hollered, walking into the small room, "I've got the best fuckin' engineer in the whole world sitting in my lobby!" He grabbed Wyatt's hand and pumped it until it ached. "Come on back; let's get you going."

As Wyatt settled into the well-worn chrome and Naugahyde chairs, he looked around Mike's office. It hadn't changed much; Mike still had his scarred, wooden desk awash with blueprints and metal parts; even the broken milling cutter still reigned as a paperweight. On the near wall, gray metal shelves, burdened with even more machined parts, sagged under their weight, making the office look more like an auto repair shop than a sophisticated aerospace house. In contrast, the elegant glass display case on the far wall still presided over the littered office, its sparkling clean panes showing off glistening titanium parts for the Mars *Curiosity* rover, Mike's pride. The air had the smell of cutting oil and Wyatt inhaled deeply, relishing the aroma.

"Tell me what's going on," prompted Wyatt.

Mike shook his head. "You won't fucking believe the mess in this industry. I know you've heard that environmentalists are bitching about carbon dioxide from jet engines, so big companies are trying to placate the public and avoid EPA fines by selling off their executive aircraft to places like Brazil. Of course overall world emissions aren't reduced by that maneuver. Nevertheless, it makes the CEO's look responsible— politically correct. Guess what that does to airplane sales?"

"Kills it. Anyone can read the trade magazines to see how serious it is," Wyatt said, shifting his burly body in the chair.

Mike stroked his huge mustache and lit a cigarette. "Hell, even the military side of business is taking it in the shorts. First there was the sequester and now they're dumping all the defense money into free birth control pills and expensive drugs for diabetics who can't figure out that obesity is bad. Hell, I can't keep up with the government bullshit. Washington is too busy buying food stamps and subsidizing housing to defend our country. With the defense cutbacks, the Taliban must be licking their chops. Typical of Washington inconsistency, the Pentagon is considering a new surveillance jet—a modified Maddox executive plane. That's the only hope for Precision Tool, but the Pentagon can't get off the fucking pot."

"Yeah, the newspapers are full of it," Wyatt said. "Say, I thought you quit smoking."

"Shee-it. A man has to have one vice," Mike said with a weak smile. "There's no time and certainly no money to chase women. Even the cost of booze is rising like a fart in a bathtub. I gotta have something to calm the ol' nerves."

Wyatt shrugged. "It's your health. By the way, I read an article in the Burbank Leader saying you've had layoffs. Bad?"

"Fuckin' A." Mike shoved the pack of cigarettes back into his cutting oil spattered plaid shirt. I'm down a third and if I don't land more work, there will be more cutbacks. My customers scramble to save money and what do they do? They pull their machine work inside to try to keep their people employed or send it overseas where labor is cheap." With a wry grin, Mike said, "I'm so desperate I've put my own sister to work as a buyer and stockroom clerk. I guess that's a hint why no woman ever considered marrying me."

A frown creased Wyatt's face. *It's the same as SAC. There's no work anywhere.* A tight knot began to form in his stomach as he realized the gravity of Mike's situation, which paralleled his own money troubles. Wyatt knew his problems were microscopic compared to Mike trying to support a staff of a hundred or so.

Wyatt set aside his self-pity. "I'm sure your sister will be a big help. Just wondering—how's your cash flow?"

"Ha!" Mike growled. "What cash flow? At least I didn't have any debts until I floated that loan to fund Optimal. I'm getting behind on those payments, but I have to pay the guys that sell me steel and cutting tools first, you know?"

Wyatt rubbed his chin, digesting Mike's words. He'd hoped to work with Mike and tackle tough problems, work out solutions and re-engage in his engineering passion. But he realized this was a wild fantasy and a folly to expect a wage. The bleak business environment had a chokehold on Precision. They were powerless. Innovation couldn't carry the day. Hard work would yield no benefits. Lady Luck frolicked in Washington, not in the bowels of limping Burbank machine shops. Wyatt shuddered. "You're in no position to hire me. This is crazy."

Mike looked at Wyatt. "Don't be so depressed, my friend. As long as we're breathing, there's hope."

Bluster can't fix anything either, Wyatt grumbled to himself. What to do? How could he help his friend? In silence, he slouched further into his chair, thinking. Suddenly, with a smile and a sense of purpose, Wyatt straightened up and leaned toward Mike. "Okay, my friend, here's the deal. I'll work for nothing—no pay. It doesn't matter what you have me do: haul chips, run errands, deburr parts—anything. I've been moping around the house every day; doing nothing. My job search keeps hitting dead ends. What good is that to anybody? Lauren has already arranged for our neighbor to pick up my daughter at school, so I'm available. At least I'd have something to do besides grump around. I need to raise steam in my life and get underway. The brain needs exercise. Just last night I was piddling around and came up with an idea for a four-degree-of-freedom holding fixture—pneumatically operated clamps. I have a few other ideas, too."

"Hell, Wyatt," Mike said. "I can't impose on you. If you come to work, you'll get paid. Not much, but whatever I can manage."

"Nope. Look at it this way; this is how I pay you back. You jumped in and sank a bundle into Optimal. It's the least I can do." Wyatt leaned back and thought: *Well, at least I'll stay busy. A good dose of science and calculus might help me set my head on square. Lack of money will have to wait.*

Mike stubbed out a cigarette, his eyes squinting in the smoke. "Suit yourself. I could sure use the fucking help. Tell you what… first you mail a kilo of anthrax to Washington."

"Now that you mention Washington, have you been following that Libertarian guy? Bellington?"

Mike lit another cigarette. "Damn right. There was a

blurb on him on the web a few days back. Did you know he goes by Frank?"

"Yeah. His real name is Ernest J. Bellington, but his campaign slogan is 'Just call me Frank, because that's what I am.' Catchy, I think."

"Sure is," Mike said, taking a deep drag on the cigarette. "He's a retired Army general who started his own communications company five years ago. Guess it's booming. They sell equipment and software to the security and military sectors. With the political turmoil around the globe, he's picked a growing market for sure."

"Kinda figures; coming out of the Army, he probably has a solid understanding of that market."

"I'll bet. Bellington already has endorsements of a number of big name CEOs and it's still eight months until the general election," Mike said. "He's running on a pro-business platform; says he'll get rid of corporate income taxes for a start."

Wyatt laughed. "How can he do that? The voters want more business taxes, not less."

"Bellington makes a point that businesses don't pay taxes, they just collect them. If taxes go up, they just pass along the cost by raising prices."

"He's right. If Joe redneck hasn't figured that out, he'll end up paying the tab. Politicians have brainwashed the voters to think big business is the villain. It's a slick scheme because people flock to the voting booths to keep reelecting the perps."

Mike slapped the tabletop. "Imagine what could happen to our country's exports if corporate taxes were eliminated. Fuckin' skyrocket, that's what. The Feds tax my profits at 39% and California dings me for another eight. If government cut those out, I'd have a huge jump on foreign competition." Mike stood and paced, looking excited. "Wanna bring jobs back to the U.S.? Flush our goddamn corporate taxes!"

Wyatt scowled. "The problem is there's about a hundred and thirty million voters and most want "greedy businesses" to carry the load. Bellington might have CEOs on his side, but they number just a few hundred. Voters will go with whoever promises the most free goodies."

"Well, those assholes had better get their fucking minds around the real world. Bellington has a fantastic track record and innovative ideas. Want more recession? Keep doing what we're doing. Want prosperity? Make changes…big changes."

"We have to elect Bellington first," Wyatt said. "But I'm afraid there's no way."

Mike sat, put his hands behind his head and kicked his feet up on his desk. "Guess you're right, but resignation isn't in my blood." Time crept as they brooded in the sullen silence until Mike jumped up, saying, "Enough of this bullshitting. Let's put you to work. I need you to design a new holding fixture for my machine center. It's one complicated fucker. Suppose that idea you mentioned would be the deal?"

Chapter 14

Eric Magana, sitting at his massive mahogany desk, hung up the phone and rubbed his hands in satisfaction, his diamond pinky ring flashing in the light.

Wayne Turnbull, one of his key connections in Washington, had just told him that funding for the new surveillance jet would be approved within 48 hours. Turnbull was an aide to a senator on the Appropriations Committee and had always been a reliable source of information. And no wonder; Eric had flown Turnbull to Bermuda for junkets masquerading as business trips, set him up with hot chicks and arranged for an expensive resort home in the Poconos for weekend soirées. Turnbull's inflated ego, couched in conceit and ravenous sexual cravings, had resulted in bundles of money for Dynamag. *Time for another favor—perhaps a case of expensive scotch or a weekend in the Bahamas.*

Rubin Berkowitz walked into the office, interrupting Eric's thoughts. He clutched a laptop and sat in a chair near the carved antique coffee table in the center of the spacious office. "What's with this panic meeting? I was in the middle of a conference call with our powder metallurgy vendor."

"Chill out, Rubin. This is way more important than a piddly supplier. Where are Chris and Ryan?"

"They're on the way," Rubin assured Eric.

Moments later, the two other engineers hustled in and settled into chairs alongside Rubin.

Eric rose and set his hands on the immense desktop, fingers splayed. "Okay, guys, I've serious good news. My connections have confirmed that funding for the surveillance jet has been given the go-ahead. Maddox will land the big airplane order in a day or two." He walked around the desk and took a chair at the coffee table. "Last week I convinced AirEnvironment to sign a letter of intent to buy our pressurization system once the government released the job. Because they already supply the entire environmental system on the civil plane, they're wired on the military version." His wide grin radiated pleasure. "This thing is in the bank."

Rubin shook his head, his lined face looking more haggard than usual. "I have to hand it to you, Eric, you get things done. Not only have you locked up AirEnvironment, but you got the FAA and DCMA to sign off our production plans and quality manual. It's a huge jump from general aviation into the military world. I hope we can manage the transition. I'm also worried because they haven't blessed the electronics and software plans."

Eric's eyes glittered as he nodded to his operations manager. "Don't sweat the problems. I'm committed no matter what. It was tough to pull this deal together—pullin' teeth if you know what I mean. Those FAA shits are as rigid as a car bumper. DCMA's even worse."

True. It hadn't been easy. Eric had to call a few markers in Washington and fork out a week in Paris for that sleazy FAA official and his wife. It had been expensive, but that's how business was nowadays: a situation where Eric was comfortable.

"Well, we can thank Chris for putting in fifteen-hour days to write the manual," said Ryan, the engineering manager. "We didn't fully understand how aircraft standards differ so much from automotive specs, not to mention between commercial and military planes. Rubin and I worked right through the weekends knocking out reams of documentation. Bought a bunch of special tooling, too."

"Get used to it because it's just begun," Eric growled. "We're in a combat zone now that Ford and GM have shut down several plants to clear their bulging inventory; over 200 days now. It's no surprise that our shipments have collapsed and nobody knows for how long. We have to assume the worst and that means going balls-out on pressurization."

What Eric would not tell his managers was that Dynamag's cash flow had dwindled to almost zero. He'd be ashamed to admit that he was panicked or that a sense of urgency brought sleepless nights. More and more, the specters of his dead father appeared, screeching, "You're shit, Eric. Fly your buddies to Bermuda and stay there! Stay out of my company!"

Desperate, Eric had pulled all possible strings and bestowed bountiful "favors" to the government officials.

It was time for his own organization to man up. There'd be no pussyfooting around and no delays. Heads would roll if there were any screw-ups. It was time to kick ass.

Eric gave Rubin a stern look, then Chris and Ryan in turn. "Tell me when the goddamn design work will be done and when manufacturing gets a checkered flag. I don't care if we're here until midnight; I need goddamn answers today."

"It's the electronics and software that's holding us up," Chris murmured, his mousy complexion more pale than usual.

"Dammit, I told you I'd take care of that. Stop making excuses!"

Eric didn't notice Chris' downcast eyes and the bulging chords of Rubin's neck as he said, "Let's get cranking on this; flush the bullshit and show me concrete plans."

Holy shit, what a friggin' babe! Eric felt a warm surge in his cheeks and pressure in his shorts as he stood, walked around his desk and introduced himself to Madison. He gestured toward the coffee table and took a seat next to her. Madison's green eyes enraptured him and her lush mahogany hair shimmered in the light. He gestured broadly as he began with small talk, "Glad you found time to visit...enjoyed our talks on the phone...yes, it's cold now, but New Jersey springs are nice."

Madison crossed her legs and bobbed her foot, drawing Eric's glance to the stylish pump, then up her shapely calf to the hemline resting demurely above her knee. "Before we get started, would you like a quick tour of our factory?" Eric suggested.

"Maybe later," Madison said, smiling. "I took a long look at your website which gave me a good sense of your operation. I've been thinking about our last telephone call and I'm curious why an automotive firm became involved in aviation."

Eric had anticipated the question and with a breezy tone said, "I'm sure you've read how the car business has faltered, putting companies like mine in a tough spot. I figure the best strategy is to diversify into other sectors. It's obvious the recent rash of worldwide conflicts will continue to expand, pressuring our government to put down rebellions, fight terrorism and even go to war if necessary. Also, I've been following Washington's rhetoric about increasing spending to juice the economy. They seem very serious which tells me the military business will be a gold mine."

"I see," Madison said, tilting her head. "They've slashed the defense budget, but I've heard they're considering a new program to convert an executive jet into a surveillance craft. If that pans out, you'd be making a smart move."

Feigning modesty, Eric said, "I have a few influential connections that keep me informed about such things. I'm told a deal will be finalized any moment."

"The jump from industrial operations into aerospace will be harrowing," Madison said, "How are you managing that?"

It sounds like she's damned good with the business stuff. Not bad for a piece of tail and a science-bound engineer at that. "Well, as you say, it gets complicated. I hired a good mechanical engineer, an aviation type. He's guiding our technical staff through the FAA and DCMA maze. Just this month, we were able to obtain certification as an aircraft system and parts manufacturer. Even so, there are lots of things to do. We need help with software and stuff like that. That's why I'm talking with you."

Madison nodded, a strand of hair falling across one eye. "I'm astonished you could pass the government's muster on such short notice."

"Oh, we'd been working on it for quite a while…just as a backup. We began development efforts for our new pressurization system two or three years ago. So it's not a last-minute thing." Eric leaned back in his chair, laced his fingers across his stomach and smiled. *A little white lie. Like a Boy Scout, I'm prepared.*

Madison smoothed her fuchsia-colored dress and looked at Eric with squinty eyes. "After we talked on the phone, I dug into the records and learned that Dynamag's design has several special features. Truly an achievement."

Eric wasn't sure he liked Madison's pointed gaze and wondered if her compliment might be sarcastic. Cautiously, he said, "I did a little research about your background, too. You worked for a small start-up, right? Optimal Aviation Systems, wasn't it?"

"Yes."

"Wasn't Optimal in the executive jet business?" Eric said, spreading his arms, palms up, pretending to be unsure.

"Pressurization."

"Oh, that's right. What a coincidence."

"Yes, isn't it?" Madison said. "Dynamag's system could be a clone of Optimal's; they're so similar."

Eric cleared his throat and squirmed in his chair. "Isn't

that odd? I've heard of simultaneous inventions before, but it's never happened to me."

With an edge in her voice, Madison said, "Leibniz and Newton."

"Pardon?"

"Gottfried Leibniz and Isaac Newton invented calculus at the same time."

"Oh. Sure," Eric said waving his hand. He worried the conversation was getting a bit testy, so he sought a diversion. "Like a little coffee or tea?"

"Iced tea would be nice."

Eric summoned Judy who returned shortly with a dewy pitcher of tea and a carafe of coffee. Eric collected himself as he poured the beverages. He couldn't understand why Madison unnerved him. Okay, she was sex in high gear, but he wasn't exactly naive in that department. He knew he'd probably bed her within a few days and the thought restored a sliver of confidence, of dominance. He pictured her legs wrapped around him as he plundered her body and saw himself grabbing a wad of that lovely hair and kissing her brutally.

But his vision was tempered by Madison's penetrating emerald eyes and pointed questions. He knew all about Optimal, the boy engineer and Madison. Not only their patent, but also credit reports, work history and even personal lives. His staff had been very thorough. Eric suspected Madison was aware of Julie Ann and the suit against her, but he hoped his gorgeous applicant hadn't considered a direct link to Dynamag. Even so, Eric felt off balance. *This is not an airhead bitch. Be careful what you say.*

One thing is for sure, I'm saying nothing about Julie Ann and the mess she's in with that damned lawyer in California.

Eric took a deep breath and sipped his coffee. He knew the electronics and software designs were on the critical path and unless the problems were ironed out, the pressurization would fold, dragging Dynamag down. He'd put his human resources staff to work, searching for electrical engineers specialized in avionics and software, but all candidates were duds compared to Madison. She had, after all, direct experience in his pressurization system. He looked at Madison sitting across from him and realized he had no serious option but her. Eric was out on a limb—he had to deliver. After all, he'd boasted to Rubin and Chris that he'd take care of it.

Under the chair, he rubbed the toe of his wing tip shoe on his sock and set his jaw, determined to salvage the project and his company by wooing and winning this green-eyed vixen. First, Eric planned to pump Madison for all the technical details about Optimal's design. He was aware of the laws against industrial espionage, but survival of Dynamag trumped playing by the rules. Besides, he had dynamite lawyers who were able to litigate until the sun burned out.

"Now then," Eric began smoothly, "let's talk about how you can contribute to our organization." He glanced at his watch and said, "Don't worry if we run a little late. I have a standing reservation at my favorite restaurant where we could chat over some bubbly and a filet. Sound okay?"

Chapter 15

He didn't waste any time, Madison thought. She wasn't surprised that Eric offered her a job that night at the restaurant.

Eric had looked supremely comfortable surrounded by the thick carpeted, gold-rimmed china elegance of the restaurant. He'd selected a bottle of very expensive Champagne from the sommelier and assumed an assured air, sitting expansively in the plush chair. To accompany the escargot, Eric had ordered a unique garlic sauce, prepared specially for him by the chef. The exquisite steak was followed by crème brûlée and a glass of forty-year-old Graham Porto. He'd chattered throughout the elegant meal, mostly bragging about Dynamag and his influential friends.

Occasionally, Eric asked what was involved in designing circuit boards or writing code, but his questions seemed offhand as if he wasn't really interested in the answers. But Madison sensed his queries were as targeted as a sniper's bullet and she answered with bravado, hoping to impress him and land a desperately needed job.

Early in the evening, Madison knew Eric had decided to hire her. The salary he proposed was astounding and she wondered if the offer was a hint of panic within Dynamag. Her immediate task would be to design the circuit boards using schematics that Dynamag already possessed. Based on what Art Weinstein had said, Madison was suspicious that the electronics might be the same as Optimal's, but until she saw the actual circuit diagrams, she couldn't know for sure. Besides, the lawyer had no proof that Magana had stolen anything. Her desperation for work, mixed with skillful rationalization, prompted Madison to accept the position on the spot.

Shaking with excitement to be taking her first trip in an executive plane, Madison boarded Eric's private jet early the next morning for her journey back to Burbank for the basics: clothes, a few textbooks and G.G., her cat. At the executive terminal, she was pleased to discover there was no check-in, no lugging baggage through the airport and no security; she felt appreciated and respected.

The flight to Bob Hope Airport was uneventful except for the trappings of the very rich. Eric had arranged for a cabin steward to serve elegant meals and marvelous cocktails. Cradled in the soft hum of the engines and the plush leather seats, Madison stretched out her feet and breathed in the lush ambiance of travel by private jet. The return trip featured gourmet food for G.G. and even a cat-box!

Back from California, Madison began to unpack, hanging several tailored blouses in the motel closet. She unzipped another suitcase, grabbed a handful of panties and bras and stuffed them into a chest of drawers beneath the TV. As she worked, G.G. rubbed against her ankles and she bent to scratch him. With brisk motions, Madison soon had her stylish collection of clothing put away.

A silent chuckle flitted through her mind as she remembered telling Eric about her pet and the need to fly him to New Jersey. When Madison explained that the cat's name, G.G., stood for Galileo Galilei, she was astonished that he'd no idea who Galileo was.

Eric had been emphatic: start right away. *No problem*, Madison had thought. Her simple life-style was unburdened by children, tennis outings or coffee klatches. There was nothing to hold her in California except her lingering love of Wyatt. Still stinging from Wyatt's brusque rejection at SAC, she embraced the opportunity to clear her head in New Jersey.

Madison knew she could get by in the pet-friendly motel room until she had a chance to locate an apartment. She planned to return to Burbank to direct the movers in packing the rest of her things and Eric promised to fly her there and back in his Gulfstream.

It soon became clear that Eric's motivation in hiring her wasn't solely her electrical engineering savvy—he'd started making romantic overtures just a few days after she'd started. One day, around mid-morning, Madison had been working with Ryan, the engineering manager, sorting out space requirements for the electronics when Eric walked in, put his hand on her waist and invited her to lunch.

They'd driven to a quiet Italian restaurant and over glasses of Chianti, Eric slid a velvet covered box across the table. "For you, my Dear. A little present to welcome you to Dynamag."

Inside, Madison found a necklace of baguette diamonds, large enough to be impressive but not ostentatious. "I can't accept this, Eric. It's lovely, but isn't it inappropriate?"

"Don't worry your little head over appearances," he said with a wink. "This is thanks for joining Dynamag—and me." He reached over, took the necklace from the box and fastened it around her neck, his fingers warm and lingering. "I don't know what's prettier, the diamonds or you."

Madison looked down at the dangling necklace, flashing and sparkling in the light. It was stunning. Even though she rarely wore jewelry, Madison admitted it looked classy. Although obviously expensive, it wasn't the value of the diamonds that impressed her; it was the idea that a man would make such an elegant gesture. Her ex-husband figured tickets to the Dodger's game was amorous. And Wyatt? Heck, he never vacated the confines of science. She remembered, however, that it was engineering and design that formed the incredible bond between them. Still, Eric's necklace was *romantic*.

With a weak shrug of her shoulders, Madison smiled. "I don't know what to say."

"Thanks would be fine."

"Okay. Thanks." Madison unfastened the necklace and nestled it in the black velvet case. "I'll save it for special occasions."

Madison nibbled on the lasagna, a habit that maintained her wasp-waisted figure. *He doesn't seem like scum*, she reflected, remembering a conversation with Wyatt. Eric was so smooth and polished; it was easy to wonder if he were putting up a façade. She peeked across the table and admired his robust tan and hard body encased in a flawlessly tailored suit. His perfect smile and clean-shaven, chiseled chin conveyed confidence and power. She couldn't help but notice the glances of other diners who whispered to their partners, "Movie stars?"

Eric took a sip of wine. "You're a great addition to Dynamag, my little Cricket. We're going to make airplane history."

"Cricket?"

"I can't keep calling you Madison; it sounds like I'm talking to an old-time president. Business has taken me to China and Japan many times and they keep crickets as pets; says it brings them luck. I think you'll be very lucky for me." Eric smiled so widely that his bright teeth flashed in the light, a bold contrast to his deep tan.

Later, as Eric drove back to the factory, Madison tuned out his ongoing rambling and thought of Wyatt. Her eyes watered as she recalled the passion that flew between them as they conceived the pressurization system. It wasn't work that joined them; it was living on the edge of ecstasy where their thoughts merged and blended, giving birth to incredible discoveries, thrilling designs and phenomenal breakthroughs. Those times fostered an awe of the creative process and she could understand Thomas Edison, George Westinghouse and Elon Musk and their passion to push back the frontiers of science and electrify the world. Madison turned to the window to hide her scratchy eyes from Eric.

Did the failure of Optimal trigger Wyatt's rejection of my love? Was he convinced the demise of the company resulted from our incompatibility, an inability to solve problems? Did he blame me? Was our identity as a couple bred in Optimal's womb and when the company died, did his love die too?

Back at Dynamag, Madison thanked Eric for the lunch and necklace and went to her office. She tapped the mouse to awaken the computer, but her thoughts returned to California.

A curious thought stirred in her mind. The key to recovering Wyatt's love, she realized, might be the pressurization. *I'll assume for a moment, that the foundation of Dynamag's design is Optimal's. No proof, but suppose.* At Dynamag, she could resurrect the system, bringing life to Wyatt's dream. She guessed the mechanical aspects of his work would be preserved by Dynamag's engineers and she had complete control over both the electronics and software. She could salvage their pressurization. Wyatt would be thrilled. Optimal might be dead, but their collaboration would prosper. A warm feeling enveloped Madison as she envisioned his gratitude and welcoming arms. *It's a long shot, but perhaps...*

March trudged into April and bathed by warming breezes, buds began emerging on the trees. The grungy brown slush that buried curbs and sidewalks all winter long, succumbed to the increasingly insistent sunlight. Madison's days bubbled with excitement as she embraced the design of the printed circuit cards and the challenges of thorny software problems.

It was peculiar, Madison thought, that Eric's angry impatience with Rubin and the schedule crises never shouldered into her office. Rather, Eric made frequent appearances and lunches together became commonplace. "Cricket," he would say, "I have tickets to a Broadway play in New York." Or he'd say, "Cricket, let's go and enjoy a weekend in the Poconos."

Madison always graciously declined his sexual propositions, but was flattered by his devotions. She savored their striking prince/princess appearance, but their relationship seemed shallow without the mental dueling she'd shared with Wyatt. She compared Eric to flat Champagne, intoxicating still, but lacking elegance. While a dark cloud of suspicion lurked in the recesses of her mind concerning Optimal's patent, Madison decided to worry about that later.

"Are you Madison McKenzie?"

Madison looked up from her work and saw a willowy young woman standing beside her desk. From where she sat, the blond looked to be all legs because her skirt hovered somewhere between indecent and pure sin. "Yes. Can I help you?"

"You bet, Sweetie. I came up from Alexandria to spend a few days with Eric, but Judy, his secretary, told me he's in Pontiac doing business today. He either stood me up or forgot. Worse, Judy also said you've been seeing him. Is that true?"

"I'm not sure that's any of your business, Miss…"

The woman thrust out her chin. "The name's Julie

Ann Kelly and you're damn right it's my business. Eric and I have been together for a year and a half and I don't need you messing with my guy."

Madison stood and faced the woman eye-to-eye. The blonde's cheeks were inflamed and little beads of perspiration sparkled on her upper lip. Moreover, her breath smelled of alcohol. Not to be intimidated, Madison crossed her arms and said, "You'll have to speak to Eric about his private life."

Madison frowned as she searched her memory. *Julie Ann? Julie Ann. The name's familiar. Julie Ann Kelly.* Then Madison remembered. Art Weinstein mentioned the name last September when they met in the attorney's office to discuss patent problems. He said she was connected with… Dynamag! And something involving the Patent Office! Her mind churning, she asked, "By any chance are you involved in patent work?"

Unsteady on her feet, Julie Ann shook her finger in Madison's face. "Don't change the subject. Are you dating Eric behind my back?"

"Like I said, you'll have to ask him."

"So you aren't denying it," Julie Ann growled.

Madison shrugged. "*I* knew he was in Pontiac today. Maybe you need to update your social calendar more often." She drew her hair back behind her ear and glared. "Incidentally, I've heard of you. If memory serves, you work for the Patent Office in Washington, right?"

It was obvious to Madison that Julie Ann was drunk, her clenched hands and lips pressed into a thin line, radiating anger. "Yeah, I work in the Patent Office. You've been talking to that smart-ass lawyer, Art Weinstein, haven't you? You know about the deposition, don't you?"

Apparently noticing Madison's confusion, Julie Ann's mouth twisted into a smirk. "Oh? You haven't? Well, let me fill you in on a few things. Your goddamn lawyer will spill everything anyway. The bastard filed a suit and hauled me in to testify; says he's going to ask the Solicitor General, Attorney General—whoever—to dig into things. Indictment he said."

"An indictment? About our patent?" Her head reeling, Madison stammered, "You stole our patent?"

Her eyes flashing, Julie Ann lashed back. "Hell no, Sweetie. I just happened to mention to Eric that my boss, the department head, got excited when he saw Optimal Aviation System's application." She sneered and raced on. "Eric wanted more information, so I helped out. When he decided to pursue things, I doled out a few 'favors' and the examiners suddenly found a bunch of errors in your application, all while Dynamag's paperwork breezed along like shit through a goose."

Seeing Julie Ann was out of control, Madison taunted her. "You copied our application and panned it off as yours, Miss skirt-up-to-your-crotch. You two ripped off three years of my life; plagiarized our innovations and crushed the man I love." Madison jabbed her finger on Julie Ann's chest. "I'm going to see you go to jail, and Eric, too. You're filth!"

Julie Ann's face reddened. "Do you take me for an idiot, telling you this? You have no proof, just a bunch of guys who can't keep their zippers up. You think they're going to come clean so you can get a fool patent? Hell, half of Washington D.C. is in the same boat and nobody ever squeals."

Maybe so, but Weinstein is a crafty old guy. He'll find a way, Madison thought. Hate enveloped her; she wanted to hurt Julie Ann, to make her pay, so she hissed, "You got one thing right; Eric and I *are* an item. Not only is he hot to get into my pants, but I hold the key to the success of his company and he knows it. The pressurization line is doomed without me." She opened her desk drawer and removed a small velvet covered box. Madison flipped the lid open and waved the diamond necklace in front of Julie Ann. "From Eric. Not bad, right? He may have forgotten you were coming to see him this afternoon, but he never forgets *our* dates." Madison snapped the lid shut and dropped the box back into the drawer. "One last thing. I'm sure Eric will implicate you and leave you swinging in the wind. Too bad for you, because the inmates and matrons in jail don't have zippers. I suppose you could always become a dyke."

Tears streaming from her eyes, Julie Ann turned away, then swung around and slapped Madison. "Bitch!"

Madison rubbed her cheek and thought; *I have a way of collecting slaps.*

The moment Julie Ann bolted to her car, Madison gathered her purse and sweater, told the receptionist she'd be leaving for the day and drove to her motel room to think the matter through.

After tossing her things on the cluttered desk, Madison went to the tiny refrigerator, selected a Diet Sprite and propped herself up on the bed, legs crossed. With a meow, the cat leapt up and hunkered against her knee. "Now what, G.G.? Tell Eric to take his job and put it where the moon doesn't shine? Ignore Julie Ann's revelations and stay at Dynamag to bring the pressurization to market? Return to Los Angeles and work with Art to sort out the legal issues?"

Eric *was* scum, just like Wyatt said. How could she continue working at Dynamag? After all, Magana had snatched their designs, ruining Optimal. Bernie and Mike, too. Eric was a world-class dirt-bag for sure.

Then again, if she told Eric what she thought of him and quit, the pressurization would be lost. Without capital, Optimal had no hope, even if they were awarded the patent. All their efforts could evaporate, leaving only the memories of those nights where they'd worked together, their minds sparkling in incredible harmony.

Another thing. Without Eric's job, Madison was strapped—she'd have to think twice before buying a pack of gum. There was enough money for an economy ticket back to Los Angeles where maybe Art could work out a legal settlement with Magana. A long shot for sure, but a worthless idea. No money, no Optimal.

Finishing the last of the Sprite, Madison rose, dropped the empty can in the trash and returned to the bed where G.G. lay curled. The cat nuzzled her hand, purred and rolled over on his back. She rubbed G.G.'s exposed tummy and a heavy pall of worry descended on her mind. How could she decide anything without talking with Wyatt? Her thoughts were a tornado of confusion.

The afternoon shadows crept across the floor and Madison glanced at her watch. *Nearly two in the afternoon in Burbank. I wonder where Wyatt is?* She guessed Lauren would be at work and decided to risk catching Wyatt at home. With a grunt, she twisted to a sitting position on the bed and picked up the telephone from the end table.

"Hello?"

"Hi, Wyatt. It's Madison. Don't hang up; I have important news."

"I don't have anything to say to you."

Madison took a deep breath. "Listen to me. This is momentous. I have information on our patent." She could hear him breathing and waited for a reply.

"What about it?" Wyatt finally said. "Get on with this."

Madison reiterated her conversation with Julie Ann, explaining every detail. "So there it is. I'm not sure if Art is making headway on the lawsuit; do you?"

"I guess he's working it, but anything involving lawyers takes forever."

"That's the problem." Madison's words began to gush. "Magana is pressing hard to get the pressurization into production; dedicating a lot of resources. He wants to ship test systems within a month or two. That will leave us out in the cold and all our work wouldn't be worth an old cassette player. There's only one way out of this mess."

Wyatt didn't respond, so Madison went on. "Suppose I stay at Dynamag and make sure the pressurization stays on track? Nobody here but me has any understanding about the electronics and software. I could keep all our ideas in place—save our pedigree."

"You'd work for that thug?"

"It's the only way to keep the design alive. Do you want to throw away everything? The innovations? Drawings? Calculations?" She waited for a reply, but Wyatt was silent.

"There's one problem, though. I can do the electrical part, but I'm beginning to think Magana's screwing up the mechanics. I'm clueless in that department."

"Where are you going with this?" Wyatt growled.

"I need you here, in Trenton. You're the only one who can sort out the mechanical design. If you and I worked together, our pressurization system would finally be realized." Madison felt elated as she raced on. "If Art can lasso Dynamag while we're putting the finishing touches on the system, we could walk away with everything: the patent, production tooling, a contract with AirEnvironment, the works!"

"You want me to leave Lauren and Timmie and move to New Jersey to prop up a slimy thief?" Wyatt snarled. "Maybe live together? Is that what you're thinking?"

Flinching from his fury, Madison whimpered, "I love you, Wyatt."

"You're out of your fucking mind!"

A dial tone droned as Madison stared at the receiver.

That very night, Madison rolled away from Eric, clutched the blankets around her naked shoulders and sobbed.

Chapter 16

The joyous shrieks of the two young girls hurtled down the hall.

Sharon, her florid face shiny with perspiration, said, "Those kids. It sounds like feeding time at the zoo." She slid a mixing bowl toward Lauren and asked, "Is the frosting smooth enough?"

Lauren reached into the maw of the oven, jabbed the cake with a toothpick and glanced over. "Looks great. See if you can find the sprinkles in the pantry, okay?" As she closed the oven door, Lauren thought, *it's great that Sharon is helping with Timmie's birthday party. Lately I've been dodging a meteor swarm.*

Sharon waddled across the kitchen. "Jenny and Timmie are really excited about the party. Just listening to them makes me want to laugh." Sharon rummaged in the shelves and said, "I sure enjoy kids. Wish I had more, but Father Time has put an end to that. I didn't have Jenny until I was 35 and Jake didn't want any more. Ha! I'm not sure he wanted *any*."

Lauren studied the toothpick, looking for raw batter. "Wyatt and I have considered trying for a little brother for Timmie, but right now our finances are in such shambles I might as well wish for the Hope Diamond. The sad part is Timmie has jumped into adolescence—grown up. There's no kids in the Morgan household any more, just a prepubescent youngster stretching for adulthood. It leaves me with an empty feeling."

Wyatt walked into the room juggling half-used rolls of crepe paper. "I have the dining area all decorated: balloons, streamers and party favors." With a smile, he jammed the depleted rolls into a kitchen drawer. He strolled over to Lauren and gave her a quick hug. "It's still a couple of hours before the mayhem begins; is there anything I can do?"

"My, you seem chipper today," Sharon said. "Did you win the lottery?"

"No such luck," Wyatt chuckled. "Besides, I never play. My collegiate math reminds me of the odds. No sense throwing away money."

With an offhand tone tinged with regret, Sharon said, "My husband blows twenty or thirty dollars a week on Lotto. I wish that were his biggest vice; he'll drop twice that much on beer."

Wyatt grinned. "Jake likes his brew, for sure." He strolled over to the coffee maker and filled his mug. "Actually, I'm in a great mood. I've sent out dozens of on-line job applications and mailed five résumés to companies that advertised in the paper or trade magazines. I even got a nibble or two. Plus, I've been working on a few fixture designs for Mike. It feels good to be busy again, you know?"

Lauren laughed. "If only you'd find the motivation to mow the grass."

Just a week ago, a tide of relief had swept aside her anxieties when Wyatt seemed to blossom, tossing aside his depression. Perhaps working for Mike flip-flopped his outlook. The return to the world of engineering had painted his boyish face with a grin. He scurried home every night with enthusiastic tales about the heat treatment of tool steel, tolerance stack-ups and other indecipherable gibberish that Lauren cherished, but couldn't grasp. They'd re-established their traditional Sunset Ritual and, over glasses of wine, the bond between them flourished. Although Wyatt had resumed his job search with zeal, nothing concrete had appeared, but Lauren, mindful of Wyatt's incredible skills, sensed a breakthrough. Joyful expectations settled in her thoughts like a mallard easing onto a placid pond.

"Wyatt, let's get the plates and silverware on the table," Sharon said. "That should wrap it up."

Over her shoulder, Lauren called out, "Tell Sharon what Art is doing, Honey."

As they laid out the utensils, Wyatt said, "Oh yes. Our lawyer, Art Weinstein, is crankin' on our patent problems. A while back he filed suit against this woman in the Patent Office and brought her in for questioning. He's saying there's enough evidence to ask the Solicitor General and Attorney General to take criminal action against the Patent Office. It won't bring Optimal back to life if we win the case, but it would be a moral victory. It's hard to explain how important this is to me. The design came from here," he said, tapping his temple. "It doesn't belong to anyone else. Engineering is my church and losing the patent is like someone ripping off the collection box—God should strike the thief with lightning!" Wyatt smacked a fist into his open palm. "I sure hope we can shove it right up their... nostrils."

"Well," Sharon said, "it seems to me if a lawyer goes to all that trouble, there must be money somewhere."

Wyatt chuckled. "I think you're right."

Lauren, overhearing the conversation, knew the underpinnings of his cheer. If Art won the case, Wyatt could shed his feelings of ineptitude and shrug off his perceived failures; he could take comfort by blaming an unscrupulous thug.

It's nice to have him back, Lauren mused as she removed the pan from the oven. She savored the aroma of chocolate and set the cake on a rack to cool.

Timmie and Jenny held court over a dozen excited youngsters. The air reverberated with shouts, the thunder of running feet and peals of laughter. The adults huddled by the kitchen counter, like penguins do when fending off a blizzard.

Wyatt wrapped his arm around Lauren's waist and beamed at the pandemonium. "Timmie's queen of the faire," he said. "It's great to see her so happy."

Squeezing Wyatt's hand, Lauren smiled. "She's a child again. These last few months she's been too serious—trying to act grownup all the time. It may sound peculiar, but I miss our little girl. Today, she's back, if only for a little while."

Resembling a chubby kewpie doll, Sharon's wide

smile radiated contentment as she watched her daughter play with the other kids. Off in the living room, Jake, her husband, sat three feet in front of the television, scowling like a cat in a bathtub. "Can you kids knock it off? We've got bases loaded with two out, for Christ's sake." He took a long pull on his beer and scrunched up closer to the screen.

Sharon shook her head and whispered to Lauren, "He doesn't even enjoy baseball, says it's a game for wimps. I guess there's no football on or that boxing—kicking thing."

Sympathy welled within Lauren and she patted Sharon's forearm. Lauren looked at Jake, and cringed at his wild curly hair jutting from his scalp and beer-belly cascading over his belt.

Wyatt rose, ambled over to a cluster of kids and squatted on the floor among them. His laughter drew Lauren's eyes to where he sat, frolicking with the youngsters. This wasn't the old Wyatt, the one consumed by work, but a man of broader horizons and affection. When Wyatt was struggling with depression, he complained that an alien possessed him, but its intrusion had left a joyful legacy. Lauren grinned. *It seems as if my husband needed a kick in the butt—a wake-up call.*

The contrast of Wyatt's happy playfulness with Sharon's comments about Jake troubled Lauren and, anxious to dispel her friend's melancholy, she said, "Let's serve the cake."

That afternoon, as the party wound down, Lauren, ankle deep in ripped wrapping paper and clinging ribbons, trundled crumb-strewn plates back to the kitchen. She saw Wyatt relaxing in his chair, nursing a tepid mug of coffee as he surveyed what he'd dubbed "the calamity." A dreamy looking smile graced his lips and Lauren's heart thumped with love for him.

Sharon and the last of the parents had collected their charges and a soft peace settled in the cluttered room when the doorbell rang. Lauren turned to answer it, but Wyatt, rising from his chair, waved her off. "I'll get it."

After a few moments, he returned, a puzzled looking scowl on his face. "A letter from the mortgage company. I had to sign for it." He slid his finger under the flap and opened it. "Notice of Trustee's Sale? What does this mean?" he asked, handing the letter to his wife.

Lauren took the letter, her eyes darting over the page and swallowed. "This is an eviction notice. They've given us thirty days before the bank puts our house up for auction!"

Stunned, Wyatt uttered, "I thought you'd been making payments."

"Just partial; I've missed the last couple of months though—I had to pay utilities and keep the web service going, now that you're job hunting. We're maxed out on the Visa card, so I had to skip a few payments." A tight knot constricted Lauren's throat as she realized they might lose the house. All at once, the sound of Timmie playing with her birthday gifts grated on her nerves.

The cords on Wyatt's neck bulged. "I thought sales of Liza's stuff had picked up. Bringing in money."

Lauren shrugged. "Emile has sold most of the easy things, but it's tapered off. He's looking at the bigger things such as the Bentley and a few of the paintings, particularly the Dali. He's searching for documentation that the art is authentic—takes time. So there's nothing certain yet."

Wyatt's shoulders slumped and his face sagged, looking dark and pained. "This is crazy. What can we do?"

Lauren waved the papers, shaking them as if the troubling words would fly from the page. "Wait a minute. Here's another sheet." After a quick look, she said, "It's a bulletin explaining a new government program that offers assistance to underwater homeowners, but it says help is limited to socially depressed areas. Here is a list of zip codes they cover." She scanned the page. "Ours isn't here."

"Damned if I'd sponge off the government anyway," Wyatt grumbled. "Screw them." He stalked to his chair and collapsed. "Why didn't you tell me? If I'd known, maybe…"

"I was afraid to mention it, Honey. You were so depressed I thought more bad news would make things even worse. I didn't see how you'd be able to help anyway."

"Gonna lose the house. I never should have hung a mortgage on it." His face twisted in misery and he slapped the coffee table with a bang. "Crap!"

Startled, Timmie jumped.

The next few week's events, like a hot wind tormenting drought-stricken farmers, harassed the Morgans. Lauren's boss told his staff that due to sagging sales figures, all overtime was canceled. Her income whittled, Lauren gave up pork roast and baked chicken in favor of macaroni and canned chili.

A debilitating lethargy smothered Wyatt once more. He'd given up his fruitless job search and sulked in his chair instead. Lauren found herself creeping past her husband, loath to engage him. Timmie, too, dwelt in her room with computer games and television or escaped to Jenny's place next door.

Three weeks after the birthday party, in early May, a speck of encouragement surfaced when Emile sold an Edwardian ring with rubies and small diamonds, worth a thousand dollars. Check in hand, Lauren drove to the mortgage company and endorsed it over to the lending officer. The official, smug behind his desk, admonished her, "We'll delay the auction for another month, but this payment hardly dents your balance. Keep that in mind."

A month later, proceeds from a three-piece nesting cherry-wood table were applied to the mortgage, but the situation remained dire.

All this Lauren was able to deal with, but it was Wyatt who drew her into the abyss. Midnights often found her red-eyed in front of the computer, seeking work for her depressed husband. His helplessness was a burden like weights on her arms and toxins to her mind. She battled the flood of bills—utilities of course, plus the plumber who cleared a sewer clog and credit card charges for Timmie's new shoes. Immobilized by these thoughts, she fought despondency by focusing on her family, her duty as a wife and mother and plodded on.

Ever since they'd received the eviction notice, Lauren had badgered Emile to estimate the Dali's value. At last he'd sent an email indicating its worth "is likely very high," but he needed more time to consult experts in London and Paris. While he employed a local auction house to handle the other items, Emile insisted the Dali to go to Europe, particularly Barcelona and Cadaqués—Dali's hometown— for authentication and appraisal. "Be patient," Emile advised. "Your mother's painting has no documentation making verification difficult. We'll have to do a chemical analysis on tiny flakes of paint, x-ray examinations… patience."

Lauren's own research on the web showed Dali paintings were selling between a few thousand dollars to well over a million. She hoped that "very high" meant salvation.

The fragrant breezes of mid-June brought a two-fold coup. First, Emile found a buyer for the turbo Bentley. As she cradled the check for over twenty thousand dollars in her palm, Lauren refused to question why anyone would pay that kind of money for a twenty-year-old car. Ebullient, she shook Wyatt who was dozing in his chair and waved the check under his nose. Wyatt's face brightened. "Damn! That will get the mortgage company off our backs!" He stood and gave Lauren a crushing hug.

A bubbly tune tickled Lauren's mind as she slipped the check and Emile's note into her purse. She told Wyatt she was going to the bank to deposit the check and would be back soon. She said nothing of Emile's evaluation of the Dali. Not yet. She couldn't bear the thought of another roller-coaster ride on Wyatt's moods if the painting didn't work out.

Buoyed by the contents of her purse and the happy twitter of songbirds, Lauren stepped into the bank and saw Lee Wong at his desk across the room. As she approached, he rose, as always, and buttoned his coat. He fiddled with his cufflinks, saying, "So nice to see you, Mrs. Morgan…Lauren."

As Lauren settled into the chair, the welcoming warmth of Lee's smile soothed her. With a nod, she said, "It's nice to see you, too. Been a while."

The perennial fountain pen crept into Lee's hand and he positioned it on the right edge of his desk blotter. His eyes seemed to twinkle as he said, "Your telephone call indicated you have good news. Most delightful. How can I help?" He leaned toward Lauren, curiosity shining on his face.

"This part," she said, "is simple. I want to deposit this into the new account." Lauren pushed the check across to Lee.

With raised eyebrows, the banker grinned. "This is a handsome sum. You don't want to hold back a little cash?"

"No. But a little advice about paying down my debt would be helpful. Do you mind?"

"My pleasure." In a matter of minutes, they'd decided to pay off most of the mortgage delinquency, and make small payments on the Visa balance and utility bills.

Embarrassed, Lauren felt sheepish because she was as capable as Lee in disbursing the funds and her cheeks flushed with the realization she was being silly. Lee had become a sanctuary for her—a generous, warm-hearted respite from Wyatt's volatile moods and she hungered for his affirmation that she was doing the right things. Lauren looked across the desk at Lee and was surprised with a flood of affection for the stuffy little banker.

Her spirits soaring, Lauren basked in Lee's approval and nurturing compliments. She was giddy as she pulled a copy of Emile's note from the envelope and handed it to Lee. "This is the *big* news. What do you think?"

After a quick glance, Lee pushed back in his chair and read the email line by line. "Did you ever suspect that the painting might be so valuable?"

"I was more hopeful than anything. With the craziness at home, I wasn't able to do more than guess. I'm ignorant about the fine-art market, so I didn't give it much thought."

Lee picked up his fountain pen and rubbed its flank with his thumb. "Is this something you can sell quickly? If the letter is accurate, the proceeds could solve your problems."

"Emile said it might take months just to make sure it's genuine. Once the Dali experts in Barcelona authenticate the painting, he wants it shipped to Sotheby's office in London for appraisals and promotions. Then it gets published in the catalogs prior to auction. It's very involved."

Wong placed his fingers tip-to-tip and closed his eyes. After a moment, he said, "That would be trouble unless you have other income. The bills keep coming, you know. With your limited income, it's possible, even likely, that you'd fall way behind on the mortgage again. Moreover, Optimal will remain stalled until the Dali situation is resolved once and for all."

Lauren nodded. "I know." She sat up straight in the chair and folded her hands on her lap. "I was wondering… is there a way…"

Lee smiled, his eyes glittering. "Say no more. You're wondering if the bank can make a loan against the Dali." He laced his fingers together and set his chin on the resulting cradle. "There's nothing I can do without a formal appraisal, but I'll work with Emile to push the process along—just for you."

"Oh, Lee. Would you?"

Lee glanced at his watch. "It's nearly closing time. Why don't we go have that cup of tea across the way and discuss it?"

Lauren blushed and her breath caught. "That would be very nice."

Once settled into a cozy booth, they ordered tea. Their discussion was supposed to be about expediting an appraisal on the Dali painting, but talk soon turned to easy banter. At first, Lee admitted he was uncomfortable socializing with a Caucasian woman due to his cloistered childhood and he'd twisted his napkin, looking embarrassed.

Lauren, normally engaging, was genuinely interested in Lee's background and family, so to encourage him, she shared a bit of her history, but, for the most part, focused on Wyatt and Timmie. Lee knew, of course, about Lauren's mother, Liza, and the financial meltdown in the Morgan home. Lauren's voice quivered when she spoke of her husband's erratic behavior and sporadic depression. Determined to loosen Lee's tongue, she rejected the sadness seeping into her mind and adopted her normal persona: perky, animated, smiling.

Lee succumbed. "Well," he said, "I was raised in San Francisco's Chinatown by my immigrant family. In high school, I fell in love with a lovely Chinese girl and was engaged for about a year when she threw me over for a Stanford guy. My troubles multiplied when I began questioning my parents' way of life because they were bound up in the rigid old Chinese traditions. So I pulled up stakes and came down to L.A. to go to school. I've been a devoted bachelor ever since."

Time flew as they exchanged pleasantries while laughter romped about their table. Lauren glanced at her watch and dabbed her lips with a napkin. "Lee," she said, "It's getting late and I need to get going, but next week we're having a Fourth-of-July get together. I'd be very pleased if you could join us."

Lee had choked on a swallow of tea and gasped. He'd set the teacup down with a shaking hand and accepted with a nod.

My usually stolid banker looks flustered, she thought.

Chapter 17

Wyatt fumed as he fumbled with a package of sparklers. They were illegal, of course, but the thought of lighting them catered to his sense of justice. The law, banning all fireworks, was simply another instance where government shouldered its way into everyone's lives. Just because some damn fool set a fire with a rocket years ago, the county solved the "problem" by passing yet another piece of legislation. He grinned, anticipating the night's defiant retribution—kids running around in the backyard waving tiny torches of liberty.

In the kitchen, Lauren sorted through yesterday's mail. "Honey, did you see this?" she hollered, waving a thick envelope. "It's from the SBA."

Wyatt set the sparklers down, went to the kitchen and picked up the letter. With a slashing motion, he ripped open the flap and pulled out a bulky pamphlet. "Looks as if the SBA has a new program, called the 'Limitless Opportunity Loans.'" He flipped through the pages, scanning the headings. "I guess somebody in Washington woke up and figured the economy had run aground, so they're going to throw a bunch of money at small businesses. Too bad Optimal is so small it's disappeared. Where was this new deal when I had a promising prototype—before that jackass in New Jersey stole my patent?"

With a wry grin, Lauren said, "New deal? As I recall, there was a New Deal back in the thirties, which you detest. Besides, we didn't have any choices except to apply for an SBA loan, right?"

"You got me there, but that's because the new banking regulations shut down lenders. I was stupid to hang our entire future on those bureaucratic idiots who can't find their butt using either hand."

"My, it's nice to see you so fired up," Lauren said, smiling. "If nothing else, politicians grab your attention. I love it when you're on the soapbox."

"Yeah, right. This mess is as therapeutic as cancer. It's not only us, but I've screwed Mike and Bernie, too. Bet they appreciate that."

With the mention of his friends, Wyatt's mind flew back to last week's phone call with Bernie, who said that Madison had called to say she's back in town...quit Dynamag and was drawing unemployment until she found work. Moreover, she'd inquired about him again.

"Goddammit, Bernie," Wyatt had shouted, "I told you to stop taking her calls."

* * *

Bare footed, Lauren padded across the backyard grass, set out the last folding chair and positioned red, white and blue napkins at each place setting. Everything was coming together nicely, reflecting her efficient nature. Even Wyatt, looking lighthearted, had set the barbeque and sliced the watermelon.

Timmie dashed from kitchen to table, putting out red plastic bowls for the potato salad along with plastic forks saying, "After we're done tonight, I'll wash them so we can use them again." Even Jenny had come early and arranged catsup, mustard and relish in a precise row on the kitchen counter.

Lauren could feel the warm breeze lift wisps of her hair as she scurried across the yard. She'd invited Bernie and Mike to come, but they were tied up today at the annual Precision Tool party. *It would have been nice to have them. Regardless, it's a great day, not too hot.*

Soon, Sharon lumbered in from next door with a Tupperware keeper of her specialty: cherry pie. "I'll put this in the fridge for now," she told Lauren. "How can I help?"

"We're in good shape." With a wave of her hand, Lauren pointed toward Timmie and Wyatt who were mounting red and blue candles into clear glass hurricane lamps. "They've been a team today, just like a two-horse hitch pulling a buggy."

Sharon laughed. "There're sure joined at the hip. Whenever I come over, Timmie is waiting on her dad. I guess that's because they're always home together while you're at work. Yup, they're very close."

Lauren looked at her daughter and husband, their noses nearly touching as they worked. *The father-daughter bond. Inevitable, I suppose, but my work schedule makes it tough for me. A clear case of role-reversal and one I don't care for.*

The afternoon shadows had grown longer when Lauren changed into her favorite bright white Calypso pants with a hint of lace on the flared legs. A collared top boasting a bold print and white sandals completed her transformation.

Sharon, having gone home to freshen up, returned wearing a floral muumuu. Jake trailed behind, scowling. "Gotta beer?"

"Certainly," Lauren replied. "They're in the refrigerator, just help yourself. Pretzels are on the picnic table outside."

As they migrated toward the back yard, the doorbell rang and when Lauren answered she saw Lee Wong wearing very un-banker attire.

"Lee! I wouldn't have recognized you. Jeans and a Hawaiian shirt?" Failing to rein in a rambunctious impulse to tease, she asked, "Did you bring your fountain pen?"

Looking embarrassed, Lee stared at his sparkling white tennis shoes. "My pen is still at home." He shifted his weight foot to foot. "Am I dressed okay?"

"Of course you are. Come in; we're in the back."

Lauren led her guest through the kitchen and into the backyard where the adults had gathered at the weathered wooden picnic table. Looking ill at ease, Lee nodded stiffly and mumbled terse sounding greetings as Lauren introduced him around. Last, she guided him over to Timmie. "Lee, this is my daughter Timshel. Timmie for short."

"Timshel? That's an unusual name," Lee said. "One of my favorite books, Steinbeck's *East of Eden*, talks about a word from the bible—Timshel."

"Lee!" Lauren blurted. "That's where we got her name! It's from an incredible scene where…"

"Where a Chinese servant and his family ponders the translation of a key word in the ancient Hebrew scriptures," Lee interrupted with an immense grin on his face. "His name was Lee, same as me."

"I know," Timmie said. "Mom told me about it; says I have to read the book when I'm older. She calls me Timshel only when she's mad. I like Timmie better." With that, she scampered off with Jennifer to play.

"She's too young to understand the nuances in the novel," Lauren explained to the disappointed looking banker. Anxious to help Lee overcome his obvious nervousness, Lauren prodded Wyatt's ribs saying, "Why don't you and Lee light the charcoal while I get the hot dogs and burgers ready?"

"Why not," Wyatt said, rising from the bench. "Lee, while we're at it, how about bringing me up to speed on the Dali."

Lauren chuckled under her breath as Lee, appearing grateful as a kid on the last day of school, said in his ultra-formal way, "Most certainly," and followed Wyatt to the grill.

Lauren turned to Sharon. "Want to help?"

"You bet." As she struggled to get up, Jake leaned toward them and whispered, "Is that damned chink gonna eat with us? I mean…shit."

Her insides boiling, Lauren thrust her head within inches of Jake's and hissed softly so Lee couldn't hear, "He's Chinese, not a chink. He's our banker and has helped us through some bad times. I'd appreciate it if you gave him the respect he deserves." She jerked her head, beckoning Sharon and strode into the kitchen.

Looking glum, Sharon tagged along. "I'm really sorry, Lauren. He can be such a turkey sometimes. Socially, he's so darned belligerent. Beer, sports and bitchin', that's my husband."

"It's not your fault, okay?" Lauren gave her friend a quick hug and said, "Here, take this plate of patties out to Wyatt."

The late afternoon sun settled behind the house, bathing the yard in shadows. Typical of California, the temperature plummeted, chilling everyone. The two screaming children played tag, weaving in and out between the adults, stopping only to ask if it was dark enough to light the sparklers. Thankfully, Lauren thought, Jake had slinked off to the living room to watch a ball game with his beer, while the rest gathered around the warmth of the dying barbeque and chatted.

With her mouth pulled into a glum looking frown, Sharon told Lauren that the donut shop was shuttering its doors. Without a job, paltry as it was, she moaned about her struggles with family finances.

"We make a fine pair, don't we?" Lauren joked, "Perhaps we can start a business to counsel destitute families."

When Wyatt's vibrant voice carried across the lawn, Lauren and Sharon turned. "I wish I was as confident as you, Lee," Wyatt was saying, "that the Dali will sell. Who, in this economy, would pony up a bunch of cash for a weird painting?"

Sharon walked over and asked with a hopeful tone, "Lee, do you expect the economy will come back?"

"Yeah, Lee…what's your prediction?" Wyatt said.

The banker drew his brows together. "I'm only familiar

with banking, but I think we're in big trouble. I've learned that my firm has united with a number of other banks to lobby Washington to adopt more restraint because there seems to be a movement in Congress to open the fiscal spigot to bolster the economy. Government is getting panicked and is considering more bond sales…adding more debt."

"That's B.S., Lee," Wyatt said. "We're just tossing the bill for our lavish living over to our kids. How can anyone with a speck of sense go along with that?"

Lee nodded. "I've been following several blogs that discuss government's fiscal policy. It's not just the banks, but large industrialists, energy firms and big pharma. They're talking about so-called 'irresponsible politics.'"

"You mean companies are banding together to fight Washington?" Wyatt asked.

"Fight might be too strong a word, but it appears to be shaping up as a cohesive lobbying effort."

Sharon looked downcast. Turning to Lauren, she said, "Well, Jake has a job, at least for now."

"Now that you mentioned politics," Lauren said, "I'll bet my husband will start pontificating about government interference and proselytizing on that Libertarian presidential candidate."

"Go easy on those big words, Dear," Wyatt joked. "You'd never guess, but for the most part, I've been listening. Lee has some interesting views on the economy. But now that you've mentioned it, Bellington and his fellow Libertarians have a lot of good ideas to fix this mess."

"Ah, yes," Lee said. "His name occasionally appears in these blogs. The Libertarians are hands-off advocates and Bellington proposes to eliminate all corporate taxes and chop dozens of regulatory agencies. It seems logical to me."

"Another thing," Wyatt said. "He's advocating a Federal Right to Work law saying workers should have the freedom to choose their own workplace representation or completely reject intermediaries. Imagine what would happen to industry freed of stupid work rules and absurd pensions?"

"Boy, I hope he's not elected," Sharon said. "I need unemployment insurance and might have to apply for food stamps. I always vote Democratic."

"Democrat, Republican—they're the same," Wyatt grumbled. "If you like what you have, keep reelecting the jerks."

"Daddy, it's dark," Timmie interjected. "Why can't we do the fireworks?"

Wyatt looked across the yard. "I guess it's dark enough. Let's do it."

Worn out from the evening's clamor, Lauren shook her head and coaxed her weary feet into the living room. Lee and the neighbors had gone home and Timmie had crawled into bed without complaining about brushing her teeth. Wyatt slouched in his chair nursing his last cup of coffee for the day. To Lauren, the silence was like balm on a sunburn. She sat in the recliner beside her husband and took a deep breath, happy that everyone enjoyed the party.

She was especially pleased that Lee actually relaxed and had engaged everyone, Jake aside. She thought it odd that Timmie seemed entranced by Lee and pestered him with questions on the way banks work, but pouted when she discovered that he was single with no kids.

Lauren had clapped her hands in glee when Timmie presented him with a sputtering sparkler and tugged on his free hand to join her running around the lawn. When Lee complied, she'd been startled by the strange sight of her stuffy banker trotting alongside Timmie, waving a bit of Americana.

She remembered that Lee had lingered as Sharon, Jenny and Jake took their leave. Wyatt had been in the kitchen tidying up when Lee approached her. It wasn't just his eyes, but his whole face twinkled as he gave her a timid hug, "I had a wonderful time. Thanks for inviting me." Her eyes met his and a wordless sensation seemed to pass between them, one of warm acceptance, of connection. She squeezed Lee's shoulders in return.

When Wyatt came in carrying his mug, Lee, with a tiny bow, said, "I'm very grateful for your hospitality. You have a lovely home and family." Lee turned to go and called over his shoulder, "Bellington—let's talk more about him later," and left.

While Lauren sat musing about Lee Wong, Wyatt stirred in his chair. "You know, that straight-laced banker of ours had some interesting thoughts on how we might work around this mess. Everyone says the Libertarians don't have a chance, but there's still four months to the election. Who knows what can happen?" He took a noisy slurp of coffee and deliberately twisted in his chair toward Lauren. "You know, I'm damned tired of moping around and grumbling about politicians. I'm through complaining. I'm gonna find a way to get Optimal back on its feet and while I'm at it, I'll see if I can convince Mike and Bernie to help make sure Bellington is our next president."

Chapter 18

"Waaa-hoooo!" Wyatt yelled, dropping the phone into its cradle. "Lauren, where are you?"

Lauren ran into the kitchen where Wyatt stood, posing like a prizefighter—hunched, fists at the ready. With a puzzled expression on her face, she asked, "What's all this racket?"

Wyatt swung his fists and dodged phantom punches crying out, "Art Weinstein just called. Remember that Patent Office employee, Julie Ann Kelly? Well, they've indicted her! He wants to meet and go over the ramifications."

"That's wonderful, Honey. When does he want to get together?"

"He suggested tomorrow at eleven. I'll call Mike and Bernie to see if they can make it. Can you get away from work?"

"I really can't. The boss and I are dealing with a sudden cash flow crunch. The auditors are coming in and he's scheduled an all-day meeting. It's pretty serious."

Imitating a boxer, Wyatt thumbed his nose and then

faked a one-two punch. "No problem, Dear. I'll meet with the guys and if I have questions, I'll give you a call. I'm not sure what Art wants to talk about, but it's exciting."

Wyatt was sweating with the mid-July heat of downtown Los Angeles as he shoved through the art deco brass door of Weinstein's office building. As he walked toward the elevators, he saw Mike waiting on a wooden bench beneath the mezzanine. Wyatt reached out and gave him a hearty handshake. "Glad you made it, Mike."

Mike stood and rubbed the seat of his pants. "This fucker is as hard as a church pew. Is Bernie coming?"

"No. Had to work. I'll bet Bernie worries he's on thin ice, just trying to hang on to his job. Doesn't want to make any ripples. Grabs a few hours pay when he can."

Mike nodded. "I can appreciate that. When I talked with him the day before yesterday, he said his company was sinking fast."

They queued at the elevator doors behind two men in Brooks Brothers suits, carrying alligator brief cases. "Fuckin' fancy place," Mike whispered, looking around the lobby. He tilted his head toward the businessmen and breathed, "We gotta a couple of dudes that belong in some fancy fashion magazine."

"To me, this place is just a musty 1920's barn," Wyatt replied. Annoyed at the snail-pace descent of the elevator, he shoved his hands into his pockets and stared at the ancient dial above the elevator. At last, the brass doors shuddered open and disgorged several starchy businesspeople. They stepped in behind "the dudes" and Wyatt jabbed the fourth-floor button. He tapped his foot impatiently as they lurched to three, where "the dudes" stepped out. At last, they jerked to a stop at four and Wyatt looked at his watch. "Hurry. It's this way."

The cramped waiting room was adorned with IKEA old-fashioned black leather reception chairs and Wyatt wondered if it had ever been updated. The receptionist, flashing her crystal blue eyes, still crouched behind the desk and pecked away at her computer with gnarly, arthritic fingers. Massive file cabinets lined the wall, prompting him to speculate why lawyers had to have different-sized paper than the rest of the world. *Self-centered egomaniacs*, he thought.

"Hello, Mr. Morgan," the receptionist said. "Nice to see you again." Looking at Mike, she continued, "And this is…"

"Mike. Mike Graham. I'm Wyatt's partner."

"Are there only the two of you? Mr. Weinstein thought there might be four."

Amused at the perky octogenarian, Wyatt quipped, "Just us. We didn't come to move pianos."

A frown clouded her face and the wrinkles became more profuse. "Oh, I get it," she laughed. "Go on in, he's expecting you. Can I get you coffee or tea?"

"Coffee for me," Wyatt said. "Mike?"

"Just water if you don't mind."

After a warm welcome by the attorney, Wyatt and Mike sat across the desk from Art who rubbed his hands briskly. "I guess Lauren and the other partner, Bernie White, couldn't make it."

"Yeah. They were tied up at work—couldn't get away," Wyatt explained.

The receptionist shuffled in, clutching a tray with coffee, sugar and creamer—not remembering Wyatt took his coffee black—and a glass of water.

"Thanks, Mom," Art said as she set her burden on the corner of the desk. "So let's begin." The lawyer handed a sheet of paper to both Wyatt and Mike. "We can work from this agenda."

Wyatt glanced at the sheet of paper and looked up at the lawyer. "Yeah, I'm curious about your phone call. You mentioned that they've handed down an indictment, but I'm not clear what happens now."

"First, the Attorney General will work with the Justice Department to launch a thorough investigation into the Patent and Trademark Office and bring charges, if warranted. The Solicitor General will get involved too. As you may recall, I have a good friend who works at the PTO and based on his input, my expectation is Julie Ann Kelly will be found guilty of fraud. There may be others involved too."

"Will there be a regular trial?" Wyatt asked.

"Yes, unless they work out a plea bargain."

"Man, a trial would take forever," Wyatt said.

Art peered over his reading glasses that perched on the end of his pudgy nose and grabbed a handful of jellybeans from an apothecary jar. "You're right. The courts are tied up because of the immense number of bankruptcies—judicial constipation if you will. The flood of new regulations governing legal proceedings exacerbates everything. Just hope for a plea bargain."

Mike shifted in his chair and pulled out a pack of

cigarettes. "We don't have any fucking control over this, right?"

Art snatched his eyeglasses from his nose and glared at Mike. Several seconds passed. "No we don't."

Wyatt hid a grin behind his hand, wondering if Mike understood the lawyer's dirty look guessing it was a toss-up between no smoking and no profanity. Mike shrugged as he tucked the cigarettes back in his pocket, and Wyatt's smile swelled wider, sneaking beyond the boundaries of his hand.

"Suppose Kelly is convicted?" Wyatt asked. "What happens to her?"

"She'll get fired and placed on probation. No jail time, though."

"Screw her," Mike said. "What happens to us? To Optimal?"

Art replaced his glasses and leaned back in his chair. "That's what I want to talk about. Here's what I know. First, the Patent Office sandbagged Optimal's application— shoved it up the chain of command for 'special reviews.' Secondly, Dynamag's patent is essentially identical to yours. Third, Kelly and this Eric Magana became romantically involved around the same time you submitted your formal patent application. Lastly, there's a company called AirEnvironment that apparently issued a letter of intent to purchase Dynamag's pressurization system before they were awarded the patent."

"AirEnvironment?" Wyatt gasped. "Hell, they were close to signing a deal with me! They told me to expect a delay until the patent thing was resolved, but I had no idea they were negotiating with Dynamag. I've been in touch with Ed Morales and he said nothing about this."

"Water under the bridge. The question is what happens next. Pure speculation now, okay? Kelly probably gave copies of your application to Magana, who put his engineers to work knocking it off. I've been in the aircraft business so I know there must have been big problems obtaining FAA and DCMA certification to manufacture the hardware. Yet somehow Magana did it. It's possible that cash was passed under the table too. We'll have to confirm that."

"That seems like a big fu...direct connection," Mike stuttered. "Kelly to Magana."

"I think it's an ironclad case," Art confirmed. "If we can prove there were irregularities inside the Patent Office, I'll file to reopen your application. I'd bet a thousand dollars to a handful of jellybeans that you'd have your patent within a week."

Wyatt uncrossed his legs and leaned forward. "You serious? I get my patent?" Exuberance raced through his mind. He felt like parents who'd located a kidnapped child: his legacy was being returned. "Then what?" he asked, fidgeting in his chair.

"That's up to you. If Kelly throws Magana under the bus, which is probable, I'll go after an indictment for industrial espionage and haul him into court. If we're right, Magana gets fined and directed to pay restitution, but that might take a year or two. Again, we'd be hung up in the courts."

Mike and Wyatt looked at each other, speechless.

"Remember guys," Art cautioned, "nothing is certain."

"Holy shit," Mike exclaimed. "You're saying there's a

chance we'd get Wyatt's patent back and a big chunk of money too?"

Wyatt felt a surge of excitement. "My patent *and* money. That puts Optimal back in the land of the living."

"Careful, now," Art said. "Any money settlement could be years in the future. Maddox and AirEnvironment can't wait for Optimal to sort out its legal problems—they'll have to go with Dynamag in order to keep their production line moving. For that reason, I don't think Magana would cave in without a fight."

Numb, Wyatt nodded.

"If Dynamag falls through, the government has to cover their bases," Art went on. "I've learned that there's legislation, or executive rule-making underway, to grandfather a couple of manufacturers of obsolete pressurization designs. Politicians can't wait to sort out the Optimal-Dynamag patent squabble if it delays the new military jet program."

"Can they do that?" Wyatt gasped.

"Of course. I don't have any particulars yet. It might take months. I just don't know."

Art picked up the agenda, pointing his finger at the last item. "One more thing. Madison McKenzie is still a partner and owns a piece of Optimal. I'm not clear what's going on, but you need to resolve the situation. Think it over."

Wyatt's breath caught at the mention of Madison's name. Off guard, he thought a moment. "What could happen if she was involved in the Magana espionage?"

"Any reason to think she is?"

Wyatt shrugged. "Maybe. She worked for Dynamag for a while. She's intimate with details of my design, particularly electronics and software." He went on, feeling his cheeks blush. "We had a falling out and Madison was mega-pissed. I'd hardly be surprised if revenge was on her mind."

"You didn't tell me that." Art rubbed his chin. "I'll check it out. If she passed along proprietary information, she could forfeit her interest in Optimal."

A broad smile spread across Wyatt's face. "I realize you're not making any promises, but you've given us hope. I can't thank you enough, Art. I owe you everything."

"Odd you should mention that," Art said, tapping his desk. "I haven't billed you a dime for my services and don't intend to. My colleagues would have me committed if they knew I'm doing this pro bono." He tipped his head toward the reception area. "Even my mother thinks I'm nuts. You might remember me saying that I started out as an engineer at Aero Commander, right? I have science and little airplanes in my blood. When you first came to my office, you impressed me with your vision and work ethic. I remember thinking I'd like to team with Optimal. Nothing since has changed my mind. My satisfaction will come when we convict the cretins who defile business and honorable people. I want Optimal to flourish and will do everything possible to make it happen. In a year, I want to be your counsel. I want to be part of the company. That will be my payoff."

As Wyatt drove north on the Hollywood freeway, Mike hollered over the din of traffic, "I remember you saying the little fucker resembles Santa Claus. No doubt now, he *is* Santa."

Wyatt laughed, a big erupting-from-the gut, laugh. "I can't get my head around it...the idea that Optimal might have a future. Hell, Mike, last year we were so close."

"I don't want to piss on your fire, my friend, but Big Brother could make Optimal irrelevant with a stroke of a pen. And there's still no money. Art said even if we connected Magana to actual criminal action, it could be a long time before we get any loot."

Wyatt banged the steering wheel with his fist. "But there's a chance! What should we do? Grovel for a piddling job in this lousy economy? Chuck our dream into a trash heap? Go on food stamps, drink beer and watch game shows all day?"

Mike crossed his burly arms in a defensive pose. "I'm not saying that, Wyatt. I'm just saying it's a long shot."

"The Mars rover 'Curiosity'—remember that?"

"Hell, yes. I made a bunch of its fuckin' parts. You know that."

Wyatt braked heavily as traffic snarled and said, "Of course." His hazel eyes, unblinking as always, flickered onto Mike's face. "Suppose you take a 375-ton rocket and launch a 2,000-pound electric car on a 350 million mile trip and hope for the best. I'd call that a long shot."

"Only a friggin' engineer could have all those numbers on the tip of his tongue," Mike laughed. "No matter, you got a point."

"Gotta have a plan. We still have our facility under lease, so we can arrange to rent the big vacuum pump; the one they repossessed. Compressor too. The burners and heat exchangers are still there, so we can tweak them to get the temperatures up to spec. Let's put our heads together and refine the design even more. Lots we can do."

"No matter. We still need money."

"We do what we can do, Mike. Lauren is working with an art dealer who says the Dali could bring in a bundle. Lee Wong is working behind the scenes, trying to push the deal though. Until that sorts itself out, we work on those two Requests for Proposal you have for that government project; they're the only ones with money nowadays. Let's grab the RFPs, burn a bunch of hours and reel in a wad of work for Precision Tool. Over the years I've prepared hundreds of proposals—enough to know the ropes. We need short-term cash. We'll find it, I know."

"You're a hard man to argue with," Mike chuckled.

"Don't fight it. Odds makers will bet there's no chance to bring Optimal back, but for me, it's all-ahead flank speed. I must save Optimal. I must. We have to find business for your machine shop—it's the only lifeline I can see." Wyatt set his jaw. "Engineers will prevail."

Chapter 19

Eric Magana had been elated when the Pentagon awarded a contract for the surveillance jet to Maddox. In short order, business flowed down through the supply chain and AirEnvironment received an order for the aircraft's environmental systems. Then, two days ago a purchase order was issued to Dynamag for the pressurization system.

But Eric's ecstasy was brief. Sitting at his desk, he stared at the contract from AirEnvironment. There it was. "Attachment B, Quality Assurance Requirements for Airborne Software." *Goddamned Rubin was right. This is a game changer.*

Rubin stood in front of Eric's desk, feet wide apart and arms crossed. "See what I mean? We're not capable of certifying stringent military software. I checked with the engineering people and my own operations staff. The only option is to sub it out."

"This is bullshit," grumbled Eric. "Certification comes later. First we have to finish the program—algorithm—code—whatever the hell you call it. We're way behind because that Madison bitch took off, leaving me swinging in the wind. You've made sure the replacement guy is racing for the checkered flag, right?"

"I think your new software engineer has a wheel in the sand. The last I saw him, he was staring at the Optimal code, shaking his head and muttering profundities like 'Wow' or 'What did she do here?' All in all, not a good sign."

Eric stabbed the intercom button. "Judy, get Lanny Greaves in here ASAP."

"Yes, Mr. Magana."

A few minutes later, a scrawny young man ambled in, scratching his mangy Che Guevara-style beard. A white cord dangled from his shirt pocket, crawled across his chest and plugged into both ears. "Morning," he said, plopping into a chair.

"Do you mind?" Eric said, pointing to his ears.

"Oh yeah. Like, I get it." Lanny tugged the ear buds, letting them fall into his lap.

"Rubin says you're working on the pressurization software. How's it going?"

"I am. I am," Lanny said, nodding like a bobble-head doll. "It's, you know, complicated. I've been studying the code on that flash drive you gave me. Like, incredible, you know? Even with the flow diagrams, I can't dope out half the logic. Tight code, man…never seen such con…what's the word?"

"Concise?" Rubin volunteered.

"Yeah. Like concise." Lanny rubbed his chin. "Incredible," he repeated.

Eric waved the troublesome sheaf of papers, saying,

"We're contractually bound to meet these software certification standards. Are we on track?"

Lanny, with a vague stare, fondled an ear-bud, rubbing it between his thumb and forefinger. "Well, like, I'm not there yet, but workin' on it. The commercial specs aren't that special—I've fiddled with it before, you know. That's not the problem."

Irritated, Eric asked, "Why don't you take a moment and tell me what *is* the problem?"

"It's the military stuff, you know. I gotta figure out the shock and vibration-resistant electronics and write redundant algorithms. Things like EMP and radiation hardness, a bunch of stuff like that."

"They designed the Optimal system for executive jets, not military," Rubin interjected. "We don't have anyone in house who's intimate with this stuff. Lanny needs help, perhaps outside contractors, to get back on track."

"You keep singing the same damn tune, Rubin," Eric scolded. "Grab Ryan by the balls and tell him he'd better take control of his engineering department. Hell, we got the FAA and DCMA to bless our quality system and manufacturing procedures, you'd think software would follow right behind. If Lanny needs help, get it. Right now." Eric was fed up with Rubin's chronic pessimism. He'd considered shoving Rubin aside into the established automotive organization while creating a new division for the aviation business. Madison had been his foremost candidate to run the new program, but she'd walked out on him. He shook his head. *Too bad, she was a sweet piece of ass.*

"Okay," Rubin said. "I'll meet with Ryan and put out

a call for a backup programmer to help—somebody with military experience."

Eric could feel his face getting red as his pulse throbbed in his neck. "No, goddammit, not 'put out a call.' Hire somebody today. Some idiot engineer from AirEnvironment is coming here next week to kick my butt and I need answers fast. Get the hell out and go to work!"

With a bewildered look on his face, Lanny rose and left, plugging in his ear buds. Rubin, his cheek muscles bulging, turned back to Eric. "I'm afraid I have another problem for you."

"*Now* what."

A hint of a smile played around Rubin's mouth. "DCMA called—they want to come back for another visit."

"Visit? What in the hell do they want now?"

"They want to see how we are progressing on the software and review the pass-through requirements to our consultants. They say to block out a couple of days to discuss the new requirements."

Weary from the cascade of problems, Eric slouched in his chair. "Just take care of it. While you're at it, keep your eye on Lanny. I'm not convinced he can find high gear."

Rubin shrugged. "Where did you find that fool hippie? Not that I'm intimate with the stuff, but he smelled like he smokes a little weed."

Eric shook his head. "He's the son of one of my FAA contacts, a guy who's handling a sensitive issue for me. As I've always said, connections matter. Of course I had Lanny checked out, and the reports say he's a good programmer."

"I'll bet he's into illicit hacking. His idea of fun."

With a dismissive wave, Eric growled, "I don't care if he screws his mother, I just need results."

A week later, the door of Eric's office swung open and a slender man in his sixties, sporting a thick mat of black hair going gray, walked in pulling a rolling briefcase. Extending his hand, he said, "Ed Morales, AirEnvironment."

Eric shook hands and waved him to the small sofa by the polished antique coffee table. "Take a seat. Coffee? Soda?"

"No thanks, I'm fine." Ed unzipped the briefcase and extracted a three-ring binder.

Carrying a manila folder that Rubin had prepared, Eric walked around his desk, sat next to Ed and lifted out a sheet of paper. "Your email indicated," he began, "that you want to review the status of our program and get a commitment when we can ship test hardware."

Ed nodded. "Right. My customer, Maddox Aviation, is getting pressed by the Defense Department to expedite flight tests. The Pentagon wants to identify any modifications needed for the military version of their jet. The boys in Washington are bragging about this new big contract, saying it will employ thousands. As you know, trouble rolls downhill and my company has to deliver prototype environmental systems before yearend."

"In Jersey, they say, *shit* rolls downhill," Eric laughed. He thought a moment and then said, "Hell, that leaves us less than five months to ship working prototypes. My engineers say the redesign is a big job." Eric stood and walked to the window with his hands clasped behind him. He was boxed in—a tiger in a cage. Dynamag's cash flow was a calamity and the only solution was to get the pressurization into production fast. The version for executive jets was nearly ready, but now he faced the prospect of diverting his engineering staff and development lab resolve the issues for the military system. *There's no way to do both.*

He turned and slid into his chair behind the desk. Eric tried to squelch any hint of desperation. "We still have to get the civil version into production."

"I realize that," Ed said. "We have to do both. Even though executive aircraft shipments are slow, Maddox has empty holes on the production line where pressurization is supposed to go. We're holding up what few deliveries there are at Maddox. They're struggling to survive and are not happy.

"I'm a general aviation guy myself," Ed continued. "I worked on small planes and executive craft all my life, but I've headed up a couple of fighter projects, too. AirEnvironment sent me here because I worked with another firm on a cabin pressurization system that's supposed to be similar to yours." Ed crossed his arms and gnawed on his lower lip, a scowl drawing his brows together. "The company was called Optimal Aviation—you may have heard of them. Went bust."

Eric squinted, studying the foreboding face across the desk. *Optimal. That's the company I screwed. No wonder he's lookin' pissed. Better be careful with this guy.*

"Yeah, I may have known something about them—not sure," Eric said, donning an innocent smile. "A lot of companies are folding nowadays."

"Sure enough." Ed hunched his shoulders. "My

management will watch your schedule like a hawk after a mouse. It's no secret that the historical pressurization supplier declared bankruptcy a few months back—big problem. At the moment, you're our only option. I'll say it again: politicians have to demonstrate bold action. Already they have expediters prowling inside Maddox, making ugly noises. If we don't want them rooting around in *our* businesses, we'll have to hit every single milestone."

What Ed didn't realize was that Eric's Washington connections hinted there was legislation being drafted to resurrect the two old-time manufactures of pressurization: bankrupt Randel Products and Garvey Airmotive which had abandoned the market. They'd subsidize them; guarantee orders; push Dynamag out of the picture. Eric had 'connections' in Washington, but not influence like the high rollers. He had to move fast to lock down the business before the bill went to the floor for a vote.

Ed opened a binder and turned to a page marked with a sticky. "Your contract has financial penalties that go into effect if delivery of the test systems is late."

Eric squirmed at the reminder of the penalty clause. *Another big-ass problem.* "I'll make sure our staff is all over this like flies on…well, you know. We'll focus on electronics and software because those are impacted big time by the new specs. But new product development always has unexpected roadblocks. I hope you can be a little flexible on the deadlines, okay?"

"Lo siento. Sorry. Everyone suffers when government puts on a happy face," Ed rolled up his sleeves and loosened his tie. "I hear that Washington is planning a big ceremony in Oklahoma City when Maddox rolls out the first test airplane The President even might come to brag how the new stimulus is bringing prosperity."

Ed tapped the table. "First, I want to review the status of the engineering drawings, software code and test procedures. Then I want to go out on the floor and take a look at Dynamag's machining capability and see how you handle shop travelers and material certifications. Last, you'll need to show me how the tool crib, stockroom and bonded stores are managed."

Two days later Ed finished his survey and they returned to Eric's office for an exit meeting. Before Ed could start the debriefing, Eric excused himself and went to his private bathroom. His shoes clattered on the marble floor, a sharp contrast to the muffled tread on the plush carpet of his office. He took a bottle of Tums from the medicine cabinet and chewed two tablets, which stuck in his throat. A glass of cool water seemed to help and Eric splashed his face, trying to clear his head. His image in the mirror painted a dismal picture where the fluorescent lights washed out his deep tan and new puffiness bulged beneath his eyes. It had been a tough couple of days and Eric dreaded sitting across from Ed to review Dynamag's readiness. Taking a deep breath, he thought, *Gotta do this. No choice.*

As anticipated, Ed subjected him to a forty-five minute litany of problems, documented by a long memo. There was nothing Eric could do except nod in agreement and toss out banalities like, "No problem. We'll get right on it."

At last, the torture session ended and Ed stuffed the binder back into his briefcase along with his laptop. With a shake of Eric's hand, Ed said, "You have a bunch of deficiencies that you'd better jump on right away. I'll be calling every day to make sure you're not falling behind. Dynamag has bitten off a big chunk and you'd better make sure you're all over things like flies on...well you know," Ed said with a sneer. He turned and walked out.

Eric stared at Ed's retreating back, dropped into his chair and shuddered. His secretary bustled in saying; "Here is the report on sales projections you wanted and a letter from your attorneys, Masterson and Leibnitz."

He glanced up and took the materials. "Thanks, Judy."

Desperate to shake his gloom, Eric drew a deep breath and picked up sales projections. His eyes skittered over the figures. Abruptly, he slapped the folder shut and tossed it on the desk. *Crap, worse than I thought.* Month by month over the past three or four years, the top line had atrophied. As car sales shrank, so did Dynamag's. The situation was far beyond the hiring freeze he'd imposed in January—it was time to slash staff—again.

Without thinking, Eric opened the bottom drawer of his credenza and removed a bottle of A. H. Hirsch Reserve bourbon and a glass. He poured two fingers and belted it down. The heat in his throat calmed him as he assembled his thoughts. He refilled the glass and decided to call a meeting with his managers to figure ways to work around the problems that the belligerent engineer from AirEnvironment had uncovered.

Ed Morales was a problem, but the big issue was implementing a big layoff. The managers, he was sure, would fight him, saying their respective departments were already understaffed. Except that goddamn Rubin was certain to remind him that prudent management would have instituted cutbacks long ago and that the pressurization project should be abandoned. Uncertainty seethed in his gut.

Eric worried that he would appear weak in front of his subordinates, but consoled himself, knowing he had no control over automotive sales volume.

He took a delicate sip of the exquisite bourbon, but a distressing thought persisted. Everyone would wonder that if he was the managerial marvel he portrayed himself to be, Dynamag should have anticipated the decline and taken firm action.

He stood and walked to a wall covered with awards, plaques and framed letters from influential people. The sight bolstered his resolve. He *had* anticipated the problem. That was precisely why he'd jumped into the pressurization—into aircraft. Every smart executive knows diversity is the key to success. That's what he'd tell his team, particularly Rubin. It wasn't his fault; it was theirs. He'd demand they fix the problems of the new project. Or else.

Determined, he went back to his desk and opened the letter from his patent lawyers. "Julie Ann Kelly," he read, "has been indicted for possible fraud in the United States Patent and Trademark Office. We suspect she may disclose damaging information about her relationship to you personally and to Dynamag in general. In view of potential liabilities, we suggest you assemble an aggressive legal team, versed not only in patent matters, but also in criminal law. Upon receipt of your request, Masterson and Leibnitz will act accordingly. Sincerely, ..."

Eric thought he heard his father's demeaning voice,

"Okay, hot shot, what good are your 'connections' now? You're in deep shit, little boy. See if you can wiggle out of this one." Eric shook his head, trying to dispel his dead father's eerie laughter. He gripped the bourbon glass until his knuckles turned white and then flung it across the room, shattering a framed commendation from the Governor of New Jersey. *This is fuckin' bullshit! First I gotta fire a bunch of workers and now I have to lawyer-up on account of a dumb slut.*

Chapter 20

Bright early morning sunlight streamed through the living room window and warmed the back of Wyatt's thick neck and broad shoulders as he read the newspaper where the headline proclaimed,

Economy Collapsing

He shook his head and took a swig of coffee. At last inured by continual bad news, he scanned the article. "... bad as the Great Depression...emergency session of Congress... massive stimulus bill...defense spending to double...the senior senator from California told this reporter that 'Inflation is better than rebellion.'...the President..."

Disgusted, Wyatt skimmed a few paragraphs when a small article on page eight caught his eye. "E.J. Bellington," it said, "the Libertarian candidate for the Presidency, will speak tonight at The National Convention of the Veterans of Foreign Wars. A retired Army general and presently CEO of a communications firm of 14,000 employees, he will address the current fiscal crisis."

Wyatt grinned. *Looks like Bellington has a chance to toss out a few new ideas. I'll watch for sure. Better call Bernie and Mike and give them a heads up; they'll want to watch, too.*

That night, Wyatt plopped on the sofa and snatched the remote. He flicked on the TV and turned to Lauren. "Thanks for picking up pizza. The speech is too early for you to fix dinner, so Pizza Hut was perfect. Timmie, I noticed, was thrilled."

Lauren set two glasses of Zinfandel on the coffee table and patted the top of Wyatt's head. "You're upsetting my biological clock having our Sunset Ritual *after* dinner." She settled beside Wyatt and sipped her wine. "I have to admit I'm interested in what Bellington will say, although I'm not as euphoric as you."

Wyatt chuckled. "There you go with your big words again." He poked at the remote until a tumultuous convention scene flashed on the screen. "They say that whenever a crisis comes up, a genuine leader shows up to take charge. Remember Churchill and the London Blitz, Admiral Nimitz at the Battle of Midway? I hope Bellington measures up."

"Are you comparing our recession with World War II?"

"We have a depression, not a recession, and if we don't straighten things out, it'll be worse than war. I'm doing everything I can to salvage Optimal, but there's nothing I can do to solve national problems—I've no power to change Washington's policies. I'm crossing my fingers that Bellington has figured out a few ways to get us out of this mess."

"We have to elect him first."

"Yeah, I know. A real long shot." Abruptly, he gestured toward the television. "Look, they're introducing him now."

On the screen, a blocky man with squared shoulders and jutting chin, strode forward and placed both hands on the podium. His gray tailored suit looked crisp and authoritative and a crew cut emphasized his weathered, craggy face. Lancing brown eyes, set in heavily lined sockets, shuttled side-to-side, surveying the audience. He raised a hand to quell the welcoming crowd's applause, saying in a rumbling voice, "Good evening. My name is E. J. Bellington, but just call me Frank, because that's what I am."

Thunderous clapping poured from the TV. Wyatt slapped his knee. "Ha!"

With a broad smile on his face, Bellington resumed. "As a retired soldier, it's a special pleasure to be with you at the annual VFW Convention."

Again, applause rippled into the Morgan living room.

"There are myriad problems confronting our nation today, but tonight I will limit my remarks to the two most pressing issues: our economy and its foundation—education.

"First, allow me to review where our nation has been. During the Second World War, we banded together and overcame two calamitous conflicts, 400,000 combat deaths and immense personal sacrifice. Emboldened by victory, we leapt into the future, prosperous and expanding. The American industrial engine, born in the agony of war, set the standard for the entire world. In 1969, the Stars and Stripes were firmly planted on the desolate lunar landscape and still reigns in regal solitude. As recently as the nineties, our technology gave the world the information age. It was a time characterized by unprecedented innovation and an unimaginable productivity boom. New words burst into our lexicon: Internet, Google and The Cloud."

Bellington paused and sipped water from a glass, his eyes dancing. Still gripping the podium, he leaned forward, as if trying to drill thoughts into his listeners' minds. "That was an era of proud people, confident and optimistic about the future. Joyful parents launched their children into society knowing their progeny would have a better life. Hard work, ambition and faith in the American way reigned supreme. It was a good time."

Wyatt and Lauren sat transfixed as television cameras panned the rapt audience who nodded and looked at one another with grim-set mouths.

Bellington leaned back and waved a cautionary hand. "Let's examine where the country is today. There is a fierce undertow of pessimism and discontent. Many grieve, jobless and helpless. Self-determination has vanished, sucked into the vortex of massive government intervention. Too often, our twenty or thirty year-olds, cringing from the storms of unemployment and crushed dreams, creep back to the safe harbor of their parents' homes."

Wyatt sputtered, choking on a swallow of wine. "That's the truth. Alex, right down the street, has two 'boomerang kids.'"

Lauren nodded.

"Who's at fault?" Bellington continued. With a harsh stare, he pointed straight into the camera. "You are. We all are. We have adopted a tragic mentality where we substitute, 'I'm entitled to it' for 'I've earned it.' So it's no surprise the politicians pander to our decadence, garnering votes while vastly expanding their empire."

He took sip of water and shook his head. During the pause, a TV camera zoomed in on a young woman, dabbing her eyes with a tissue. A murmur crept through the crowd and people shifted in their chairs. Bellington took a deep breath, letting the stunned silence in the auditorium wash over him.

"Good grief," Wyatt murmured. "He's laying down serious cards!"

"It's become fashionable to complain," Bellington went on, "and shun responsibility or action. That has to stop! We must decide whether to rededicate our lives to the American ethic, or turn our backs and tumble into a lethargic nanny-state. It's your call. To those who wallow in self-pity and victimhood, I suggest you leave this honored gathering of veterans who fought for our liberty. As to viewers at home, flip the channel to a silly reality show. For those who remain, I will propose a path out of our dilemma."

Resembling an Alaskan totem, Bellington stood erect behind the podium, hands at his side, and gazed at the sea of astounded looking faces. "First, each of you must revisit your own moral code. Ask yourself if you want guaranteed opportunity or guaranteed mediocrity. Do you seek freedom to follow your own path or bondage by a suffocating government? Will you embrace the invigorating principles of the Founding Fathers or choose to reside in the world of the nameless, the mundane and the slothful?"

"Goodness," Lauren breathed. "He's an incredible speaker."

Bellington tapped the podium with his forefinger. "What actions would I take to resolve these things, you ask?"

Wyatt and Lauren sat mesmerized as Bellington ticked off problems and solutions to resolve them. One by one, he spoke of high unemployment, the exploding national debt, massive over-regulation, union intransigence, high corporate taxes and even proposed a complete overhaul of the educational system.

Wyatt turned up the volume on the TV and murmured, "This is like a salvo of sixteen inch shells from a battleship."

Once again, the speaker pointed into the camera. "You, the voters, must reject big government. We must stop paying people not to work. Extravagant unemployment insurance, housing subsidies, the burgeoning food stamp program and welfare are incentives to stay home and watch game shows."

Bellington shrugged, his cufflinks flashing in the harsh spotlights. "We recognize that people run into a streak of bad luck now and then. I believe private organizations can help better than government intervention and here's an example: there is a well-known church that provides for their needy, but along with assistance, they impose an obligation to pay back; to avoid 'the evils of the dole.' No free ride. You get help; you owe help. That makes sense to me.

"There you have it," he said, straightening his tie. "*We* are to blame for the decay of our country and must change our ways. *We* must reject the creature comforts we've embraced by commandeering other people's wages. *We* must stop piling debt onto the backs of our children.

It is time to decide if we're conquerors of our destiny or lemmings racing into the void. That's what I see."

He fixed a stern gaze on the audience. "Next January, I hope you'll call me Mr. President. For now, just call me Frank."

Several seconds passed in silence and then a ripple of applause swelled into a torrent of exultation. The cameras darted from one joyful face to the next as a commentator tried to capture the emotional scene in a rush of jumbled words.

Wyatt was dumbfounded. As if in a trance, he reached for the remote and snapped off the TV, squelching the babbling news anchor.

"Incredible," Wyatt whispered. He took Lauren's hand. "I don't know what to say."

"Absolutely the most inspiring speech I've ever heard," she said. "I've never seen a politician with the courage to say those things."

"Bellington isn't a politician; he's an Army general and an industrialist. He's spent his life making organizations work, not chasing votes. Rightfully, he blames the situation on us, the electorate. Trouble is, there are far more people looking for a free ride than diligent workers."

Lauren nodded. "You're spot on —we've become a nation of hangers-on. But what is so unique with this speech is Bellington's challenge to our morality. He proposed bringing back our traditional 'rugged individualism' and blowing off a homogeneous egalitarian society."

The jangling telephone startled them. Wyatt picked up the receiver. "Hello?"

An impassioned voice boomed from the phone. "That

guy is fuckin' right on! He's got a set of balls an elephant would envy!"

"Mike," Wyatt smiled, pointing at the receiver.

"I guessed," Lauren giggled. "It looks as if our friend 'Frank' has lit a fire."

Wyatt chuckled, then spoke to Mike. "What? Yeah, he says he wants to redo our schools."

"A strong workforce would jack up my business," Mike bellowed. "Bellington was correct when he said the foundation to our economy is education. When business was good and I was hiring, most job applicants couldn't add a grocery list, much less calculate an offset on a taper. I had to train them, which took lots of time and money. In today's economy, I can't afford any training. I'm screwed and they're screwed."

Wyatt laughed. "Yeah, educators are more interested in coddling their students than teaching. 'Don't critique little Johnny,' they say. 'It'll destroy his self-esteem.' Thinking about it, we've a meeting with Art next week; let's kick the speech around then. I want to read what the newspaper analysts have to say."

"I don't need to read any goddamn paper. My mind's made up."

Wyatt smiled. "In a week." He hung up, reached for the wine bottle and topped off their glasses. "Bellington sure has *me* thinking. Why do I have to wage war on the Building and Safety Department, the SBA or the FAA? Why do crazy regulations and petty inspectors block every turn? Why do I have to accept the screw-ups of bungling bureaucrats in the Patent Office?"

"Complaining will get you nowhere, Hon," Lauren said with a quick smile. "Just relax and do your best."

"Relaxing is not my long suit," Wyatt growled. "I can't just sit back and wait for fate to drag me under. I gotta do something." He paused, taking a sip of Zinfandel. "You know, I've been talking with Mike and Bernie about helping to get Bellington elected. It's time to move. There has to be a local committee where I can volunteer. I'll work a phone bank, help set up rallies, whatever they need." He rubbed his hands together. "I wonder if Mike and Bernie would jump in too?"

He leapt from the chair and hurried to his office. Wyatt shook with impatience waiting for the computer to boot up. *Optimal is my child and a crazy witch in the Patent Office has strangled it. All my life I have striven toward my fate as an engineer. Stupid public administrators have passed judgment on my skills and stolen my future. I cannot, I will not accept that fate. I may recover my patent; I may raise enough money to restart my company, but the enemy remains: politicians who promote the culture of victimhood. They deceive hard working people and buy votes masquerading as benevolent protectors. They're killing the economy and our way of life. I have worked for my destiny and I deserve it. I will achieve it.*

At last, the computer screen flashed and Wyatt went to Google and typed in: "Bellington volunteer committees."

* * *

Across the country in New Jersey, there was a different reaction. "This Bellington guy is an idiot," Eric grumbled, turning off the TV. "I don't know why they give him air time. Ideas like that could bring our whole system down."

"Don't get so upset, Lovey-poo. It was just a silly speech. Let me pour you a nice glass of bourbon; you need something to take off the edge."

Eric watched as Angela rose from the sofa like a wisp of smoke, her seductive figure shimmering beneath a slinky silk gown. He smiled as he accepted her offering: his favorite bourbon in a crystal tumbler etched with "Dynamag—Your Partner." He sniffed the aroma and took a sip. Eric's gaze fell on Angela's bare feet, crept up her leg, then hips and finally rested on her firm, pointed breasts straining at the gown's filmy fabric. *Angela damn near killed me last night. She has more twists than a pretzel—puts that Madison broad to shame.*

Eric took another sip and mulled over Bellington's speech. "Maybe it *was* a stupid speech, Angela, but the crowd seemed to get into it." With a dismissive wave of his hand, he said, "No matter, they're just a bunch of shell-shocked old farts. They'll never elect a Libertarian, that's for sure."

"Didn't you mention that a friend of yours in Washington, the Commerce Department guy, suggested you watch the telecast?" Angela said, drawing back a strand of fine blond hair from her cheek. "Didn't he say the polls showed increasing support for a change in Washington?"

"Yeah, but I don't see why he's worried. Bellington just spouts a bunch of fancy words. He ignored the big new stimulus package moving through Congress and the expansion of the defense budget. Hell, the new Maddox surveillance jet is going to put my company back in business. The President just signed off on that new agency, the Department of Industrial Management, which will prohibit all future layoffs. They're even working up new legislation to force companies to rebuild their staff to pre-recession levels. Unemployment will evaporate and the voters will go back to their television sets."

"But didn't you just lay off a bunch of workers? Won't you have to bring them back?"

"Are you nuts? That same Commerce guy, the one I flew to Vegas last weekend, figured a way for me to dance around the law. I'm lean and mean and plan to stay that way."

Eric took another swallow of bourbon and wiggled with pleasure as Angela fondled his ear lobe. His thoughts jumped to his father. *Yup, connections matter, don't they, Daddy-Dear.*

Chapter 21

Wyatt sputtered at the backup on the Harbor Freeway off-ramp. "This is crazy. We're going to be late for our meeting with Art and the guys."

"Be patient, my Love. The traffic jam isn't going to disappear because you're in a rush," Lauren scolded. "We're in the middle of downtown L.A., you know."

She's sung that tune dozens of times, he thought. "Got it, but it still drives me nuts." With quick, nervous drumming, he rapped on the steering wheel. "The morning newspaper says inflation has hit double digits and the Office of Management and Budget projects the deficit will exceed two trillion. Two *trillion*! That's crazy. I'm bouncing off the walls."

"I can see that." Lauren reached over and gave Wyatt a calming pat on his arm. "But remember what they said last night on TV—Bellington's poll numbers are surging since his speech last week. That should be encouraging."

"True enough. When I signed up at Bellington's field office, the manager was thrilled with the latest trends. My computer skills are going to help the campaign for sure; their work is really tech-driven. Surprised me. When I called Mike and Bernie about volunteering for Bellington, they jumped onboard. It's not that we're pressed for time: I'm out of work, Mike's business is sputtering and Bernie's hours have been cut back to a couple of days a week."

Immersed in thought, Wyatt nearly struck a pedestrian who slapped the fender and flipped him off. Lauren, her feet jammed against the floorboard, gasped. His hands shaking, Wyatt crept through the intersection and once more was submerged in stalled traffic.

Twenty minutes later, Wyatt bolted from the elevator and glanced at his watch. "Dang, fifteen minutes late." With a wave, he scurried past the receptionist and hurried into Art's conference room with Lauren in his wake. A quick look confirmed his fears; they were the last to arrive. "Sorry, everyone. Traffic was a bear."

"We've just been chatting," Art said. "Not a problem." He grinned as his mother, with mincing steps, came in with a steaming mug of coffee for Wyatt. "As you can see," he chuckled, "Mom knows you well. Before starting, can we get you anything, Lauren?"

Lauren shook her head, so Art began, pushing his rimless glasses high on his nose. "It's nice to finally meet Mr. White. I understand you've been a principal for some time."

Bernie flushed. "A very small participant, I'm afraid. I worked with Wyatt at a small firm before he started Optimal. I'm still there, but my schedule is off-and-on. Business is very slow."

"And Mr. Wong," Art continued, tilting his head toward

the banker. "Lauren tells me that you've been handling the finances for Optimal. She thought it would be appropriate for you to attend."

Lee Wong smiled, pulled a fountain pen from his pocket and set it on the conference table next to his note pad. "It's been my pleasure."

"And of course I've met Mr. Graham. Good to see you again, Mike." Art clasped his hands together and said, "I've uncovered a few interesting developments, but before I jump in, perhaps Wyatt will fill us in about his conversations with AirEnvironment, a potential customer, and Maddox, the large airframe manufacturer."

Wyatt cleared his throat. "I've had phone calls from both firms. They're worried who owns the patent rights— the rights Magana stole from us. The AirEnvironment attorneys think Dynamag could lose protection if the authorities go after them."

"Just so everyone knows," Art interrupted, "this morning my colleagues informed me that a clerk in the Patent Office, Julie Ann Kelly, was indicted and has plea bargained, implicating Eric Magana and Dynamag. This casts a shadow over the status of the pressurization patent."

"Wow!" Wyatt hollered, sitting upright in his chair. "I knew they indicted Kelly but didn't realize a judgment had come down. Now Optimal can light off all boilers— sorry, navy lingo—if Dynamag loses manufacturing rights." A rush of joy brought a broad smile to his lips. Pressurization, his inspiration, his creation, was coming home.

"There's another wrinkle," Art said. "I remember that Nick Nolan, AirEnvironment's buyer, insisted on extremely detailed information while negotiating prices with Optimal last year. Right, Wyatt?"

Wyatt tugged his ear and searched his memory. "Yeah. He wanted prices broken down by individual part and demanded a number of key engineering drawings so their staff could evaluate airworthiness."

"Simple malarkey," Art growled. "I was suspicious then and virtually certain now: Nolan fed that information to Dynamag. This is another link to a case of fraud and industrial espionage." He pushed back in his chair and laced his pudgy fingers across his belly. "Bottom line: we have an excellent chance of recovering Optimal's patent."

Bernie's wrinkles crowded together in a scowl. "But a patent isn't business. With the economy the way it is, I could be laid off from SAC any day and I'm sixty-three. Optimal is my only lifeline."

"I understand," Art said, "but we should ask why Maddox and AirEnvironment are digging into Optimal's readiness—something is stirring their soup. We know the military has placed a big airplane order with accelerated deliveries. Consequently, any production bottleneck at Dynamag will pressure Maddox and AirEnvironment to either resolve the case promptly or develop a backup."

"Besides," Wyatt said, "There's more talk that China has been nosing around, looking for bids on business jets. Their economy is hanging on. Huge potential. A big commercial order would save SAC and Optimal."

"If I might," Lee began. "Our research division at the bank just issued a bulletin saying China has been wrestling with their internal transportation problems. Recent riots in remote western provinces have illustrated the difficulties of officials reaching troubled areas quickly. Even with their push for more high-speed trains and expanded airline service, businessmen fret over inefficiencies in public transportation."

"Everyone has heard about the train crashes," Wyatt said. "Not exactly a confidence builder."

Lee nodded. "Increasing reports suggest China is in negotiations for a large number of Maddox jets. One of the prominent stock brokerages has raised Maddox's rating from 'neutral' to 'buy.' That's good news for us."

"Hell," Mike exclaimed, "If that comes through along with the military version of the plane, we could be talking hundreds of aircraft."

"Hundreds of pressurization systems," Wyatt corrected.

"Didn't I hear that India is investigating a purchase of planes too?" Lauren asked.

"True," Lee agreed. "The report mentioned that also, but our analysts lack hard information to confirm anything. Still, one never knows."

"Let's hope all that business materializes," Bernie said.

"There's something else," Lee ventured, tugging on his shirtsleeves. "As you'd expect, the banking business has its fingers on the pulse of industry and I'm seeing an interesting phenomena. A coalition of big corporations, called the Alliance for Industrial Might, or A.I.M., has launched serious queries about expanding into China. In the past, only individual companies sought business, but now, there's a highly coordinated team of American industrialists directly engaging the Chinese government. A major stumbling block, however, is our Commerce Department's policy that restricts outsourcing, supposedly to preserve domestic jobs. As a consequence, A.I.M. is fielding a large lobbying effort in Washington. Wyatt, I believe, is correct in saying China could be a credible opportunity."

"Yeah, but our government has to get out of the way," Bernie groaned. "That isn't going to happen as long as the voters think we're shipping jobs overseas. They don't seem to understand that trade creates new markets."

"Fucking on point," snapped Mike, tugging on his mustache. "We need results fast, not two or three years down the road."

Wyatt nodded his head in agreement. "We'll see if things turn around after the November elections."

"Okay, okay people," Art grumbled as he glared at Mike. "We're getting off track. AirEnvironment and Maddox seem serious to ascertain Optimal's ability to start production. We need to clarify the key issues. Let's put together a package that evaluates the status of the engineering, determines what's required to complete certification of Optimal and lists what's needed to assure the facility and machinery are ready to go. And perhaps our biggest issue: where will we get funds to resume work?"

Wyatt drained his coffee mug and set it down with a thump. "We were very close to getting certification on the civil configuration; it's the military system that's new. We've nobody to develop a hardened design for the circuitry and redo the software. We'll have to recruit an electrical engineer experienced in military specifications."

"Is that difficult?" Art asked.

Lauren raised her hand. "Given the state of our

economy, you'd think there would be thousands of unemployed engineers."

"You'd think so," Wyatt agreed. "Regardless, good ones are as rare as supersonic turtles." Wyatt knew the task of replacing Madison was daunting. Her replacement might take months to figure out where she left off and learn the new requirements. Time was critical as Art noted. Delays would give Washington time to pass proposed legislation that would grandfather the old-style equipment and exclude Optimal's.

"Regarding the facility and machinery," Mike interjected, "we still have the office under lease and, thanks to shitty bookings, I have extra room at my factory. The necessary metalworking machines are in place, but we need to get the repossessed test equipment back. There's a small inventory of leftover parts, so in general, we're lookin' pretty good—just a few gaps to fill in."

Art removed his glasses and rubbed the bridge of his nose. "That leaves the gorilla—money. Lauren, what's the situation?"

Lauren laughed mirthlessly. "It's simple. There's no money. We're broke. The only reason we're holding on is I'm able to sell a few items from my late mother's estate. I'm getting daily calls from Optimal's creditors, but there's no way to pay, even token amounts. Without settling their accounts, it will be impossible to resume business with them—a big problem if we manage to resurrect Optimal." She turned to Wong and nudged his shoulder. "Lee has been working on this problem. Maybe he can explain."

With an embarrassed looking frown, Lee pushed his fountain pen a few inches on the table. "The most promising is the Dali. As I've said, I've been coordinating with Emile Beaulieu, an art dealer I've worked with for years. Sotheby's has booked a big art auction next April and we're trying to tie up all the loose ends by then. The process is very complicated because Emile thinks the painting could be a forgery." He shrugged, palms up.

"Are we talking big bucks?" Bernie asked.

"Substantial."

"Let's not forget that if a judgment goes against Dynamag, Optimal could recover damages, but timing is anyone's guess," Art said.

"That's the problem," Mike grumbled. "We need upfront bucks to buy castings, recover the pumps and pay off our vendors."

"That certainly brings pressure to obtain funds fast," Lee murmured, tapping his pen on the note pad, "Emile and I are pushing to expedite the appraisal process. I'm working hard on this, but it just takes time."

"I'm appreciative you're taking this on, Lee," Lauren said. "I just *know* you're going to slay the dragon." With a brisk wave of her hand, she said, "I'm going to nominate you to a seat on Optimal's board."

Lee shook his head, looking confused. "Dragon?"

"Just a saying, Lee," Wyatt laughed. "And I'll second my wife's motion to elect you to the board."

With an affectionate grin on his face, Lee turned to Lauren. "I'm just a simple banker with a knack for numbers. I'm afraid I'd be useless in strategic business matters."

Art frowned. "A quick source of funds would certainly solve a lot of problems, but it doesn't seem to be in the cards." He pressed his lips together. "We simply *must* find some capital right away." He looked at Wyatt. "Regardless, we should get a formal response back to AirEnvironment ASAP now that the patent situation has changed. It's even more urgent if the pending legislation in Washington goes through and obsoletes Optimal's design."

"Right," Wyatt acknowledged. "Ed wants a quick assessment. If things look good, he said he'd come out for a quick meeting. If we could put together a letter in the next day or so, I'll bet he'd be on Optimal's doorstep within a week. He really sounds worried."

"Draft something tonight and email it to me," Art ordered. "I'll look it over for legal aspects and you can shoot it off tomorrow."

Wyatt nodded. "Will do. Looks like our money problems won't go away for a while; maybe something will come up."

"It had better," Lauren whispered.

"One last thing," Art said. "I'm digging into Madison McKenzie's involvement in Optimal. There was a non-compete clause in the operating agreement of the LLC. Standard boilerplate. She's still a partner, but not for long if my suspicions are valid. Don't worry about that; I'm all over it like frosting on a cake."

Anxious to avoid a discussion concerning Madison, Wyatt jumped in, saying. "Well, I guess that wraps it up. Anybody want to add anything?"

Lauren nodded, "We have the technical talent and drive to make Optimal work, but we always lacked one critical thing: money. If we can hold on, perhaps Lee may has found a way for us—in the long term, anyway," she said, grinning.

Lee blushed and muttered, "It's not me. Your mother will save the company. She's the hero."

Lauren stared at her hands. "Very true. Mother was skeptical of Optimal at first, but began to understand the glory and challenge of a start-up and of Wyatt's passion for an idea. Now, a year after her death, her legacy could save the company." She sighed again. "Liza's gift."

They crowded into a booth of a noisy downtown restaurant, bubbling about Art's news. Wyatt was famished, the heartening developments bolstering his appetite.

Patiently, the waitress managed to extract their lunch orders in spite of their incessant jabbering. The enthused chatter swirled around the booth until the plates were served and became muted as everyone devoured their meals. As the clatter of utensils diminished and bellies filled, conversation resumed.

"Indicted. Magana's up a creek."

"Espionage—could mean big money."

"Patent's in our pocket."

"Anything else besides the Dali, Lauren?"

"Gotta find a new software person."

"We'd better move fast to find a good engineer and programmer."

That last comment jarred Wyatt from his ruminations over Madison's replacement. He'd been speculating how things would be if she'd hadn't fallen in love with him—remembering their exquisite rapport as they worked together. Feeling panicked, he wondered if there was a way to get her help for a few days without making big trouble again. He'd worked hard to reassure his wife that his "indiscretion" was a blunder, apologizing and bringing her bouquets of roses. But if only he could find a way for Madison to... *Don't go there*, he brought himself up short. *But I have to do something.*

"What? Oh, a new circuit board designer?" Wyatt said, his thoughts returning to the group.

"We need more than a designer," Bernie said. "You'll have to find the most brilliant electrical engineer in the world who can program too."

"The fucker will have to be a saint if we expect him to get along with us," Mike joked.

"One who'll work for peanuts," Lauren said.

Lee smiled. "Not a problem—I can count nuts as easily as dollars and cents."

Everyone laughed. Lauren reached across the table and gave Lee a high-five.

Chapter 22

An early August heat wave clutched Burbank and a shimmery mirage hovered around the foothills of the Verdugo Mountains as Ed Morales of AirEnvironment and his companion strode into the stuffy offices of Optimal Aviation Systems.

"Welcome Ed," Wyatt said, a little too enthusiastically. "Good seeing you again."

"Same here. Let me introduce Pete Sykes, our senior buyer."

Pete tilted his head with a confident grin. He looked to be in his late fifties with gray hair, a gray complexion and a pronounced comb-over.

Puzzled, Wyatt shook hands. "Pleased to meet you. Are you replacing Nick Nolan?"

"I'll explain," Ed interrupted, his curt manner softened by a slight Mexican accent. "Nick was reassigned. It seems there were ethics-related questions concerning his dealings with an East Coast company. Pete is here to assure everything is on the straight and narrow."

It looks like Art was right—Nolan was on the take, Wyatt thought. "No problem. Come and sit. Sorry the heat's so bad. Our little window air conditioning can't keep up with California summers." As they sat, Wyatt mulled over Ed's comment regarding Nick's 'ethics' issues, remembering Art's comments of an East coast firm. *Dynamag? Maybe.* He tugged his mind back to current business and asked, "What can I tell you about Optimal?"

"I've studied the report you emailed last week," Pete said. "It looks like you could resume operations on short notice. Our company is concerned that deliveries of the cabin pressurization system from the current supplier is uncertain."

"Dynamag?" Wyatt ventured.

"Off the record, yes. I know you're aware there's litigation regarding intellectual property."

Wyatt nodded.

"Further, Dynamag is having difficulties obtaining software certification and meeting production deadlines," Pete said. "We're worried they might default on their contractual obligations, which would put AirEnvironment in big trouble. Ed and I are here to resolve two things: your ability and willingness to resume operations and to negotiate tentative pricing. This will be on a contingency basis, you understand. Budgetary for now."

"Of course," Wyatt said. "My email pretty much sums up our capabilities about production. Assuming we can clear up the patent question, we are fully committed to getting Optimal back on its feet."

"You're sure?"

"Cross my heart," Wyatt grinned.

"Good," Ed muttered, flipping open his laptop. "Let's go over a few questions I have about castings, machine workload and qualification tests. We also want to check your facility to see for ourselves the condition of the equipment and instrumentation. Most importantly, we need a reading on the design status of new circuit boards and an estimate of work needed to complete the software. Everything is complicated by the fact there are two systems: the commercial one for executive planes and the other for the military surveillance jet."

"Yes," Wyatt replied. It's the military version that will be the most trouble."

"Well, let's see what we have," Ed said.

An hour and forty-five minutes later, Ed entered the last note into his computer. "That's it, Pete. Looks to me that Wyatt's could start manufacturing hardware soon because engineering on the mechanical stuff is in hand. But the big issue is electronics and software. Optimal isn't staffed for this since Madison left—she's the double-E that did the original electrical work; but she's no longer with Optimal."

Ed turned to Wyatt. "There's another wrinkle in all this; the FAA has informed my office that they're considering a new ruling about airborne software on flight-critical equipment such as pressurization. That, plus the special characteristics of military electronics, means you have to locate a solid replacement for Madison. Do you have a plan?"

"I'll use the standard stuff: agencies, ads, word-of-mouth." Wyatt replied. "The unemployment picture is getting worse, and you'd think there would be gobs of engineers needing work. But there are 100 million working-age people who've withdrawn from the workforce. How many electronic engineers? Who can guess? In spite of that, I hope to locate a hotshot or two, presuming I'm able to wean them from unemployment payments and food stamps."

Pete chuckled. "I see your point. Well, better get on it. There's no time."

"Sure," Wyatt said. "I'll put out feelers right away and hit it hard as soon as I get my patent back."

Pete waved a piece of paper, fanning his glistening face. "That leaves pricing. We need to estimate recurring and nonrecurring costs."

"I've made a few notes on that," Wyatt nodded. "While certification of the commercial system will be easy, we'll have to do a lot of redesign and generate new software for the military jet. I'm guessing there will be substantial nonrecurring costs."

"Okay," Pete said. "Let's haggle over that first."

Wyatt paused. "I'll have to limit pricing to ballpark figures. Inflation is going crazy and the election could turn everything on its head."

Both Ed and Pete bobbed their heads.

"Bellington is on the fringe," Ed said. "Even so, he may have a chance. That would shake the nuts from the trees."

"Well, he's got my vote," Wyatt growled. "We've seen what politicians have done to business. To our country. With that thought, let's work up some numbers."

An hour later, they had agreed on budgetary costs. Ed and Pete were gathering up their belongings when Pete turned to Wyatt and said, "There's a lot of loose ends. The patent situation needs to be resolved and you need an engineer or two. Your big problem is funding. Optimal has to come up with quick money for the flight test systems, but tooling and inventory for long term production will require a major investment. You've indicated Optimal doesn't have the cash to assemble even the three test systems, much less get into full production."

Ed scowled. "Pete's right. This goes nowhere without money. Right now you haven't any answers. Be sure you keep us in the loop about funding."

Wyatt stood at the window and watched as they drove away. Although Optimal was in good shape technically and the patent issue was moving, there was no money in sight—not until the Dali sold and that might take months. Wyatt felt like a lawn mower had churned through his head. Over and over Ed's words battered him: "Goes nowhere without money."

Chapter 23

Eric trudged through Dynamag's lobby crowded with garish skeletons, gargantuan spiders clinging to expansive webs and a six-foot ghost that moaned when he passed. He hated Halloween, or any other holiday for that matter, but his airhead office staff insisted on adorning their areas with tacky symbols of the season. As he unlocked his office door, Eric considered an edict banning all decorations for the upcoming Thanksgiving and Christmas holidays… they wasted precious time and added nothing to the bottom line.

As he sat in his immense leather chair, Judy Severinson rushed in, a harried look on her middle age face. "Here's the day's agenda, Mr. Magana. You've scheduled an urgent meeting with Rubin first thing. At 9:30, Skip will give you the new sales projections. Engineering wants to update the status on the pressurization design at 10:15, Russ will brief you on OSHA's emission issues at 11:00 and for lunch, you've penciled in Ms. Angela Ascencio. After that you have…"

Eric tuned out the droning voice of his secretary. He dreaded facing that pompous, know-it-all Rubin and explaining their cash crunch. Eric figured his operations manager would probably gloat and play the "I told you so" card and demand another brutal cutback. Without a doubt, Rubin would insist he fire that pot-smoking, air-drum playing electrical engineer. But Eric couldn't can him—the kid was the son of a key Washington connection. He was stuck.

Already he'd cut janitorial service to once a month and the last layoff had emasculated the production floor. Eric released several sales people and outsourced half of accounting. Now, the damn lawyers, like buzzards on a carcass, were obliterating the bank account—just because that bitch, Julie Ann, had dodged serious trouble by fingering him. Even Nick Nolan had called to complain that he'd been shoved aside and grumbled that swarming lawyers hassled him daily. *I guess she nailed him, too.*

He sighed and waved his arm at Judy. "Send in Rubin."

That afternoon, Eric opened the medicine chest in his bathroom and opened a bottle of Tums. He chewed two tablets, thought a moment and gobbled another. *Antacids are becoming a habit.*

The morning had been a calamity. Rubin's tirade had been predictable; a livid battle that flared at the top of their voices.

Then, confirming his fears, sales continued to slide. "Hell, what do you expect?" Skip had yelled. "You've cut the sales staff as if it were a gangrene-laced leg."

His morning business struggled on with Ryan, the Engineering Manager, who choked and sputtered at the news. "Fire them? We look like idiots, Eric. I just hired those engineers to bail us out."

"I know," Eric had responded, feeling mortified. "Just keep Lanny, okay?"

The morning schedule wrapped up when Russ vacillated and ducked every question Eric posed about fumes from the paint department. "Doesn't *anyone* have answers?" He'd hollered.

After Ryan left, Eric picked up the phone and called Maxine, an official at the EPA who audited Dynamag's environmental procedures and monitored paint emissions. As he waited for the call to go through, he visualized her. She was tall, almost six feet, had the figure of a Barbie Doll and flaunted stunning long black hair. They'd met three times over the past year, and he'd tried to wheedle her into being more "understanding" concerning Dynamag's paint fume emissions. Offers of sex—his first choice—a trip to Jamaica or cash ricocheted off her like bullets hitting armor plate. She was impervious. *She's got me by the nuts and she's twisting. Give someone a little authority and...*

"Maxine Whittier's office, Peggy speaking."

"Is Maxine available? Eric Magana calling." He knew it was fruitless, but it was urgent that he resolve the problem: the cost of the vapor recovery equipment for the paint booth was mind-boggling. When she answered in her sultry, purring voice, Eric implored, cajoled and pleaded for relief, with no luck.

"I have to be squeaky clean, Eric," she said. "The election is just around the corner and politicians of all colors are digging up dirt. Everyone, from the Office of the Administrator on down, is nervous about the shake-ups in Washington. That damn Bellington has exposed another scandal. This time he's accusing people inside the EPA of taking bribes. Too close to home to dole out favors."

"Bellington? Don't worry. He's a friggin' Libertarian who'll never get elected, everyone knows that."

"Don't be too sure," Maxine cautioned. "It's only a week until Election Day and the latest Fox poll shows Bellington neck and neck with Stanford."

"Hell, Fox is so biased, you can't believe any of their garbage."

"Heard of A.I.M.? That alliance of big companies? They're making serious waves, donating wads of money to elect your so-called 'unelectable' Libertarian and his congressional followers. It's the huge companies: manufacturers, big oil, the banks and construction. They're acting like a big crowbar, prying loose every sympathetic official we've cultivated over the years."

"I know," Eric whimpered. "Even car makers have joined in. I don't know what they're thinking."

"I don't care what *anybody* is thinking," Maxine laughed. "Republican, Democrat or Libertarian. No matter. I have a cushy job and I'm not going to jeopardize it. I've another call; got to go."

"But my business is on its ass. I need…"

A dial tone droned in Eric's ear and, in slow motion, he eased the phone back in its cradle. All at once, a snatch from Bellington's speech popped into his head. "Where have the good-paying blue-collar jobs gone?" Bellington had asked. "When you're driving, look around. In 1950, it was rare to see a foreign car. Today? American cars comprise a meager 45% of total sales—and then only if you count Chrysler, now owned by Fiat in Italy."

But the most troubling sentence the Libertarian had uttered was, "The reason for our high unemployment is hiding in plain sight. Under union leadership, we have lost our passion for work."

So what if union shops are to blame with their idiotic work rules? I bust my ass every day, Eric thought. *I'm on top of things.*

He stared into space and then noticed the wall clock; he had only 35 minutes before meeting Angela for lunch.

Even though the restaurant was cool, Eric felt clammy. He grimaced as he downed his third bourbon on the rocks. "Terrible stuff," he complained to Angela. "They don't have my brand."

He shoved aside his half-full plate of seafood linguini and waved at the waiter for another drink.

He couldn't shake his anger at Julie Ann and his lawyers. "You'd think my 500-dollar-an-hour attorneys could get me off. Instead, they made me plea-bargain—admit to being an accomplice. At least I wasn't sucked into a trial."

Eric ignored his lunch companion and pondered his problems. The call with Maxine aggravated his despondency that lingered from the disastrous deposition two months ago. During those proceedings, Lanny, that smelly, hippy engineer he'd hired, confessed to using Optimal's drawings and Madison's code. Eric's lawyers tossed up their hands, saying that their case had just blown up. A trial, they advised, would be a blunder; so he'd agreed to schedule a meeting with that conniving Optimal lawyer and work out a settlement.

Eric swirled his fresh bourbon, rattling the ice cubes and scowled. Predictably, tragedy had struck at yesterday's afternoon meeting with that slime-ball attorney. Weinstein, with the breezy acquiescence of Dynamag's round-heeled lawyers, foisted a disaster on him. Now, he'd have to relinquish the manufacturing rights for the pressurization system to that sophomoric schoolboy at Optimal. They invalidated his patent, leaving the door open for Optimal to reopen its claim—a certain victory for Wyatt whatever his last name is. He remembered the glitter in Weinstein's eyes as he slapped the table saying, "Now, let's talk about damages. My client has suffered severe financial setbacks warranting compensation."

Eric's lawyers had glanced at one another and huddled. They balked, of course, but he knew it was pure posturing. Like a fencer, Weinstein thrust and parried for an hour as Eric's legal team bobbed and weaved. In the end, they capitulated, agreeing to another meeting to work out the details. It was going to cost him plenty. There had been mention of liens and sale of assets to cover the tab. That bastard Weinstein had even suggested that he sell the Gulfstream to raise money. His lawyers had nodded; one saying, "There's always Chapter Eleven bankruptcy."

"I'm thinking Chapter Seven," said another. "Dynamag's cash flow is nil and prospects suck. I'm thinking the only way to raise cash is liquidation."

Sitting across from Angela and clutching his chilled old-fashioned glass, Eric felt the bourbon churn in his stomach as he weighed the consequences. His vision of a diversified Dynamag, capitalizing on the big military jet order, was demolished. His financial reserves were depleted and accounting, fighting cash flow troubles, stretched payments well past 90 days.

His real irritation was Julie Ann. Because of her plea-bargaining treachery, the bitch avoided major legal retributions. They fired her of course, and levied a small fine. But nothing else. Of course she'd never work in government again which pleased Eric, but there was a downside—he'd lost a reliable connection inside the Patent Office.

Worse, that morning when he walked through his factory, the workers halted their chatter and looked away. Eric figured the news had leaked; they were gossiping about his disastrous gaffe into aircraft. Flushing with humiliation, he'd retreated to his office, wrestling with strange feelings: embarrassment, inadequacy and confusion.

With a shake of his head, Eric ordered another bourbon.

Angela gulped the last of her Champagne. "Did you hear what I said? Is this legal fuss going to make us give up our weekend in Rio?" she asked, fluffing her platinum hair. "I've already gone to The City and bought three gorgeous new outfits for the trip."

As the waiter laid the check by his elbow, Eric recalled an invoice for jet fuel that Judy handed him as he was leaving for lunch. The fixed base operator wanted the balance of his account paid off before gassing up the Gulfstream with another $30,000 load of Jet-A.

"Happy now, little man?"

Startled, Eric looked around and his eyes jerked to a stop on the surface of his bourbon glass. There, shimmering on the amber liquid, was his father's face. "Gonna ride that jet plane to Washington and bribe your connections?" The face sneered. "Gonna explain the bankruptcy to your babe? Cancel her trip?"

Eric thrust his finger into the whiskey and as the image shattered, he thought he heard his father cackle.

Suddenly, Eric had to quell a surge of tears; his world had crumbled.

*   *   *

Wyatt topped off his coffee mug and walked up behind Lauren, who was fixing dinner. He set the mug on the counter and rubbed her shoulders and kissed the back of her neck.

"You'd better stop that, Honey, if you're expecting something to eat tonight."

"Suppose I say that I'm hungry, but food isn't on my mind."

Lauren tilted her head toward Timmie sitting at the dining table, thumbing her handheld game console. "You better find a diversion for your daughter first."

Wyatt chuckled as he took a big slurp of coffee, and lowered his voice. "Kids can be a serious drag sometimes. The good news is she's a real sound sleeper, so later tonight…"

He leaned against the counter top. "New subject. Things are going crazy at Bellington's field office. The poll numbers are getting better every day. They have me working on a spreadsheet that tracks voter profiles. It's similar to exit polling, but aimed at swinging the votes, not figuring out what happened after the fact. Also, Mike and Bernie are putting in a couple of hours every evening on the phone banks. I'm getting very optimistic. It's exciting to be doing something instead of just bellyaching."

"It's nice to see you diving in. I always enjoy your soapbox tirades against politicians, but it's better to get involved."

"I'm learning a lot." Wyatt waved a small pamphlet and said, "They've published excerpts from a recent speech: Bellington's stance on education,"

"I'll put the potatoes in the oven to bake and you can tell me about it," Lauren said. "Let's go in the living room."

"You won't believe this stuff, Dear," Wyatt said. "Let me read a couple of paragraphs, okay?"

"Sure; we have forty-five minutes to dinner," Lauren said, slipping out of her apron.

"Here's what Bellington says." Wyatt wiggled deeper into his chair, sipped his coffee and began.

"In the past, the best educational system in the world propelled our workers and leaders. America has accumulated 343 Nobel Prizes compared to 88 for the runner-up, Great Britain. Once, when we revered the teaching profession, only the very best aspired to the awesome obligation of creating the stuff of the next generation. Even today, like the afterglow of the Big Bang, foreign students still apply to our universities in droves."

Wyatt turned to Lauren. "That's true. UCLA is full of them, particularly in engineering."

Continuing, he read, "The government's own statistics show our high school seniors rank nineteenth in the world in math, behind such countries as Slovenia and Lithuania.

In science, we're sixteenth, behind Iceland and the Czech Republic. For every engineer we graduate, China produces five and India four. Seventy percent of U.S. engineering doctoral degrees are awarded to foreign-born students. Forget about degrees in Gender Studies, Theatre or Art History. Those majors lead straight to McDonald's or the welfare line. America has traded our historic zeal of the hard sciences for the comfy feel-good pursuit of egalitarian blather."

"Egalitarian blather?" Lauren chuckled. "And you accuse me of using fancy words?"

With a shrug, Wyatt said, "Kinda over-the-top, but you know me and engineering. Science is my foundation; it's what I live for; it nourishes me. When Einstein spoke of his work, he said, 'I seek the face of God.' For me, God resides in the Periodic Table of the Elements and calculus."

"Bellington's words are depressing," Lauren said. "But what can he do?"

"Ah-ha," Wyatt laughed, waving the booklet. "Here's what he says: 'Unions have resisted changes in education, even though the world has been yanked upside down by advances in science and technology. Vouchers are one answer. Let parents select good schools where teacher pay is tied to student success. When schools grant tenure, they divorce performance from security. You'll find no tenure in industry, for a good reason. Abolish it.

"Let's encourage our universities to recruit promising youngsters from foreign lands to come and study science. Along with their degrees, grant them citizenship and let us join them in their exuberant march into the future as Americans."

"That's controversial stuff, Dear," Lauren said, cradling her chin in her hand. "He's taking on teachers' unions and immigration as well. That won't bolster his election chances."

"I'm not so sure, but it's refreshing to hear bold new ideas to deal with our systemic problems."

"True enough. Like they say—if you like what you have…"

Wyatt smiled. "Yeah." He stretched and yawned. "Mind if I change the subject? Didn't you say Emile made a nice sale today?"

"Yes. The sale surprised me. It was an antique Haviland Limoges dinner service for eight. It went for $3,650. It's a nice sum, but it won't even cover half our credit card bill."

"I hope it can hold off the bill collectors for a few days. Still, we're just squeaking by. I don't know what we'll do if we get the patent. There's not a dime to fund the test systems. Optimal's on hold. With AirEnvironment demanding hardware by year-end, it could kill us if the Dali sale takes until April. I sure hope it's genuine."

Wyatt was raising his mug to his lips when the phone rang, interrupting him. "Hello? Oh, hi, Art. Got news about yesterday's meeting in Jersey?"

"Sit down, Wyatt," Art instructed. "I'm going to rock your world with good news. I just spent the day with Dynamag's attorneys writing up the final terms of yesterday's meeting with Magana. To summarize, Dynamag will forfeit any claims to the patent. I'll reapply at the Patent Office and get your application in motion. I expect Optimal will have the patent in no time. Also, Dynamag cedes all manufacturing rights to you. They're out of the pressurization business. Lastly, they acknowledge you're entitled to damages. We've set up another meeting to iron out the specifics of the settlement. You'll get a very substantial sum, I'm sure. The only problem is Dynamag is running on fumes...no cash. It may be a long time before we see actual money."

"Good grief, Art! You're a miracle worker!" Covering the mouthpiece, Wyatt yelled, "Lauren! Art has nailed Dynamag to the wall!"

Wyatt picked up his mug and paced back and forth as the lawyer explained every detail of the meeting. Thirty minutes later, Wyatt sank in his chair saying, "I can't thank you enough, Art. We owe you big time. Someday we'll make it worth your while. Someday..."

"There's a long way to go, but today was big," Art cautioned. "Sorry. Gotta run. I have a plane to catch."

Wyatt switched off the phone. "Lauren, listen up. There's a lot of news." Excitedly, he briefed his wife on the conversation, concluding, "I can't believe it. Optimal has clear sailing. All we need is the Dali."

Lauren rose and gave Wyatt a warm hug. "Patience, my Love, it's just a matter of time."

Feeling awkward, Wyatt said, "One more thing. In the meeting, Art learned that Madison gave Dynamag our code. He's going to sue her for industrial espionage. He says she'll lose her interest in Optimal."

"Serves her right." Lauren walked over to Wyatt and kissed him. "I believe you were saying something about later tonight. Let's get dinner on the table and then Timmie to bed."

Three days later, Optimal received a contract from AirEnvironment for three systems, contingent on passing quality surveys by DCMA and the FAA. The delivery date was shoved out to early April because of government delays and specification revisions, which brought little comfort to Wyatt; the task ahead was complex and the schedule daunting. And there was no money.

Chapter 24

The morning of Election Day was dreary and fogbound. Wyatt whistled a spirited tune as he unlocked Optimal's door. A frigid wave of musty air greeted him when it swung open. "Place smells like a mausoleum," he said to Lauren. Timmie, given a day off from school, followed them. Wyatt went to the wall thermostat and turned on the furnace, which came to life with a soft huff. He flipped on the overhead lights and said, "Mike, I see, has piled a few crates of parts on the work bench over there."

Lauren shivered and snuggled deeper into her coat. "It's a good thing I had the gas turned back on. It's downright cold today." In the dim light that stole through the grimy front window, Lauren drew her finger across a bench top, leaving a shiny streak in the dust. "Mike is no house-keeper, though." Lauren snatched a paper towel from the dispenser on the wall and wiped down the stools and chairs, making them habitable for the first time since Ed Morales surveyed Optimal last summer.

Wyatt looked around the room. The forlorn sight

depressed him, a reminder of the abandoned rock quarry that bordered the I-5 freeway: grimy and gray, with weeds growing up through crevasses in the machinery. He slipped his arm around Lauren, drew Timmie to his side and they stood in silence. "The place may look dead, but we'll bring it back," Wyatt said at last.

Timmie leaned her head against Wyatt's chest. "It's not so bad. I'll help clean. Can you bring the vacuum and duster from home? Soap, too?" She slipped the paper towel from Lauren's hand, went to the window and wiped away a large cobweb. "Yucky."

Wyatt strolled over to the hot-air test stand. "Everything's here, ready to go. Altitude chambers too. Now that Emile sold that dinnerware, I'll call and see if I can get the compressor and vacuum pump reinstalled. That will drain our reserves, but everything could be running within a week. Can we swing it?"

"You bet. With Art's news and the P.O., we'd be stupid not to go for the brass ring. Forget the credit card bills," Lauren said, her perky face beaming. "Emile has brought us a bit of cheer, even though it's 'Like snow upon the desert's dusty face'—Omar Khayyam if you didn't recognize it."

"Big fancy words and now a silly kind of story—poem—whatever. You read too much." Wyatt picked up a pressure gage and dusted its face. "Now that Dynamag's scuttled, this little guy will be hard at work soon." Wyatt caressed the burners like he was petting a puppy and stooped to study a sticker on a temperature readout. "We'll have to re-calibrate everything before…"

Mike burst into the office and bellowed, "The patent!

You're getting the fucking patent and an order too! Oops, Timmie. Didn't see you."

"Hello, Mr. Graham. Don't worry…I know a bunch of those words. I'm not allowed to use them, of course."

"Of course." Mike turned to Wyatt. "I couldn't believe the news when you called. You got the manufacturing rights and the patent. They'll have to pay damages too. We're in business!" He glanced around. "Where's Bernie?"

"He said he wanted to vote before coming over. Have you voted?"

"Damn right," Mike said. "First in line. Today's the day. It's Bellington or disaster. They're expecting a huge turnout."

"Last night's news said the latest polls are showing Bellington three or four points ahead," Lauren said, smiling.

"I thrashed around all last night, thinking about the election and Optimal," Wyatt said. "Not only is Optimal on the launch pad, but the last few weeks have been nuts at Bellington's field office. Bet I've put in a hundred hours setting up their computerized call lists and tracking programs. I even made a few dozen campaign calls myself. You and Bernie have been working the phones, too. We've put a bunch into this. If Bellington wins, our business would take off at flank speed. If not…well, head winds." He took a seat and crossed his legs. "This is an odd political campaign. Usually, the unions and political machines dominate everything. This time, however, the big news is A.I.M. Seen those TV commercials they sponsored? Hammering on the economy? Saying industry makes jobs, not deficit spending? I've never seen such a unified front."

"We'll see if people listened," Lauren said. "More to

the point, we'll see what they decide: hard honest work or sticking out their hands."

"The Libertarians complain about our national debt," Wyatt said. "The government's unfunded liabilities exceed a million dollars per taxpayer. One of the volunteers mentioned that everyone carries debt—mortgage, car payment, that sort of thing. My reply? 'Who pays off your car? You do, of course. Who pays the national debt? Nobody…it just keeps growing.' So I pressed the point. 'Your children and grandchildren will have to pay the interest,' I said. 'Over $300 billion a year. It's our kids who'll be forced to pay for our extravagant lifestyle.' Guess that put him in his place."

Lauren laughed. "And the guy was working for Bellington? It sounds like he's working for the wrong candidate…he'd be better off on welfare."

"Hey, don't knock welfare—I'm on it," Bernie called out as he shuffled through the door looking bent from fatigue. He gave Lauren a big hug and shook hands with Mike and Wyatt.

"Don't forget me," scolded Timmie.

Bernie gave her a quick squeeze and turned to the others. "Sorry I'm late; the lines at the polling booth are a mile long. For once, it's not just Democrats and Republicans—hell, they're the same; but Libertarians represent a real option. It's going to be a wild ride."

"I'm sorry to hear SAC laid you off, my friend," Wyatt said. "Grim news for sure."

"Yeah. SAC has almost shuttered its doors. As much as I hate to say it, right now unemployment insurance looks good."

"Precision Tool is in bad shape, too," Mike said. "I managed to pull in a little work last week. Wyatt helped with an RFP—a proposal—and we won the competition. That helps, but I still have time to take off a few hours. Sad. Not my habit."

Wyatt waved everyone into chairs that Lauren had situated around the conference table. An effervescent sense of purpose and enthusiasm surged in his mind. He realized the huge grin on his face belied the serious business he wanted to discuss, but problems had smothered him for a long time. He would forgive himself for a bit of exhilaration.

"Okay, guys, I'll summarize my phone call last night. The patent problem is going to evaporate and AirEnvironment has placed an order with a couple of contingencies—I guess they've nowhere else to go. Bottom line: if we can put together a little cash, Optimal is ready to launch. However we need a plan."

Bernie scooted his chair closer to the table and grinned. "I think I'll apply for a new full-time job: handy man for Precision Tool—right beside you, Mike. I'll do it for nothing which is about what I've been making as a part-timer the last few months."

"Bullshit," Mike growled. "I can always use a top-drawer manufacturing guy. I'll pay you too. Get you off fucking unemployment."

"But you just said things are tough at Precision," Bernie protested. "You can't afford it."

"He's right," Wyatt said walking to the counter to make a pot of coffee. As he returned, he decided the time was now. "Bernie has a point, Mike. Lauren and I have talked a few things over, knowing how things are with your business.

You've said it yourself: job shopping is tough. How can you compete with the Chinese where wages are four dollars an hour? The only way we can survive is to develop unique products and get patent protection. That's why Art's news on the pressurization patent has me pumped up."

Mike rubbed his chin and scowled. "What are you saying? You wanna set me up with some proprietary gizmo?"

Wyatt nodded. "Actually, we're considering something more. You have an incredible manufacturing facility and I have a gift for engineering design. Sounds like a case of a sprocket and chain—they mesh. I bet we could put together one hell of a company. A merger, if you will."

Time hung heavy in the air as Mike scratched his stubble. Timmie ceased her aimless wandering around the shop and sidled up to Wyatt with a quizzical look on her freckled face. She jumped when Mike banged the tabletop with his fist, saying, "Might work! As you say, everyone is exporting machine work to low wage countries. It's killing shops like me. It makes sense that a business has to have an innovative product line to survive. Optimal and Precision—horse and carriage, Mars and Curiosity…"

"Isaac Newton and calculus," Wyatt bubbled.

Mike laughed. "I don't know about that."

"We're in this together," Lauren said. "We have a financial stake in Optimal."

"But a merger is in the future," Wyatt said. "Right now we have a short-term panic: how to find money to deliver a system by early April."

"If I might belabor the obvious," Lauren interrupted. "We don't have a customer, not in a formal sense, anyway.

AirEnvironment is anxious, but their purchase order requires we certify our facilities before we can deliver hardware."

"Leave it to an engineer to overlook a small detail such as that," Wyatt mumbled with an embarrassed grin. "I'll call that new AirEnvironment buyer, Pete Sykes, today. Coordinate with my buddy Ed, of course. I'll fill them in on our thoughts and estimated schedule."

"There's no time to waste," Mike grumbled. "We have to light a fire under this job right now. Time's running out. Remember that new rule the FAA is drafting, Wyatt? The one that would invalidate your design and resurrect that old stuff of Randel Products and Garvey Airmotive?"

"Bet your sweet fanny," Wyatt murmured. "We have to beat them to the punch."

Like a tennis fan, Timmie's eyes bounced from her father to Mike and back. Her studied look grew more intense by the moment. Conversely, Bernie had little to say and seemed to melt into the background, a weary smile lingering on his lips.

Wyatt felt a surge of his old confidence return and without realizing it, took command of the meeting. "Forget the FAA's rule-making for now. Let's start with Precision Tool. Mike, we need to get ready for the quality surveys…a big job."

"Hell, Precision was already certified," Mike said. "but the expanded requirements means I'll have to change my quality manual, procedures and even record keeping."

Wyatt nodded. "I'll help."

"Will the military version require any design changes?" Mike asked.

"Might." Wyatt suspected the requirements had changed, but until he saw the new specifications, there was no way to quantify the revisions. He decided to talk with Ed right away. "I don't expect big mechanical changes—just plating specs, quality control records, that sort of thing."

"We'll need to understand the cost impact before we commit firm prices to AirEnvironment," Lauren said.

"Yup," Wyatt grunted. "Mechanical design isn't the biggie; it's the electronics and software."

"Big problem." Mike said.

Wyatt leaned back in his chair and put an arm around Timmie, who looked transfixed by the proceedings. "In this arena, I'm like Ronald McDonald trying to do computerized stress simulations. Fighter aircraft have to resist very high vibration, radiation, EMP and all that garbage. Software certification is to higher standards, too. I just don't have a clue."

"Although it's military, maybe surveillance aircraft can get by with easier requirements," Mike suggested.

Wyatt shrugged. He felt as useless as a ship in dry-dock and realized how much he'd relied on Madison. The thought gnawed at him. In spite of the pain she'd caused, she was a dynamite programmer. Finding her successor would be tough. Once again, he considered contacting her to work with the problems, but he shook with revulsion. Clearing his head, he said, "We'll have to hire a new electronics guru right away. Any ideas?"

Bernie stirred. "I know a guy who worked for a local machinery manufacturer. He did their electronic controls and programming. Laid off, I think."

"Get hold of him," Wyatt commanded.

"I can place ads on Monster, Craigslist and all those other sites," Lauren offered.

"Daddy looks for jobs in the newspaper," Timmie said. "Could we do an ad there?"

"You bet, Timmie," Wyatt said, smiling. He walked to the coffee pot and filled his mug. Returning to the table, his mind clicked as he led the discussion, carefully delineating the problems and probing for solutions. He could feel the team coming together, challenging every difficulty and committing to each task with conviction. Wyatt was giddy. He was reviving Optimal bit by bit. After nearly a year, things were on a roll. He was back.

"Okay," Wyatt said. "It looks as if everyone has their action items, right?"

Everyone murmured their agreement, even Timmie, who'd assumed responsibility for the cleanup and putting the small parts bins in order. Everyone smiled and looked at one another, radiant and confident.

"Too bad Lee Wong couldn't break away," Lauren lamented. "He's the one who might make long term funding possible."

"Be sure to phone him. He'll appreciate a briefing," Wyatt suggested. "One more thing. Let's pull Lee and Art together and get them thinking how we might coordinate a merger between Optimal and Precision." Wyatt grinned. "Me? I'm going to write a want ad for the electronics guy, glue myself to the tube and watch the election returns. Big day for Optimal. Big day for America."

*　　*　　*

Lauren looked forward to calling Wong and giving him an update. Warmed by his devotion to Optimal, she became conscious that his attention wasn't pure business. In his awkward and shy way, Lee's affection for her was increasingly apparent and the thought pleased her; it was nice to be liked.

A vision of Lee Wong's gentle smile came to mind and Lauren realized the banker had been a beacon for her the past few months. Wyatt's tumultuous moods tore at her and their marriage, in many ways, lay tattered. Her husband seemed to be two people: one an ineffectual, yet affectionate father, and the other a depressed monomaniac. She feared which might appear. But Lee was a harbor in a storm. His kindness and modesty were tranquilizers for her fragmented mind and his steadiness and clam demeanor drew her to him. A refuge.

She understood Lee's attraction to her. He lived an isolated life, adopting a safe routine contained in the predictability of bachelorhood and banking. Lauren had always nestled in the cradle of his expertise and generous assistance and, by revealing her personal travails, she'd made him a confidant. *He means a lot to me.*

Abruptly, Lauren tossed thoughts of Lee aside. *Stop this. My husband is in trouble and it's my duty to stand by him. Timmie too.*

She turned back to business. While excited that Optimal was recovering and welcomed the prospect of teaming with Mike and Precision Tool, Lauren was ambivalent about the meeting earlier that day. She worried over Wyatt's turnaround and remembered the way engineering once consumed him. She recalled tension in the house as

Timmie drifted away from her father, whose interaction with his daughter hadn't been harsh or critical, just one of neglect. His love of science left little room for diversions. Like his family.

Conversely, Lauren marveled at Wyatt's focus and his innate mastery of engineering. His skills set him apart from the mediocre throngs of average Joes and she worshipped him.

But in the last few months, Wyatt had battled massive setbacks, which jolted him from his usual mindset. He'd hugged her more often, and they'd come together as peers, struggling with "the situation." Somehow, Lauren felt closer to Wyatt, but on a different plane. But a return to his old ways? Today at the meeting, she saw his narrow focus on engineering return; even his gestures were emphatic like before.

However, Timmie's recent bonding with Wyatt made Lauren feel left out, even jealous. Unemployed, Wyatt was at home while she was away at work, an obvious disadvantage for her, although she rejected the notion she was in competition with her husband for Timmie's affection. Perhaps money from the Dali would allow her to quit and become a full-time mom. Lauren mulled the idea and tried to think how she might reconnect with Timmie. *Perhaps we could do homework together, romp in the park and maybe catch an afternoon movie.* Anxious for action, an idea came to her. *I'll check to see if it's too late to get Timmie back into soccer. She would like that.*

Chapter 25

Heavy dew clung to the trees and shrubs as Wyatt, shivering with the chill, scurried across the driveway and snatched the newspaper. He peeled off the plastic wrapping as he stepped through the front door.

In disbelief, Wyatt starred at the headlines:

Stanford Wins, Bellington Concedes

Last night, he'd fallen asleep in front of the TV waiting on sluggish returns and listening to pompous commentators. At one in the morning, he'd given up and collapsed in bed knowing Bellington was trailing, but the votes from Texas and California weren't in.

Now, in a trance, he made a pot of coffee and tried to read the article describing the close victory for Stanford. He filled his mug, shook his head and then set the mug down without drinking.

Lauren padded into the kitchen wearing her bathrobe and slippers.

"How could the polls be so wrong?" Wyatt grumbled,

waving the paper. "It looked to me as if Bellington could squeak through."

Glancing at the newspaper, Lauren pressed her lips into a grim line. "It's not a mystery. In my college psych class, the professor explained a fundamental problem with polls. Everyone wants to please the interviewer, to answer questions in ways they figure the pollster wants to hear. In this case, the voters were probably ashamed to admit they wanted Washington charity, so in public, they climbed on Bellington's honorable-sounding bandwagon. But in the privacy of the voting booth…"

Wyatt turned her explanation over in his mind. "So you're saying the typical voter is a weak-kneed, two-faced pickpocket."

"Seems like it."

Wyatt slapped the newspaper and growled, "Well, the turkeys will get what they wanted. Look at this." Showing the front page to Lauren, he pointed to a large article:

Dollar Falls

Lauren nodded. "It doesn't bode well for the business. A weak dollar will heat up inflation."

Wyatt shrugged. "Nothing we can do now. This article says Washington is pushing through another massive stimulus. That should pump up the stock market bubble and assure Maddox's military jet goes into production. Even so, I'll give it a year before everything collapses."

Lauren followed Wyatt into the living room and sat. She folded her hands in her lap and stared at them. "So what can we do?"

"We have a contract with AirEnvironment for the test systems. No alternative but to keep pushing and hope for the big production order."

"I guess." Lauren shifted, tucking her legs beneath her. Her pert nose wrinkled and her freckles drew together. "We have a lot of loose ends. For instance, Mike's machine shop is in trouble. I think we should meet, figure out how we can help cover operations for the next few months and then draft an agreement. In April, when the Dali sells, we might have enough money to open the door to a genuine merger."

"You have my head spinning as fast as a destroyer's turbines," Wyatt complained. "We should focus on the near term. Sure, let's talk to Mike, but the immediate panic, besides money, is to find a top-notch electronics engineer, one that's up to speed on military design."

Lauren rose and beckoned with her finger. "Well? We've drafted the ad; let's polish it right now. We can post it on a dozen websites by tonight."

Wyatt laughed. "You're a real pushy broad, aren't you?" He stood, wrapped his arm around her waist and said, "Better place it in the *Burbank Leader* and the *Times,* too. Can't ignore Timmie's suggestion. Don't need any guff from her."

Bernie tottered through Optimal's front door balancing a large carton of components and said, "Here are several spare housings, Wyatt. Now that we're gearing up, Mike wanted you to inspect them to see if we can salvage any." He set the box on the end of the conference table and dropped into a chair, mopping his brow. "I don't care if it *is* late November, it's still damned hot."

Wyatt rummaged through the parts. "These need modifications, but they'll be minor machine work. Not a big problem."

"Well, we need only three sets for the first shipment." Bernie glanced at a maze of papers that buried Wyatt's desk. "What's all that mess?"

"It's the new specifications for the military system. I'm going insane trying to figure out how to fix the electronics and software. Changes are massive. I'm a football fullback in a ballet. I haven't any idea what I'm reading."

"Didn't you post the programmer job on the web last week?"

"Closer to two weeks back," Wyatt replied. "Had a couple of interviews. Both guys were awash in theory but couldn't recognize a hot soldering iron if they sat on one. I showed them several of Madison's algorithms and they were mystified. I screened them by phone, of course, and asked if they had military experience. Both assured me they did. Weird. I'm guessing they play around with those stupid computer games, but neither had a knack for practical stuff."

Bernie laughed, "Maybe they meant war games like 'Call to Duty.' My neighbor's kid plays it by the hour."

Wyatt shook his head.

"Any more prospects?" Bernie asked.

"I've tried to reach that engineer you mentioned—the guy who was laid off. His wife said he's back East visiting family. Returns next week. Other than that…"

"We'd better do *something,* Wyatt. Even though they extended the deadline, we have to hump."

"You think I don't know?" Wyatt cradled his head in his hands. "I'm desperate. No matter how much I churn water, there's only one person who can save our bacon—Madison. She knows the design and could dive in just like that," he said, snapping his fingers.

"So? She's in town. Call her."

"Come on, my friend. You're aware we had a falling-out. It's all I can do to mention her name, much less look her in the eye again. Put us in the same room and you have gunpowder and matches. Lauren often talks about being between a rock and a hard place; that's where I am. My choices? I can be stubborn and allow Optimal to get torpedoed once more or beg Madison for help. For now, I've decided to prey for a miracle—without Madison."

A week had passed and Wyatt's anxiety skyrocketed. He had three more interviews—three more strikeouts. He made no progress on the electronics and the shipping deadline surged a week closer. His only hope was the engineer Bernie recommended. Wyatt had finally connected and arranged for an interview the next day. It loomed as the last gasp effort.

Even though the weather had turned nippy, Wyatt sweated as he prodded the computer keys, seeking solutions to a difficult algorithm. *This is insane. I keep getting error messages.* He squirmed closer, his nose inches from the glowing screen and hoped his display of intensity might intimidate the computer.

"Hello, Wyatt."

He looked up and there, silhouetted against the glare

from the window, was the slinky form of Madison. With tentative steps, she approached and fixed her stunning green eyes on him. "I hear you're in trouble."

Wyatt coughed, gasping for breath. "Madison! What the hell?"

"May I?" she asked, gesturing to a chair next to his desk.

"Uhhh." Wyatt muttered. "Yeah. Sure." Hate and distrust swirled in his mind, but her soft smile and demure manner disarmed him. "What do you mean, 'I'm in trouble?'"

"Bernie's worried about you. He told me you mentioned my name—you wanted help to sort out software glitches and PCB design."

"Goddamn him. I don't know how many times..."

"Don't blame Bernie. I bought him lunch, schmoozed him and lathered on compliments. You should know; when I turn it on, men turn to putty. He's a great guy who worships you and wants to lend a hand. He told me you couldn't see any way out of the redesign problems without me. Right?"

"Maybe I said that," Wyatt growled, "but there's no way we can work together again."

Madison nodded. "I've changed. Sure, you remember me as a predatory bitch and perhaps that was true. But now, I've become resigned to the fact that you, Lauren and Timmie are a devoted family. That doesn't mean I don't love you—I do. More than ever. But if I interfere, it might destroy you, your family and whatever relationship might evolve between us. My only solution is to love you from afar—the way I love the pioneers of my science: Galileo

Galilei, Michael Faraday and Nikola Tesla—that handsome devil. Bizarre perhaps. Even perverted. But there's no alternative."

Speechless, Wyatt tried to gather his thoughts.

Madison pulled her shimmering hair back and tucked it behind an ear, not in her usual coquettish way, but resembling a shy schoolgirl. "There's another aspect to this. One you will understand. Like you, I'm imbued with my craft. In science. Together, we have scaled glorious heights in our quests. I want to preserve my legacy, to have you think warmly of me whenever you see a Maddox jet whispering overhead. I have come today to help, to help preserve and complete our work."

Astonished, Wyatt sorted through Madison's words. Collaborating, he knew, they would have a chance to conquer the new specifications on time. Optimal would be saved, at least until they delivered the test systems. "Glorious heights," she'd said and Wyatt smiled at the recollection. All he had to do was say "yes," and he'd demolish an impenetrable barrier.

With a patient look, Madison crossed her legs and tilted her head to one side.

She seems so...angelic, Wyatt thought. *The aggression is gone. Her offer sounds earnest and genuine. Why not take her up?*

Madison jiggled her foot and lifted an eyebrow.

Wyatt clenched his fists. *You idiot! Lauren would have a fit!* About to dismiss Madison, he shuddered with the realization that Optimal was ready to go under, mined by his ignorance. Madison could save the company. Was there a way? Perhaps she could come during the day while Lauren was at work; he didn't have to tell his wife. Then he remembered…he'd scheduled an interview the next day with an applicant who sounded great on the phone—Bernie's guy. With a sense of relief, he decided not to decide. "Tell you what, Madison. Let me think it over, Okay?"

"Sure." She rose and stepped to the door. "I'll be in touch." With a saucy glance over her shoulder, she winked and left.

Chapter 26

The next morning, Wyatt set aside thoughts of Madison and concentrated on supervising the installation of the huge vacuum pump. He poked the large red "STOP" button on the control panel and the roar of the pump faded. He gave a thumbs-up sign to the installers who collected their tools and drove away. *Well, that obliterates the bank account.*

He glanced at his watch, noting he had twenty minutes before an interview he'd scheduled with Singh. Hunched over his desk, Wyatt pushed aside a pile of résumés. The ads had been running for only two weeks, but responses inundated his desk. Most had no experience in military electronics and fewer yet were skilled in both circuit design and software. He'd conducted a number phone interviews since the fruitless face-to-face sessions last week, but only one had been encouraging: the guy Bernie had mentioned. Ravinder Singh was his name. He spoke with the soft lilt of a native of India, but his English was clear. Importantly, his apparent technical skills were complimented by refreshing enthusiasm. As a lark, Wyatt googled "Ravinder" and discovered it meant "God of Knowledge." *Good omen*, Wyatt mused.

While he waited, Wyatt browsed through his email inbox, finding a dozen more responses. Abruptly, he shuddered. One read: "From: Madison McKenzie. Subject: together again?" She was following up on yesterday's conversation. Wyatt's fingers poised over the reply key. With a grunt, he set his jaw and struck. "Don't push. Give me a few days." The computer made a whishing sound when he jabbed the send button. He was ashamed to see he was shaking.

"Mr. Morgan?"

Wyatt's head jerked up and standing there was a tall dusky young man who extended his hand. "I'm Ravinder Singh. I plan to work for you."

Wyatt had to smile at Singh's audacity. The applicant was neatly dressed in Dockers and a striped dress shirt. His shiny black hair was trimmed and, unlike current fashion, was clean-shaven.

Wyatt stood and shook hands. "Pleased to meet you Mr. Singh, Wyatt Morgan."

"Please. My friends call me Rav."

"Rav it is." Wyatt waved him to a chair. "I'll ask the question everyone says to avoid. Why don't you tell me about yourself?"

With a nod, Rav replied, "Good question and the only one I've rehearsed." A wide smile revealed bright, perfect teeth. "It's obvious I'm from India. My parents brought me to the states some sixteen years ago when I was ten. I'm a Cal Tech grad and worked on a couple of NASA projects. I did contract work with Lockheed...that's where I gained experience in military work. They laid me off with a bunch of other people when the project was canceled."

"I thought defense spending was booming. What happened?"

"Washington moves in mysterious ways."

Wyatt had to laugh. "Got that right." Warming to his task, Wyatt tilted back in his chair and crossed his legs. "If I'm correct, Singh is a Sikh name, right?"

"Most people don't know that. Yes, I am…well sort of. My parents are hardcore. Father has the beard, wears a turban and even carries the Kirpan—short sword. But I grew up here; this is my country. Kids rebel, you know, and I became an *über*-American."

"And your father?"

Rav shrugged. "Sikhs are warriors. He's tough to change."

For over two hours they talked science and engineering. Rav's grasp of the nuances of design startled Wyatt who likened the man's mind to the vigor of a squall at sea. They settled into a virtual dual, challenging each other and dashing electrical schematics and logic diagrams on scrap paper with bold pencil slashes. An outsider would have compared their discussion to a championship tennis match…rapid cannon-like serves and bull's-eye returns. Characteristically, Wyatt's passion for engineering swept him away. Rav was a catalyst that ignited Wyatt's zeal for innovation and his mind whirled in a world of ecstasy.

The cherry on the sundae? Rav was a certified solder technician.

Breathless, Wyatt asked, "Plans for dinner?"

"I was planning to dine with you tonight."

Once more, Wyatt laughed. "Good. Let me call my wife, Lauren. She's the accountant, strategic advisor and my direct boss," he winked. "Together, we'll work out the terms of your employment over a steak."

* * *

In the dim light of the Mexican restaurant, Lauren chuckled under her breath as Rav ordered a Margarita, blended, with salt. Somehow, it was odd that an Indian would order tequila and Baja-style camarónes.

Wyatt wanted to go to IHOP, but Lauren pointed out that an up-scale restaurant was more suitable for an interview. Wyatt gave in, but insisted that Rav be allowed to pick his favorite cuisine. So, Guava Garden it was.

Lauren leaned back in the booth, sipped her drink and listened to Wyatt and Rav banter. She didn't understand a word…something about EMI susceptibility, but it didn't matter. Their excitement was contagious, and she found herself drawn into their fervor. Once again, Lauren swelled with pride listening to her husband flex his engineering prowess. Rav, it was apparent, was no slouch in the science department either. *They're like two little boys in a sand box,* she mused.

It was Wyatt who diverted the conversation to the real purpose of the meeting: pay, duties and title. "Enough of the fun stuff, Rav. I'll bet Lauren has a few business related questions for you."

"I'm puzzled, Rav," Lauren said. "With your obvious talents and education, why would you want to join a two-person firm with only one contract…and that with contingencies?"

Rav laced his meal with Tabasco. "As you know, I learned of Optimal through Bernie White. He's a fascinating man, saturated with love of manufacturing and gilded with an astounding work ethic. He's a man to listen to. When Bernie described Wyatt as an impassioned engineer with a world-class mind, I listened. He told me about the extent of your commitment to Optimal…to the point of bankruptcy. *That* is conviction. *That* is belief in your capability. *That* is the kind of man I want to work alongside. I want to be on the ground floor of a blossoming new company… like Steve Wosniak and Apple." Nodding toward Wyatt, he continued. "My conversation with your husband today has convinced me I'm on the right track. There's a big hole in Optimal's capabilities and I'm the one to fill it."

"I don't know about all the 'world-class' bull," Wyatt said, "but you seem to be a perfect fit…military electronics, software, you name it."

"Well, then," Lauren said, "let's talk about pay."

"I'm good with a small salary and a bonus dependent on Optimal's success. Okay?"

Wow. We have a winner, Lauren thought. "Okay."

* * *

Rav reported to work the very next morning and they poured over the specifications, comparing the new requirements to their existing programs and circuit cards.

"Who is this Madison?" Rav inquired, shuffling

through a pile of documentation. "This is fantastic work. Trouble is, I'll need several weeks, maybe more, to dope out her stuff before I get down to work."

"We don't have weeks," Wyatt replied. "We have to start revisions before Christmas."

"Look, Wyatt. There are hundreds of pages of code, dozens of complex schematics and gnarly Gerber files. I can't digest all that before Christmas. Can we get this Madison person to lend a hand? That way, I could get up to speed faster."

Wyatt blanched. He'd pondered the same idea for several weeks and knew Madison was the only answer. Wyatt had to respect Rav's take on the scope of the job. The kid was probably on target unless he was an Einstein and Isaac Newton rolled into one. "Madison used to work for the guy who stole my patent—Dynamag. Lauren is adamant I never speak to her again. You sure you can't handle this yourself?"

Rav rubbed his smooth tawny chin and rummaged through the papers. "There's too much here. It's subtle. Clever. Complex. If you want to start the new programming by Christmas, I'll need help."

I'm screwed, Wyatt thought. He rose, walked to the tiny kitchen area in the back of the shop and topped off his coffee. He could not face Madison—that was certain. The April deadline seemed insurmountable and if Optimal slipped the schedule, he would hold up an entire airplane program. He slurped a slug of coffee and scalded his lip. *Gotta be a way.*

As he returned to the table, an idea came to him. He'd have Rav and Madison work over the phone. Lauren would never know and he wouldn't get involved directly. Perhaps she'd have to spend a little time at Optimal to test actual hardware, but he'd find an excuse to be at Mike's those days. *There's no other way. Has to work.*

Wyatt scooted his chair close to Rav's and explained his approach. He didn't mention, of course, his plans to avoid a face-to-face confrontation with Madison or how to pay her. His hand shook as he picked up the phone and dialed her number.

Over the next few days, Rav's appearance evolved from preppy to jeans, flip-flops and tee shirts touting rock-and-roll concerts he'd attended. He'd established a working rapport by phone and email with Madison and progress had been satisfactory. Wyatt developed a nasty rash on his chest, attributable, he supposed, to the intense tension created by Madison's phantom presence.

One morning, Wyatt discovered Rav waiting at Optimal's door in the predawn darkness, anxious to begin work. After a brief negotiation, they agreed on new working hours: five in the morning to nine at night. Wyatt gave Rav a key.

The days had flown, and it was only a week and a half until Christmas. For the season, Lauren had placed a tiny artificial tree in Optimal's window—its anemic glow washed out by the office lights. Oblivious to the decoration, Wyatt rose from his desk and poured another cup of coffee. In the far corner, Rav bent over his computer, wrestling with the final Gerber files for the hardened PCB's. Exhausted, Wyatt took a deep breath and settled back in his chair, embraced by the late night silence broken only by the soft hum of fluorescent lights.

With Madison's remote assistance, progress had been meteoric; problem upon problem had fallen under their onslaught. In spite of the esoteric requirements of military specifications, the electronics became more compact... more elegant. Even Madison's software flowered under Rav's touch.

So far, Madison's collaboration with Rav didn't require her presence at Optimal, although according to Rav, she kept insisting that she come. When he heard this, Wyatt tried to throttle his fear and cautioned Rav, saying, "Madison would be disruptive if on-site." He didn't explain his rationale beyond the fact she'd worked for a competitor.

That afternoon, he stopped at a drugstore and bought a tube of ointment for his rampaging rash—nerves he suspected.

Squinting in the resin smoke rising from the soldering iron, Rav bread boarded circuit cards and subjected them to rigorous tests under the glowing amber Cyclops eye of the oscilloscope. Wyatt heaved a sigh of relief when Rav said Madison wasn't needed for the tests. If Rav was curious why Wyatt was vehement about keeping Madison away, he didn't say anything.

Happy to discover his mechanical design just needed a few tweaks to bring it into conformity, Wyatt released dozens of refreshed drawings to Mike. Finally, after numerous emails and conference calls with AirEnvironment, the government procurement agency agreed that the nine-g combat turns demanded of fighter jets didn't apply to surveillance craft. *Damn government...can't decide what it wants,* Wyatt fretted. Because of the confusion, delivery of the test systems slipped another week. Even with the delay, it would take a miracle to deliver hardware on time, a realization that grated on Wyatt.

Mike and Precision Tool, with a flurry of activity, reworked updated parts and heaps of hardware began to collect on the workbenches. Frantic, Wyatt slapped together subassemblies, checking for proper fit and function. As time crept toward Christmas, Wyatt and Rav often worked past midnight, guzzling coffee and rubbing blurry eyes. Bernie, although fighting encroaching arthritis, labored alongside Mike and Wyatt with eagerness.

Perhaps the biggest development of the week was news from the FAA. They, along with the NTSB, decided Optimal's inflow control valve was not the cause of the fire that grounded the test aircraft nearly a year ago. Suddenly, they were cleared for flight tests.

That night, as Wyatt sank into bed, he slyly peeked at Lauren, searching for a hint she knew of the clandestine arrangement with Madison. Seeing only weariness, he vented, "A year! Darn near a year! It took that long for them to figure out my valves weren't even on the plane that caught fire. They're a bunch of sloths with their heads up their…nostrils. I must be insane. Here I am, banking on a government program to salvage Optimal. We've reelected the same idiots in Washington who'll continue to screw up the economy. I just wish Bellington had won—I'd feel better."

Lauren stirred. "I heard on the news that the industrial alliance, A.I.M., is making big waves. They sent another delegation to D.C.—there are rumors about an ultimatum."

"Yeah, I heard that too. I don't know what's going on. Don't guess they can do much...nothing that'll help us."

"Odd word to be tossing around...ultimatum," Lauren murmured.

Chapter 27

It was early morning and Wyatt staggered blurry-eyed to breakfast. At the dining table, he found two wrapped gifts, crowned by cards, sitting by his cereal bowl. "Happy Birthday," Lauren and his daughter crowed in unison. Wyatt blushed—he'd forgotten again. A sheepish grin was warm on Wyatt's cheeks as he rationalized his absentmindedness, muttering that in matters he considered trivial—like his birthday—more important things took over. He felt the redness in his face deepen when he read the cards, hand drawn, elaborate and embarrassing in their sentimentality.

The large gift box contained a pastel coral dress shirt and a contrasting tie. "For those high-powered business meetings you'll have at AirEnvironment and Maddox," Lauren boasted. When Wyatt unwrapped the small box, he found a medium-sized strap wrench needed to assemble the pressurization outflow valves. He was mystified that Lauren found the strange tool and how she even came up with the precise size required. Wyatt shook his head in amazement, guessing his wife was clairvoyant. It never dawned on him that she simply paid attention to his utterances, even about strap wrenches.

As he drove through the streets of Burbank toward Optimal's facility, Wyatt chuckled and his heart swelled with affection for his family. Buoyant, he whipped into a parking spot at Optimal and bound through the door. There, he found Rav testing the communications circuits between the inflow control and the outflow valve. Rav didn't notice Wyatt's noisy entrance and judging from the thin grin on his face, it looked like things were going well.

Wyatt sat at the desk and picked up his action-item list. He was behind—way behind. One reason was he'd spent the previous afternoon at Precision Tool working with Mike incorporating dozens of revisions to holding fixtures and preparing for the pending government surveys.

Mike had appointed Bernie "Head of Operations" and Wyatt had a flash of fondness for the old guy as they worked side-by-side once again. The deep lines in Bernie's face had softened and he moved with a vigor that had abandoned him in the quagmire of SAC's troubles. Although it was only mid-December, just a month since Bernie had joined Precision, Wyatt could see several improvements. Bernie had rearranged the inspection area to reduce slack time and accumulation of parts between stations. "Kanban," he'd said, "refers to a Japanese term for 'Just in Time' production techniques. I've reduced the queues and set up a roadmap to show the flow of parts through the department."

"He's looking at my mill department too," Mike said. "Never knew of this Kanban crap before—too busy making fucking chips. Bernie has kicked the shit out of my costs. I should have hired the ancient one years ago."

Wyatt sensed a frenzy as machinists coaxed their lathes to go faster, blue chips hissing from carbide tools. The howl of pneumatic deburring grinders blended with the screech of air nozzles blasting metal chips from milling cutters. Workers shouted to be heard above the din.

Mike looked possessed. In addition to the pressurization hardware, the new contract swamped the machines making their operators irritable. Mike raced from machine to machine, explaining datums, clarifying tolerances and helping with setups. From time to time, caught away from his office, he'd duck into the quiet of the restroom to badger suppliers on his cell phone: seeking status, demanding faster delivery or begging for reduced expediting fees.

Mike took a rare breathing spell behind his desk and explained to Wyatt that he'd gone back to the casting supplier that made the original parts. Minor mold changes were needed, but thankfully the revisions were simple. "Glad we stayed with investment castings. If we'd gone ahead with die castings, we'd have to cough up a fucking fortune for alterations."

Mike picked up a PERT diagram and groaned at the demanding schedule. "I'm balls to the wall. To get everything done on time, we're working right through the holidays...except Christmas day." He tugged on his mustache and grimaced. "Gonna cost a wad in overtime pay. I've temporarily brought back a few guys I laid off, but can't rehire anyone permanently because nobody knows what's happening after we ship in April."

Wyatt nodded. Rav and he faced the same time pressures, except there wasn't any extra pay.

The rattle of the telephone interrupted Mike's

preoccupation with the schedule. With an irritated looking scowl, he snatched the receiver. "Hello. Mike here." After a moment, he handed the phone to Wyatt. "It's Art. He wants to talk to you."

"Hi, Art. What's up?" Wyatt nodded and suddenly hollered, "You sure? It's a done deal? Hot damn! If you weren't so ugly, I'd run over there and kiss you!" Wyatt's mind staggered as he passed the phone back to Mike. Part of him wanted to roar with laughter, but another side brought tears to his eyes.

Mike replaced the receiver and stared at Wyatt. "What?"

"It's ours. They granted the patent to us this morning." Wyatt's breath shuddered in his throat as a salty taste tickled his lips. Tears came in earnest.

Mike leapt up, and grabbed Wyatt from his chair. Stretching around Wyatt's barrel chest, Mike pounded Wyatt on the back. "You did it, you fucker! Why in the hell are you blubbering?" In spite of Wyatt's bulk, Mike lifted him off his feet and danced around the desk singing a discordant version of ABBA's *Bang-A-Boomerang*. Panting, Mike set Wyatt on the corner of the desk, clutched him by the shoulders and looked into his eyes. "You deserve this, my friend. You've earned it. We're going for the moon!" With a wink, he said, "Let's go tell Bernie."

In defiance of the rigorous schedule, Wyatt declared Super Bowl Sunday a holiday. It wasn't because he was an avid football fan, it was simply because everyone had worked to the point of collapse.

True, he'd caught a glimpse of the Rose Parade when

he grabbed a mid-morning lunch at home before returning to work, but the sports page, listing collegiate bowl game results, went unopened. Lauren's Christmas tree silently wept dry needles on the carpet; ignored by manic humans dashing to other business. When Wyatt dozed off while working on a critical stack-up analysis at Optimal, he declared, "This is silly. It's time to sleep in a day, make a batch of popcorn and guzzle a beer."

So everyone, even Lee Wong, met at Wyatt's to watch the Super Bowl. Bernie fell asleep during halftime and Mike lasted until halfway through the third quarter. That evening, Wyatt couldn't remember who'd won.

Early the next morning, the push resumed.

Lashing rain heralded the arrival of early February and two roof leaks added to the panic at Optimal. Spent coffee cans provided the expeditious solution, and being a weekend, Timmie volunteered to empty them when needed. While Wyatt and Rav labored over their computers, Lauren paid bills and updated her general ledger, clearing up a pile of neglected papers.

Timmie, who'd learned to operate the label printer, tagged plastic bins and filled them with small parts. "Daddy, what does #10-24 UNC-3 x .375 mean?" she asked.

Wyatt, completely engrossed by a failure analysis problem, waved off the question and scratched the rash on his chest. So Timmie shrugged, pasted the label and dumped a box of screws into the bin. The incessant spatter of the watery assault on the roof obliterated her tuneless humming.

As darkness blotted the rivulets on the window, Wyatt and Rav hunched over a computer, entering a refined program into a microprocessor. Lauren cradled Timmie, spent and grumpy, in her lap. A large paper cup, empty except for a few cubes of ice, sweated next to a sheet of discarded wax paper that once embraced a Subway sandwich.

Wyatt didn't hear his wife struggle to open an umbrella and leave, hugging Timmie close to her side. He didn't notice the storm abated a few hours later. He didn't notice the wall clock that crept toward midnight. He and Rav, immersed in exotic code, put their heads close together and rejoiced in their craft, their journey toward solutions and their bond in science.

The ten days following that rainy night proved exceptional. Although Stanford's inauguration three weeks ago plunged Wyatt into despondency, a number of events bolstered his spirits. First, he'd resolved nearly all the design issues. He abandoned differential equations and Solid Works to focus on the delivery deadline, to work with Mike and Bernie on fabrication techniques and selecting subcontractors and vendors for aneroids, springs and other specialty hardware. Rav, with Madison's clandestine help, had resolved the problems with the electronic circuits and began to coordinate with the PCB house and the third-party software certification firm.

It was still early on a Tuesday evening when Art Weinstein and Lee Wong ambled in, both lugging briefcases. Prompted by Art's startling news that Optimal had been awarded full patent rights to the pressurization, Wyatt decided to call a meeting to discuss a formal arrangement to integrate the two firms. He rubbed his hands together as everyone settled around the table. Wyatt chastised himself and tried to scuttle a weird vision: he as a corporate tycoon. Thankfully, he was dressed in jeans and a sport shirt, not his new coral dress shirt.

His queasiness was, in part, triggered two days earlier, when Lauren reminded him they had discussed inviting Art and Lee to join the company as advisors...sort of like a board of directors. Because Mike had already made a significant cash investment in Optimal and Bernie a lesser one, the newcomers had offered to invest too. Both wanted to be partners. So, as Timmie crouched at a bench in the corner of the room to cut out Valentine cards for her school friends, the new Board of Directors began deliberations. Wyatt relaxed in his chair, pleased that Lauren, Art and Lee did most of the talking; finances were beyond him. They reached a broad agreement in less than an hour where Art and Lee would invest cash in Optimal, providing sufficient funding to complete the initial test systems. Money for the production effort, gargantuan in comparison, remained unresolved. "One step at a time," Art cautioned.

Once more, Wyatt was overwhelmed with emotion. The specter of defaulting on payments for the vacuum pump and compressor vanished. They could renew the lease on the facility and squeak by on payments to vendors. He knew relief would last only a couple of months, but the blade of a guillotine plummeting toward his neck had jammed halfway down. He gazed at the group, now enhanced by Art and Lee, and thought of one of his favorite movies: *Band of Brothers*. Yes, they'd come together as brothers. Wyatt bit his lip to quell a strange overwhelming sentiment.

Everyone took on tasks: to list the estimated value of inventory, prepare a cash flow analysis and draft a new LLC operating agreement. After setting the date for a follow-up meeting, talk changed to the long-term fate of Optimal/ Precision Tools.

Wyatt stood and stared out the window. Speaking over his shoulder, he said, "Sounds great, but don't count on anything. Ed Morales at AirEnvironment told me yesterday that the FAA will announce a new ruling soon that could trash my pressurization concept. Everything we've done could sink to the bottom of the ocean. Worse, they plan to grandfather in my competition—companies with old technology. Even though one is bankrupt and the other has abandoned the pressurization business, the FAA is moving to save them. Must have connections in Washington. Call it crony capitalism, graft, corruption, whatever. If the ruling is implemented, we're screwed."

Lee Wong scowled. "There's more. The Commerce Department might impose new rules to limit business with overseas firms, telling the voters that government action will save their jobs. Our business with China might be in jeopardy."

"FDR did that in the early thirties," Art said. "The only thing it accomplished was extending the depression until the beginning of the war. Stupid."

"Remember that corporate organization I've been following?" Lauren said. "I've read they're rapidly expanding. According to the news, big oil has jumped in along with large construction equipment builders and even agriculture. Their delegation in Washington is getting very aggressive. Newscasters are hinting they may strike. Lock out the workers."

"That's what I'm hearing too," Lee said.

Wyatt closed his eyes. *What can they accomplish? The public has spoken. Stanford is President, not Bellington. There's nothing to do except ship the test systems and hold on. I may not have to sweat the Dali or funding production.*

Chapter 28

February's weak morning sun struggled through the window at Optimal and found Wyatt making adjustments on the hot-air test stand. The huge compressor grumbled outside and the gas burners increased their bellowing as he turned up the heat. The pipes glowed dull red as the thermocouple indicated 1,020 degrees, 1,040 and finally 1,050 degrees, the design point. Pleased, Wyatt watched to see if the reading was stable. Rav, recording data on the computer, nodded, looking satisfied.

"Good enough," Wyatt said, securing the burners and compressor. "Now, I have to go over those new specs and decipher the revised quality requirements before Jason and Karl get here. They'll want a copy of Optimal's updated quality manual. While I'm doing that, you sort out those final software problems. Once you're ready, we should test the algorithm—make sure it's right."

Rav nodded, walked to his desk and sat in front of his computer. "It's great we have orders for both civilian and military hardware. Trouble is, we have to deal with two sets of regulations: the Defense Department and DCMA, plus civilian authorities: the FAA."

Wyatt scowled. "It's giving me fits."

Hunched over the purchase order from AirEnvironment, Wyatt tried to decipher the legalese. In the morning's dim light, the harsh glare from the fluorescent desk lamp cast stark shadows, making the fine print difficult to read. Setting two specifications side-by-side, he slid his index fingers down each page to the heading "Quality Assurance Terms" and squinted, his mind searching for understanding. As expected, testing, record-keeping and calibration standards had been expanded far beyond established practice. Frustrated with the tedious task, he began updating Optimal's Quality Assurance Manual.

Regardless, Wyatt knew everything was falling into place: last month Art had obtained the patent for Optimal, Art's and Lee's investments temporarily band-aided their financial hemorrhaging and now they had a tentative commitment for the test systems. The next step was the full production order, as many as 120 systems—if only the Dali would work out. All they had to do was perform. But first they needed certification of both facilities, which depended on the day's meetings.

Wyatt glanced at his watch. Karl Leechmann from DCMA and FAA's Jason Meil were due in an hour, looming like two incoming torpedoes aimed squarely at Optimal's hull.

Wyatt was haunted by a vivid recollection of Leechmann when, three years ago, they battled at his old company, SAC. Leechmann was a niggling perfectionist who found dozens of picayune infractions that tied up the company for weeks.

Wyatt recalled the pompous bodybuilder strutting around throwing vindictive barbs at everyone. When Leechmann came today, Wyatt suspected he'd be grilled over trivia, but vowed to prepare the best he could.

More worrisome, he learned the pumped-up hulk would audit Precision Tool after finishing at Optimal. Mike's company was already certified, but extensive regulatory modifications required fresh reviews for everyone. Mike, who always focused on precision tolerances, timely deliveries and cost control, had no tolerance for piddly stuff such as paperwork. Wyatt's head throbbed with the thought that Leechmann might trigger Mike's violent temper.

As with Leechmann, Wyatt had worked with Jason Meil at SAC and knew the inspector was a microscopic minded dolt who fell back on "The Book" because of his inability to construct a rational thought. Worse, the man was a crook who'd tried to force him to hire his son.

As with all FAA inspectors, Jason wielded immense power over the companies he surveyed, and flaunted it. While Wyatt was confident he could slog through the nitpicking and demeaning cracks of Leechmann, he feared Jason's corrupt ways.

Rav, across the room, gathered papers, his laptop and cell phone and walked to the door. "I'm running over to the PCB house to explain the new quality pass-through requirements. I should be back by two."

"Fine." Wyatt lifted the last copies of the updated quality manual from the printer and inserted them into a binder. He set them on the conference table next to calibration records and a summary of material certifications.

As Wyatt was placing coffee cups alongside the paperwork, Karl Leechmann and Jason Meil walked through the door together, chatting like good friends. Their camaraderie surprised Wyatt. They paused long enough to accept Wyatt's offer of coffee and then continued their conversation as they sat at the conference table.

"Stanford sure creamed that weirdo Libertarian," Karl laughed. "Already Washington has announced new spending. My office has tossed together new budget proposals—pumped it up good. There's talk about big pay raises, too."

Jason ran his fingers through his thinning hair, his pudgy pale body contrasting with Karl's muscular, shirt-stretching muscles. "The FAA, too. Big changes comin', right?" Jason said. "I've been told a new ruling will obsolete these fancy computerized pressurization systems like Optimal's. Put you out to pasture if it goes into effect this summer as planned, right Wyatt? I'm not sure why we're even bothering with today's audit."

Wyatt grimaced. Before, the new rule was rumors, but Washington was apparently on the attack. For unknown reasons, the FAA was moving to kill Optimal and set up his competitors. *Some deep-pocketed lobbyists with connections,* Wyatt thought. His hands knotted into fists and he struggled to resume breathing.

With a glib wave of his hand, Jason continued. "Commercial aviation might be sinking out of sight, but the FAA is hiring hundreds of inspectors to enforce the new regulations. With luck, I'll get a promotion to Section Head."

Karl grunted. "From what I see, the only turds in

the soup are those Ivy League CEOs putting the arm on Congress. Call themselves 'The Alliance' of something-or-other. The bastards are running dozens of TV ads and digging up dirt on politicians they despise. They're pushing Congress to put a hold on new legislation and rule-making until they conduct a comprehensive review."

"No way; they're powerless—they've no authority. I remember someone saying elections have consequences. They're over a barrel, right?"

"Uh, fellows," Wyatt interrupted, his thoughts reeling. "Should we get started?"

With an irritated glare, both inspectors turned to Wyatt. Karl shrugged. "Why not."

For the next three hours, Karl and Jason swamped Wyatt with terse questions, harsh criticisms and numerous deficiencies. Wyatt's head swam with contradictory regulations where DCMA and the FAA demanded different report formats and conflicting pass-through requirements to subcontractors. They even mandated separate stock rooms to isolate military hardware from commercial parts. Exasperated, Wyatt protested, explaining there wasn't space, but was soundly overruled. *What do they want me to do, conjure another thousand square feet?*

As Wyatt expected, at lunchtime Jason suggested they go out to eat. Even though he knew he was expected to pick up the tab, Wyatt drove past IHOP and went to The Plaid Bear, a very upscale restaurant.

The waitress, a homely mid-twenties woman with stunning legs and a short ruffled skirt, had barely introduced herself when Jason ordered a double martini. Karl went for the house white and Wyatt settled for his usual coffee.

After they ordered, Jason drained his glass and signaled for another drink. "I've been with the FAA over twenty years and I've never seen such craziness. Every company I audit tries to weasel out of the regulations and gripe they can't keep up with the changes. Same at DCMA?"

"Sure is," Karl replied. "Probably worse. The Defense Department just issued a bunch of new rules to get more control over incompetent manufacturers. Industry always fights the rules so I have to thump heads. Keeps me busy."

Wyatt listened silently, uneasy being left out, but scared they'd resume their harangue about Optimal's shortcomings. How was it, he wondered, that government hobbled creative people with useless regulations? Did Karl and Jason think he'd release reckless designs that would jeopardize human life? Did they assume he was inept and needed parental guidance? Did they really believe they were able to direct his efforts more skillfully than he? Unable to sort through the questions, Wyatt sighed. *I feel as if I'm getting mugged all over again.*

The two government men talked throughout the meal, barely acknowledging Wyatt's presence. Jason was into his fourth martini when he turned to Wyatt. "You guys are small potatoes. What—you got two, maybe three employees? Hell, one of those is your wife," he snickered. "It's insane, but even the big guys don't realize I can shut them down, right? I got my checklists and if they screw up on even one item—bang—I got 'em by the nuts. Right, Karl?"

"Well, I wouldn't say it exactly like that, but if someone really messed up…"

"Damn right," Jason slurred. "These stuffed shirt

executives don't realize how much responsibility we have. Got muscle to enforce it, too. Everyone expects to get certification right away, right? 'Delays cost money,' they say. I don't give a shit about money. I got my checklist—that's all I go by." He tossed off the last of the gin, chomped on the olive and smacked his lips. "I go by the book. Last week, a chief engineer wanted me to stay late to work on a serious screw-up. 'No way,' I said. 'I'm paid for forty hours a week. Don't get overtime pay, right? But I try to be helpful,' I told him. 'If you could help me out—ya know what I mean—I could put in an extra hour or two.' The dummy had no choice, so he forked over a couple hundred—cash of course. Checks leave a trail."

Wyatt couldn't believe what he was hearing. Even Karl looked uneasy. Jason, of course, had tried a similar stunt when he pressured Wyatt to hire his shiftless son. When Wyatt declined to play along, Jason "discovered" a rash of new problems, such as a misspelled word in a test report and a smudged calibration sticker on a pressure gauge. Wyatt took a sip of coffee and shuddered.

"We're overworked as well," Karl said. "I'm paid O.T. on critical programs. I thought the FAA did too."

Jason shrugged and grinned. "You know how it is."

Wyatt set his credit card on the check and waved at the waitress. As she came to the table he noticed Jason leering at her legs. "You guys ready to get to work? It's pushing two." Wyatt wondered why he bothered if he would lose his business by summer, but decided the only option was to continue with Optimal as long as possible.

The afternoon's inquisition wrapped up by three and

in desperation, Wyatt scrambled to document test reports, explain procedures and jot down action items.

Glancing at his notes, two items in particular roiled his stomach and aggravated his rash.

Karl had rejected Optimal's management plan for controlling the source of raw materials. "Government forbids purchases from certain adversarial countries," he said "You have to document where all materials come from. The original source, not just your supplier."

"How in the world can I do that?" Wyatt had grumbled. "Steel from China might go through a dozen hands before I buy it."

"Not my problem," Karl said. "You figure out how to do it; change your procedure and resubmit it."

Wyatt stifled an urge to throw a stapler at Karl's smug grin.

The second issue involved Jason. "New rulings can be very involved, Wyatt," he'd said. "These tough calibration standards in particular are complicated, right? Rather than get bogged down, I have a friend who can pull together a good procedure for you. Saves a lot of trouble."

Furious, Wyatt stalked to the coffee pot and filled his mug. *What does he take me for, a moron? There's no doubt who his 'friend' is. It's him, wanting to clip me out of money.* He spun around, about to yell, but restrained himself. *Calm down. He's got me by the throat.*

Later, as the inspector's cars disappeared around the corner, Wyatt strode to the window and screamed: "Idiots! Dolts! Damn government vampires!" His outburst echoed in the room, but he didn't feel better for it.

Wyatt dropped into his desk chair, exhausted. His mind reeled with countless action items levied by Jason and Karl.

The jingle of the phone jarred Wyatt back to the present. "Oh. Hi, Rav. What's up?" Suddenly, he jerked upright. "Madison? She's coming over?"

"Yeah," Rav said. "She called, insisting we test the new algorithm we've been working on. We have to install it in the valves and run them together. I'm on my way back and expect to meet her at Optimal in twenty minutes."

A wave of panic washed over Wyatt. Frantic, he slammed the phone into its cradle and stood, but dread immobilized him. Abruptly, he remembered Jason's last words: "We're at Precision Tool in the morning. I hope to hell he's in better shape than you."

I know. Jason and Karl are headed for Precision tomorrow. I'll go see Mike and try to sweep the minefield.

He snatched his keys and bolted to the door.

Chapter 29

The boisterous early evening crowd stared at the overhead television sets, transfixed. The L.A. Lakers led their division midway through the basketball season and the patrons at Sammy's Sports Bar leapt to their feet, booing a close call. "Ref must be blind," Karl growled. Jason shook his head in agreement and drained his beer mug.

Mike, both elbows on the table, cupped his chin in his hands. He had no interest in sports and was clueless about the rules, much less standings. The no-smoking laws of California pissed him off, so Mike slipped an unlit cigarette between his lips. He shifted it to the other side of his mouth and reflected on the day's survey at Precision Tool. He was frustrated because his shop had passed many quality audits over the years, including NASA, the toughest of all. Although he'd expected a rough time, the fucking inspectors found a way to dun him with dozens of infractions.

As a scowl settled beneath his immense mustache, Mike recalled the marathon session last night when Wyatt had come over to help him get ready. They'd worked until two in the morning tweaking procedures and organizing records. *This is fuckin' crap*, he thought. *I'm in the business of cutting chips, not screwing around putting together a shitty encyclopedia of useless paper.*

"Half-time," Jason announced. "I need another beer."

Mike glanced at his own mug, still nearly full, and said. "I'm good. You guys like another platter of wings?"

"Sure, they're better than most," Karl called out above the din. "I think I could live on bar food. Another beer would help wash 'em down."

Mike waved at the waitress who pranced over to their table wearing little more than short-shorts, a tight tee and a big grin.

Jason waved his empty mug and said to the waitress, "Hit me again, Honey. More wings too." After she'd wiggled off, he turned to Mike. "You didn't do too bad today. At least you have a real company, not like that grubby hole-in-the-wall of Wyatt's. It's a mystery why AirEnvironment, a well-known established firm, would even fool with Optimal: a third-string facility and a troublemaking owner."

"Maybe it's because he has an extraordinary product," Mike grumbled. "Maybe AirEnvironment didn't have any options because the only established supplier of pressurization, Randel Products, went bankrupt."

"No wonder," Jason said. "A buddy of mine, who used to inspect them, said they were seriously on their ass. He couldn't believe how screwed up their records were; damn little material traceability, lacked…well, no point in going on. They simply didn't measure up."

"I knew them, too," Karl said, wiping sauce from his

mouth. "They tried to capitalize on the opportunity after that big manufacturer, Garvey Airmotive, spun off their pressurization line, saying they couldn't deal with the latest regulations."

"Hear what you're saying, Karl?" Mike asked. "Garvey, a multimillion dollar corporation, turned their back on good business because of fuckin' government rules. So did Randel. Do you see a common denominator?"

"Hey, if you can't get it right, shut the doors," Jason sneered. "What's weird is that this new ruling on pressurization—Airborne Safety Standards, they call it— will qualify both Garvey's and Randel's systems. I'll make sure they've got their act together before I allow them to ship squat."

Mike, feeling his blood pressure rising, grumbled, "You guys ever question how new regulations shut down an innovative company such as Optimal and resurrect two has-beens?"

"Not our call," Jason said. He leaned back in the chair and laced his fingers behind his head. "You don't see it, Mike, but FAA's management is all over my butt to show results. If I give a company a clean slate, the boss thinks I'm skating. Right, Karl?"

"Yup."

"Every day, we issue new rules, advisory circulars and airworthiness directives, right?" Jason said. "It's my job to enforce them. When there's an accident, the FAA teams with the NTSB and digs into the case. If they find I overlooked a rule, even a piece of documentation, my ass is grass. I gotta be very, very careful, right?"

Mike's cheeks bulged as he ground his teeth. "So your

job is to dance around any kind of risk. Go by the book. You avoid making judgments of any kind, even when the safety of the public might be at stake."

"What do I know about safety?" Jason shrugged. "Washington tells me where to look, so that's what I do."

Mike looked at his clenched fists, nestled on his lap, and tried to control his temper. *This guy is a fuckin' Neanderthal.* He felt powerless to deal with either inspector. His world of logic, bold action and objective thinking was neutered by arbitrary rules and mindless obedience. As Jason ordered yet another beer, Mike flexed his fingers and took a deep breath. *Chill out. I'm a mouse in a hawk's claws.*

"Jason's right," Karl said. "We just follow the rules. It makes our job easy. You guys, the industrialists and entrepreneurs, are nuts working your butts off with no guarantee of success. Look at me. I put in my 40, draw a good salary and will retire with full pay and Cadillac-style insurance for the rest of my life. What do you have? A company on the ropes and an ulcer? You're inches away from following Randel into bankruptcy unless you shape up and get certification. Not only do you worry about Precision Tool, you gotta make sure your suppliers to toe the line, too." Karl shook his head. "Why pound your head on the wall when you could have a sweet job like mine?"

"Now that you mention suppliers," Jason said. "Metalcast, that casting house you've been using, isn't working out. I've checked them out and their inspection records, X-ray and penetrant data are a total mess. I don't see how I could ever approve them." He took a big swallow of beer and continued with a sly grin. "There's a good foundry in the South Bay that I've already certified. If you want to move things along, you'd better place your casting orders with them, right?"

"Good advice," Karl said.

"I just happen to have their business card," Jason said, handing one to Mike. "They're called Fallon's Foundry. Give them a call."

His mind numb from the audacity of Jason's proposition, Mike took the card and tucked in his shirt pocket. He'd been doing business with Metalcast for years and knew it produced excellent castings—castings that resided on Mars and numerous aircraft. Once again, rage ravished his gut and Mike clamped his arms against his chest to stop trembling.

Jason drained his mug and waved for another. He sucked the meat off a chicken wing and wiped his mouth with the back of his hand. "Karl, did you hear that Washington is getting tough on all the big airframe manufacturers, holding them responsible for any deviations from the rules? The FAA has leased a new building and staffed it with a bunch of lawyers. They're scrounging for trouble in airplane companies and have already asked me for names of firms and individuals that haven't fully cooperated in my surveys. I have to admit, I helped them out, right? Bet we're gonna make a few waves."

"That's right," Karl said. "The web says Maddox Aviation has been smacked with a big fine. Nobody's saying why, but that should get everyone's attention: Boeing, Textron, Bombardier, Airbus, the works. I figure it's another dose of job security."

"Damn right," Jason hiccupped. "That big bunch of corporations, A.I.M. they call themselves, is raising all kinds of questions. They whine that Washington is killing the airplane business. Bullshit! If you ask me, it's time we get these manufacturers under control."

Mike was seething. He'd come to the sports bar hoping to smooth things over, work out a few compromises and get moving toward certification. As he listened to Karl and Jason, it became clear they had no interest in cooperating or certifying his company. To them, success was finding problems, prolonging investigations and avoiding risk. In their view, his reputation and skills were voided by the new regulations. They subjected him, not to an honest audit, but to an arbitrary inquisition. They might as well burn him at the stake.

His temples throbbing, Mike banged his fist on the table. "You ass-holes are fucking crazy. If it weren't for guys like Wyatt and me, you'd have nothing to inspect. Government thugs make a living off hard working people who take risks and create products the world needs. The FAA's and DCMA's mission is to find fault with other people's work. You bastards contribute NOTHING! I have to kiss your ass because you can close my doors any time. Well, I'm not going to kiss ass anymore." Mike reached into his pocket and pulled out a key ring, separated one and slapped it on the table. "Want to shut me down? Here's the key to my place. Take it and explain to your bosses, AirEnvironment and Maddox why I don't deserve to be in business."

Neither Karl nor Jason moved, but stared wide-eyed at the key.

Several nearby patrons glared at Mike and then turned their eyes back to the game.

"Take it, fuckers. Lock my doors! No pressurization, no airplanes! Take it!"

Time crept and neither inspector moved. Overhead, the television sets flickered as the game resumed. Like radar antenna, the faces of the crowd locked onto the nearest screen. Moans, groans and cheers blended—a choir.

Mike stared at his adversaries and then deliberately retrieved the key. "You're both spineless turds." He took his wallet, extracted a twenty-dollar bill and dropped it in a puddle of beer. "This will cover my eats. Pay for your own meals for a change." Shaking, Mike rose and stalked out, leaving Karl and Jason with their jaws hanging open.

The only lights on that night at Precision Tool were the security fixtures, dim and sparse. Mike hunkered behind his desk in the gloom and pondered the day's events. *I've fucked myself for sure.* He'd felt exuberant striding out of the bar, like a prizefighter standing over a fallen foe, but reality had settled in. He'd kicked the two guys he needed for survival right in the nuts. They didn't have the balls to padlock his place, but they'd get even by sandbagging his certification. He might as well start making roller skates or bottle caps; his airplane business was finished for sure. Death would not be clean and quick, but lingering, agonizing. Still, it felt good teeing off on the fuckers.

But Mike's habit was to take action and pulverize roadblocks, not dwell on problems. He rocked back in his chair, put his feet on the desk and thought. Karl, he knew, was a coward, afraid to make decisions—a guy who hid behind the rulebook. Sure, he'd be a pain in the ass, but was so locked up in the cage of DCMA dogma, that troubles would be entirely predictable. Mike could deal with that.

The real villain was Jason. He wasn't very bright, but he had power: a very dangerous combination. Moreover, he dwelt in a world of dishonesty and slashed through small companies like ragged chips whirling from a drill press.

And today, Jason had pressured Mike to throw business to an unknown foundry, a company where Jason would probably get a kickback. *Something fuckin' odd about this foundry business,* Mike thought.

He'd worked with Metalcast for years and knew both the FAA and DCMA had certified them in the past. True, the last few months had seen a rash of new rulings requiring exhaustive record-keeping and huge alterations to procedures, testing and manufacturing processes. Still, Mike knew Metalcast wouldn't brush aside regulatory changes in their industry.

Mike stood and walked over to the glass enclosed case of Mars Curiosity parts he'd machined years ago. He flipped on the display lights and studied the gleaming metal as if trying to suck inspiration from them. *Time to get my ass in gear.*

He walked back to his desk, grabbed a small note pad and jotted:

- Call Donnie at Metalcast—check quality control and records.
- See Wyatt in AM. Emails, etc. re. Jason's son? Need evidence.
- Call Morales at AirEnvironment. Help from their H.R. dept.?

- See Art—any legal stuff?
- Email Jason— get him to document this foundry caper.
- Google Fallon's Foundry.
- Bellington or A.I.M.—can they help?

Mike peeled the list from the pad, stuck it in his shirt pocket and smiled. *Don't get too comfy, Mr. Jason Meil. I'm all over your ass.*

Chapter 30

It was another typical Saturday morning. The rumble of the big vacuum pump faded and Wyatt fussed, waiting for the vacuum to decay in the cabin tank. He addressed the hulking white vessel, saying, "I'm going to install a big dump valve on you to speed up tests. You're holding me up." When the pressure gage finally dropped to zero, Wyatt yanked the door open, released the over-center clamps and removed the outflow valve. "Looks good, Rav," he called out. "All it needs is an adjustment on the rate orifice."

Rav didn't look up and continued to rummage through trays of resistors. "Great. I'm getting the hang of calibrating these electronic cards. I'll have another to test in a minute."

Even though the springtime weather was still cool, perspiration glistened on Wyatt's clean-shaven face. After installing the second outflow valve, he went to the hot-air test stand and pushed a large red knob and the massive compressor thundered to life. "I'm going to do an end-to-end system check. Hand me a new electronic package, okay?"

It took twenty minutes for Wyatt, with Rav's help, to bring up and stabilize the air temperature. The burners radiated a stifling heat and Wyatt broke out in an earnest sweat. Resembling a tightly executed football play, they brought the data acquisition online, adjusted altitude, set flow rates and swept through the formal acceptance test procedure. Wyatt pursed his lips, elated that the system proved flawless. Rav's eyes glittered above a wide, ivory smile as he downloaded the data onto a flash drive in preparation for comprehensive analysis later that evening.

"One down, two to go," Wyatt muttered as he secured the burners, but left the compressed air flowing to cool the bleed-air valve. Impatiently, he licked his finger and tapped the valve. The resulting hiss told him it was still too hot to handle.

Rav shut off the vacuum pump, vented the big tank and began switching the outflow valve.

"This thing is smoking," Wyatt complained. "It'll be twenty minutes before I can change it out."

Rav chuckled. "Relax. Have a cup of coffee. Grumbling isn't going to cool it off any faster."

"My wife tells me that every day."

"Shrewd lady," Rav said. "Come help connect the new electronics module. There's a lot we can do while waiting."

Wyatt twisted a ferrule, removed a connector from the "black box" and reflected on Rav's amazing design work. Madison's electronics and software required substantial modifications and Rav had to spend hours on the phone with her working through the problems. Three times Wyatt scurried over to Mike's when Madison came to Optimal for tests. Despite Wyatt's near hysteria about his ex-partner's visits, Rav conquered all the issues as easily as Henry Ford had cranked out Model T's.

As the days passed, Rav grooved to thumping rap music, bobbing his head and tapping his foot with iPod buds stuffed into his ears. Yet somehow, elegant computer code spewed from his mind and ingenious Gerber files blossomed under his touch, birthing extraordinary printed circuitry. Now in his mid-thirties, Wyatt felt old watching the younger engineer blaze through tasks looking brisk and alert, even at the now-routine midnight hour.

At last the bleed-air valve had cooled enough so Wyatt, cradling it with a rag, removed it from the test stand and installed another. "Let's see if we can finish this second system before Lauren shows up with lunch, okay?"

Rav removed an ear bud. "What?"

"Let's light the afterburner and try to finish the next system before lunch."

"No problem." Rav entered the final settings into the computer. "I'm ready with the outflow tank," he said, closing the hatch and turning on the vacuum pump. "These valves have the old style castings, so we'll have to redo everything once Mike brings over the redesigned ones. But this way we'll get a jump on any hitches that might turn up."

Wyatt dragged his forearm across his sweaty brow. "Right on. There's less than a month to ship qualification hardware. No time to screw around." He jerked open a ball valve sending compressed air surging through the pipes and lit the burners once more. Exasperated, Wyatt waited for the temperature to rise, creeping from 500, then 600. He was tempted to bellyache, but recalled Rav's admonition:

"Grumbling doesn't make things go faster." He bit his lip. 750, 800….

*   *   *

The front door burst open belching a wave of chilly air. Lauren stepped in carrying a Crockpot of chili and set it on the conference table. Timmie trailed behind with a large bowl of salad while young Jenny and her mother, Sharon, followed holding a cake in her pudgy hands.

"The feast has arrived," Sharon giggled. "I brought Jenny along…hope you don't mind. She's never seen the place."

"Fine," Wyatt grunted, engrossed in the test. "Give us a minute."

While the women scurried to set up lunch, Wyatt and Rav hunkered over their work, oblivious to the clatter of glasses and soft murmurings. Lauren tidied up the place settings, pleased how neat everything looked. The chili was one of her specialties and she knew Wyatt would devour it by the gallon.

Contented, she sat and watched her husband twiddle valves, jot gage readings and peer through the Plexiglas window of the cabin tank. He moved purposefully, directing Rav with a wave of his hand or a grunt. Lauren swelled with pride at the sight of her husband: talented and dedicated. She glanced at Sharon and was warmed to see her friend transfixed by the engineers at work, immersed in the growl of the compressor and roar of the burners. Even Timmie and Jenny stood side by side, watching. "Like Star Wars," Jenny whispered, looking wide-eyed at the control panels.

"Finally, that's it," Wyatt said, shutting off the burners.

Rav secured the vacuum pump and began venting the big tanks. "Everything looks cool, man, really cool," Rav exclaimed. "I'll go over the numbers later tonight. I don't see any problems, though."

Wyatt slapped the tabletop. "Hot damn! We have one phenomenal system! AirEnvironment will think we walk on water." He set his clipboard on the conference table and walked to his wife, his nose twitching like a bunny rabbit. "Glad you brought your chili, Hon. I could eat a horse."

Lauren spooned the chili into leftover Valentine's Day paper bowls, decorated with red hearts, while Timmie filled plates with salad. Everyone settled around the table and brandished their utensils. Rav went to his desk, took a bottle of Bandar sauce and splashed it on his chili.

Lauren was astounded. "Not spicy enough?"

Seeing Lauren's quizzical expression, Rav said, "They call this monkey sauce. Indian cooking is super spicy and I can tell the chili is too mild for my taste because it didn't set the paper bowl on fire."

"Have it your way," Lauren laughed.

While Wyatt attacked the chili, Timmie took his cold coffee, dumped it and rinsed out the mug. With a flourish, she filled it with fresh, steaming brew and set it by her father's elbow. "Here, Daddy. Are you ready for a piece of Sharon's cake?"

"I'll need seconds on the chili first, okay?"

"Let me." Timmie took Wyatt's bowl and filled it. "I'll cut a piece of cake anyway." With Sharon's help, she sliced a large chunk of cake and scraped up laggard frosting, smearing it on the plate's edge. After sliding the plate alongside Wyatt's mug, Timmie stood by his side, her eyes following his spoon—bowl, mouth, bowl, mouth...

"Timmie, don't pester your dad," Lauren admonished. She gathered up a few spent salad plates and tossed them into the trash.

Wyatt shoved aside the remnants of the chili and proceeded to demolish the cake.

Sharon, daintily licking frosting from her spoon, said to Lauren, "I remember you were discussing a merger between your company and Mike's—Precision Tool, right? Are you still working on that?"

Nodding, Lauren said, "It's almost a done deal. Art, our lawyer, is wrapping up the final agreement. We're very excited about it."

Like a conductor of a symphony orchestra, Wyatt waved his fork. "For once, Mike was a pussycat. I figured we'd get into a major gun battle over a name for the combined company, but Mike said a name like Precision Tool was too limiting. We changed Optimal Aviation Systems to just Optimal Systems, dropping the reference to aircraft because Mike thinks we'll diversify."

"What's 'diversify' mean, Daddy?" Timmie inquired, leaning over her father's leg and staring into his face.

Wyatt ruffled the child's hair. "Come on over while Rav and I get the next system installed in the test stand. I'll explain as we go." He put his arm around her shoulder and walked across the room. Jenny tagged along and with an earnest look, listened to Wyatt explain the word as he and Rav went to work.

Lauren and Sharon gathered the dishes and put away the leftovers.

"Little Timmie is growing up fast, isn't she?" Sharon said. "She's nuts about Wyatt I can tell. That's nice. You're lucky to have Wyatt."

I am, Lauren thought. Wyatt had adopted a new attitude over the past few months. Last November he was devastated by the election results and she had to prod him to interview for a new electrical engineer to replace Madison. But once Ravinder was in place, Wyatt seemed to shed his melancholia and grapple with Optimal's future with enthusiasm. Unlike before, he didn't confine his newfound eagerness to engineering. Over the Christmas holidays, Wyatt shadowed her, offering to peel potatoes or vacuum floors. Their Sunset Ritual became a warm and romantic time—time the old Wyatt seldom found. For Lauren, the Zinfandel tasted smoother and the chats more engaging and intimate. They touched often, Wyatt patting her arm as he passed and pecks evolved into fervent kisses, often giving way to passion. In bed, their lovemaking sometimes left her in tears of contentment and togetherness and they always cuddled until she fell asleep.

Lauren chuckled under her breath. *Sex,* she thought. *Who'd think an accountant and an engineer could "get it on?"* There was the time two days before Valentine's when Wyatt arranged for a babysitter explaining they should beat the rush and celebrate a couple of days early. He'd presented her with a frilly card and took her, not to a restaurant as she expected, but to a motel where a bouquet of red roses and a bottle of premier Zinfandel awaited. *Wow!*

But she wasn't the sole object of his attention. Contrary to his typical monomaniacal focus on engineering, Wyatt showed genuine affection for Timmie: joking, helping with school assignments and yelling encouragement at soccer games. It struck Lauren that her husband, for the first time, noticed he had a daughter. He even gave serious consideration to his daughter's insistence to get a cell phone. "Like all my friends," she'd argued.

Lauren turned and saw Wyatt talking to Timmie and Jenny, but couldn't hear what was being said. Wyatt, wearing a big grin, snatched Timmie and gave her a big hug. She worried that her daughter, in her nascent maturity, would bolt from childhood leaving a void in the Morgan household—in her life. *Maybe I'll quit my job and spend more time with my daughter. I'll see what Wyatt thinks.*

She rose and walked over to a stool next to Wyatt. He was twisting a wrench when Jenny asked, "What does all this stuff do?"

"Well, this equipment helps people in airplanes keep warm and gives them air so they can breathe."

"Is it hard to breathe in an airplane?"

Wyatt set aside the wrench and squatted on his hams, nose-to-nose with Jenny. "When an airplane is high, it gets much colder than your freezer at home and the air is very thin. Engineers like Rav and me design valves and things to make riding in an airplane real cozy and nice."

Lauren had to smile as her husband tried to explain the glories of engineering and a few basic facts of fluid dynamics to the ten-year old. Timmie stood alongside her dad, looking proud and nodding from time to time, suggesting she already knew everything being said. Rav stopped working, smiled and leaned on the edge of the bench. Even Sharon seemed rapt as Jenny bobbed her head, her face screwed up in obvious concentration.

"Here comes Santa Claus," Mike boomed, bounding into the office carrying a large cardboard carton. "Now we can start kitting the qualification systems."

Wyatt leapt to his feet and beckoned to Rav. "Help clear this table. We'll start putting together subassemblies here."

Mike trundled the armload of parts over and set them gingerly on the table. "This is just a start. Next week, I'll start machining the new castings."

"Castings?" Wyatt said. "I thought you were still knocking heads with Jason, our government goon, over your casting supplier."

"Grab yourself a cup of coffee, my friend," Mike said, dropping into a chair. "I've news." His eyes twinkling, he waited until Wyatt topped off his mug and sat. Lauren and Rav drew up stools to listen.

Abandoned, Sharon and the kids wandered to the back of the shop to examine the huge array of gages, valves and plumbing.

"When was it? Around a month ago?" Mike began. "The FAA and DCMA did that survey, remember? Jason said my casting outfit, Metalcast, was so sloppy with their record keeping that they'd never get certified. Well, the next day I dropped in on Metalcast and found out they were *already* blessed by the FAA. Jason was fuckin' full of shit. Then, you," Mike said pointing at Wyatt, "searched your email strings and phone notes that proved that Jason tried blackmail to get his kid hired at Optimal." Mike thumped the tabletop with his fist. "I even called a buddy from the A.I.M. field office who said he'd check it out. I don't need to set a magnesium fire to tell me the tool is dull, so I called Art for a little lawyerly advice. He said he'd already asked one of his colleagues to contact the FAA."

Lauren laughed. "I bet you could subdue an army single-handed if you wanted. Has Art heard anything back from the FAA?"

"Just that we have their attention. Fucking big time. I figure we've got Jason by the throat, so I went ahead and placed an order with Metalcast."

"I never thought I'd appreciate a lawyer," Wyatt said, shaking his head. "Gotta hand it to Art."

"Now that you're talking about legal things, Mike," Lauren said, "we heard that Madison is embroiled in her own court proceedings. Nothing is determined yet, but Art said that he'd bet all his jelly beans that Madison's partnership in Optimal is history."

"If only Washington would get off our back," Wyatt grumbled. "That new FAA ruling, Airborne Safety Standards they call it, goes into effect in a few months. Unless A.I.M. finds a way to stop it, the Feds could pull down our house of cards on a whim."

"Let's worry about that later," Lauren said. "We have a deadline to hit; that should be our focus."

"Well, let's get going," Mike said, slapping his thigh.

With a nod, Lauren rose, took the chili bowl to the bathroom in the back of the building and rinsed it.

Wyatt walked to the test stand and began installing the last valve. He sensed a cool breeze on his back and turned to see the front door was open. There, framed by the afternoon sun, stood Madison. "What the hell?" Wyatt gasped.

Madison looked startled. "My God."

Rav looked up from his computer. "What are you doing here? You were supposed to come *tomorrow.*"

"I…I," Madison stammered. "I though you said today."

Wyatt took several steps toward Madison. "You'd better leave. Now." His neck felt clammy and his belly boiled in acid.

"You!" bellowed Lauren, striding across the room. She planted her feet and glared at Madison. "What in the hell are you doing here?"

"I must have made a mistake and…"

"Damn right you made a mistake," Lauren yelled. "Get out! Get out now!"

Wyatt went up to Madison. "Do as she says."

From the back of the room, Sharon and the kids looked wide-eyed as Madison spun and tripped out the door.

His face livid with anger, Wyatt stared at Rav. "How did *that* happen," he growled.

Rav shrugged. "Mix-up. It's the new circuit board we're supposed to test."

"What's going on?" Lauren demanded, her face florid and eyes blazing. "Tell me Wyatt!"

Sweat broke out on Wyatt's brow as he tried to collect his thoughts.

"Wyatt? Give!"

"I don't know how to explain," Wyatt stammered.

"Just start, goddamnit!"

Sharon gathered the two children and hustled them out to the sidewalk while Mike and Rav retreated silently to the conference table.

With a choking sound, Wyatt cleared his throat. "I…we couldn't figure out the electronics and programming soon enough to make the deadline. Got way behind schedule. Rav needed help, so we…"

"You went to that bitch for help?" Lauren hissed. "How could you do such a thing?"

His mind crippled by heartbreak, Wyatt turned to Rav and whispered, "Crap."

"It's my fault, Lauren," Rav spoke up. "I needed too much time to figure out the circuitry and software, so I persuaded Wyatt to enlist Madison's help. We did it by phone—she never worked with your husband—just me."

"If that's true, then tell me why she came here," Lauren snarled.

"We had to test things. On our equipment," Rav admitted. "She's been here maybe three or four times, but Wyatt always left—never saw her."

"That true?" Lauren demanded, whirling to face Wyatt.

"Yeah." He shuddered as he collapsed in his chair. "Couldn't figure out what to do. She was the only way. Rav and I made a deal, like he said." Wyatt's lips quivered as he covered his eyes with his hands. "Sorry."

With a disgusted scowl, Lauren faced Mike. "I suppose you were on in this *deal* too?"

Mike nodded. "Yeah."

"Bernie?"

"Yup."

"Everyone was in on Madison's arrangement but me, huh? Real nice!" Lauren snatched her purse and marched to the door. "I'm taking Sharon and the kids home. How am I going to explain this calamity to Timmie? To Sharon?" The door slammed like the crash of a lightning-bolt.

Chapter 31

Two days had slogged by since the scene with Madison. Lauren, rage inundating her mind, still refused to speak to Wyatt and when talking to Timmie, referred to "your father" rather than "Wyatt" or "Dad."

When Wyatt came to breakfast on the third morning, he looked like a bedraggled Cocker puppy that had been abandoned in the rain. Listless, he pushed corn flakes around in his bowl and silently beseeched Lauren with moist Cocker eyes. When Lauren's anger persisted beyond endurance, he made awkward attempts to explain. "You know what Rav said...I never saw her...we were in trouble." When his attempts faded like morning mist, he donned a pathetic Cocker puppy face.

Finally, Lauren wavered. Truth be known, she was embarrassed by her rage that day.

So they talked—exhaustive rambling talk. On the forth evening, a bottle of Zinfandel reappeared, and they talked. The next night, a flickering candle bathed their faces, and they talked. As they explored and debated over wine and basked in candlelight, Lauren, at long last, yielded to Cupid's arrow.

Lauren was satisfied that Wyatt hadn't gotten involved with Madison. His mania for achievement and Optimal drove him to seek the only option he was able to visualize—Madison. He'd arranged with Rav to tackle the design problems while excluding him from technical decision-making—an arrangement that must have been agonizing.

Lauren understood why Wyatt couldn't tell her—the explosion in front of Madison attested to her towering volatility. Still, Lauren found it difficult to accept the notion he couldn't face her with the facts.

Dancing candle shadows highlighted Wyatt's fatigue and, downcast, he apologized, vowed to cut off Madison for good and never again hold anything back. For her part, Lauren was ashamed by her violent temper and promised to rein in this new aspect of her personality.

A touch of vanity shouldered its way into Lauren's thoughts. What did everyone think of her rant? Did Mike and Bernie deduce the real situation? That Madison seduced her husband? Lauren explained that her obvious hatred of Madison was because Little Miss Green Eyes fled to Dynamag. Because the witch jumped ship to a competitor, a traitor. But were Mike, Bernie and Sharon convinced? *I'll never know.*

It was day six when Lauren drew a deep breath and like Japanese cherry blossoms dropping to earth, harmony settled into the Morgan household once more.

*   *   *

After a frantic week had passed, Wyatt stretched out on his recliner and took his first morning sip of coffee while Garfield wiggled between his knees, purring with obvious contentment. He slipped the plastic wrapper from the Sunday newspaper and blanched at the headlines:

Industrialists Threaten Washington
Stocks Plunge

"Washington—The Alliance for Industrial Might issued a strike ultimatum that threatens to shut down dozens of large corporations unless legislators and the President rescind the new regulations and heavy taxes recently enacted to address the economic crisis."

Wyatt's throat constricted as he read the article. The biggest oil companies, huge banks, the Big Three auto manufacturers, grocery chains, communications giants and even the aviation sector had banded together saying they would cease all operations effective April thirtieth unless their demands were met. He swallowed: corporations never banded together the way labor unions had for years. In the past, companies were powerless to defend against the onslaught of agencies such as the IRS, the Commerce Department and, of course, the FAA. Inevitably, firms acquiesced to the demands of Washington, but this was different. A.I.M. had amassed the power to quash the nation's economy.

In demeaning rhetoric, the newspaper screeched: "Bellington, the defeated Libertarian candidate for the Presidency, has assumed leadership of A.I.M. and is promoting anarchy." As he read this, Wyatt drew a hopeful breath. *Anarchy? Seems to me old Frank is kicking a little butt. About time.*

Not so fast. Wyatt knew that if Maddox closed its doors, AirEnvironment would follow. That would kill any hope of getting Optimal on its feet. Suddenly, Wyatt's world teetered on a bizarre battlefield: industry vs. Washington. Suppose Bellington carried through? Suppose the President called his bluff? There were just six weeks until the A.I.M. deadline, six weeks of uncertainty, six weeks of terror. He trembled and Garfield, disturbed from his slumber, gave Wyatt a harsh stare.

"Yes, I know about the ultimatum," Lauren said, poking cloves into a ham. "There's nothing else on the news. We've been through this before. I realize you're upset, but we have no control over either A.I.M. or Washington. Why don't you just relax and give me a hand getting ready for the dinner party? You can start by shucking those ears of corn."

Wyatt bit his lip. Lauren was right; there was nothing to do. But after he saw those headlines, his mind churned, imagining a litany of disastrous scenarios: A.I.M. strikes and the economy crashes, Washington declares martial law to control massive looting, Bellington gives up and Congress passes new laws prohibiting industrial collusion and leveling huge fines, the President issues an executive order to cancel federal purchases from members of A.I.M....

Wyatt shook his head and picked up an ear of corn. "It just seems that no matter what, we're screwed."

"I'm more sanguine," Lauren said, flashing a reassuring smile. "Politicians always make sure they get reelected. That means they'll reach a deal and life will go on. Although A.I.M. and Bellington may strike for a day or two, stockholders will rebel if they decide confrontation isn't in their interest."

"But they're on board so far."

"Sure, they think the government will make concessions. But what if a strike drags out? The world economy will collapse and everybody loses. The way I see it, everyone has motivation to find a compromise."

"You're making the assumption that Washington will have a rational moment. That hasn't happened since Lincoln."

"Wyatt, you can be such a drag," Lauren scolded. "There's lots of things going for us. Why don't you think of those?" She set the ham in a pan and squared her shoulders, suggesting the subject was closed. "When you're done with the corn, set the table. Everyone will be here soon."

Wyatt wasn't in a party mood, but he decided to give in to his wife's love of entertaining. So he tried to look mellow as their guests jostled up to the dining table, augmented with three leaves and a card table. Invasive chitchat grated on his nerves and everyone's animated expressions looked false and exaggerated. *This is supposed to be a mind-blowing celebration about the patent and our pending merger, but if Washington tries to pull rank or we don't get certification, this could turn into a funeral.*

Lee Wong raised his wine glass, pulling Wyatt from his desolation. "If I may, I want to make a toast." He paused, waiting for the others. "To our extraordinary group and to success. We've captured Wyatt's patent and the merger between Mike and Wyatt is coming to fruition. For now, there's even a little money in the bank. Most important, Wyatt conceived Optimal during the year of the Dragon—very auspicious—we are destined to overcome every obstacle."

"Fucking right on," Mike burst out. "Oops." Blushing, he turned to Timmie at the end of the table. "Sorry."

"Don't fucking worry about it," Timmie giggled.

"Timmie!" Lauren yelled.

The table shook with laughter and even Wyatt had to snicker.

As the uproar faded, Bernie said, "For me, Optimal is a new start and I feel young again. Mike doesn't know it yet, but I have a few ideas for specialized tooling that will speed up production. At SAC, I wasn't allowed to try new things or to incorporate advances in machining technology. But now, after we get FAA and DCMA certification, I'll dig into Lean Manufacturing. It's as if the clouds have lifted."

Once again, everyone raised their glasses, even Timmie, who had a goblet of water colored with a splash of wine.

Wyatt frowned as he gnawed a chunk of ham. *Bernie has blinders on—he's thinking about fixtures when the Dali could fail to get a buyer in this lousy economy. That would sink any hope of going into production. The government could scuttle our ship if they carry through on that damn FAA ruling. Hope to hell Bellington knows what he's doing.*

"You're a key player, Bernie," Art said. "The merger of Optimal and Precision Tool will create immense possibilities. We've pulled together all the key elements and, thanks to Lauren's mother, we're going to be properly funded. I think we should lift our glasses to Liza."

"Hear. Hear," everyone chorused.

"Moreover, I have a bit of interesting news," Art continued. "This afternoon I learned that Madison McKenzie has admitted to industrial espionage, been fined and lost all rights to her partnership in Optimal. Guess I turned up so much hard evidence; it didn't even go to court."

Wyatt met his wife's look and nodded.

"Serves her right," Lauren said. "At last our team is ready to go."

*   *   *

While Art was gloating over his success, Madison was sulking just a few miles away. The drapes in her apartment were drawn, creating a dark cave as depressing as her mood. When she brushed her teeth that morning, she noticed dark circles under her bloodshot eyes, making her look haggard and old. Her clothes were wrinkled and hair disheveled. Stained by spilled wine, a sheaf of legal paperwork sat at her elbow serving as a coaster for a goblet, smudged by stale lipstick.

Madison rose and tottered to the refrigerator to pour another glass of Chardonnay. When returning to her chair, she inadvertently stepped on G.G.'s tail, sending the terrified cat howling to a refuge under the sofa.

Thoughts tumbled in her head like laundry in a dryer. As much as Madison tried, she couldn't hate Wyatt. She loved him. They were soul mates linked by passion for science and innovation. It was obvious both were brilliant engineers, gifted beyond words. But together, they became a gestalt where ideas reverberated like low notes in a pipe organ. When working side by side, they fed off one another and innovations were dragged from the realm of mere possibility and thrust into reality. When linked, they became perfection.

Even working in the shadows, as she'd been the past few weeks, Rav had been a conduit for collaboration with Wyatt. Sure, it was holding hands with gloves on, but the thrill remained. She'd taken a step closer to him.

But he was married that milquetoast bitch. He clung to her; he wouldn't leave her—the bastard.

Then there was that calculating, devious lawyer. So what if she'd signed the LLC paperwork? Does anyone read the fine print? The criminal lawyer that Weinstein hired almost seemed gleeful as he waved the "No Compete" clause under her nose. Why did Weinstein have to file the damn lawsuit and depose her? Why had the new attorney threatened her with big fines? Sure, she'd worked for Dynamag. So what? She gulped half a glass of wine and her acid-ridden stomach rebelled. Why argue over the code? It was her program, her algorithms. How could it belong to Optimal when it sprang to life in her head?

She had to cash a rubber check to buy an hour's advice from an attorney who suggested she make a deal. So she had, giving up all rights to Optimal and her design work in exchange for a small fine and probation. The decision left an empty feeling in her stomach—another tie to Wyatt had been cut. Piece by piece her life was being decimated. No job. No Optimal. No Wyatt.

Madison took consolation that Eric had taken a worse beating at the hands of that tyrant lawyer. Eric was nothing but a worthless slime-ball with a big factory. She'd gone to Dynamag thinking to get Wyatt's creation into production and ultimately win him over. *I'm a damn fool,* she thought. When she'd walked out of Dynamag the last time, Eric had screamed at her, "Bitch, whore!" No wonder he was mad; the deposition snared him, too. With a hollow chuckle, Madison recalled that Dynamag would have to pay the enormous legal fees. A tight smile came to Madison's lips. *Live by deception, die by deception.*

Madison finished the wine and went for more. Rather than fill her glass, she decided to drink straight from the bottle. As she collapsed in her chair, Madison's thoughts turned to her sudden poverty. She was broke, living from one unemployment check to the next. Before, she was confident she could land a job, even in the lousy economy, but now, with the judgment of industrial espionage against her, who'd want to hire her?

She tipped the bottle and a trickle of wine ran down her chin. Tears welled up and joined the Chardonnay. *God almighty, I love him so.*

Chapter 32

There was only a smattering of lathe operators at their machines in Precision Tool's shop, now Optimal Systems. Mike had finished fabricating all the pressurization parts and lacking backlog, had cut back working hours and furlough thirty more workers. The occasional hollow clatter of a wrench or squeal of a cutting tool seemed to echo in Mike's ears—his place had the atmosphere of a morgue, not a vibrant manufacturing house.

The last pushrod in the CNC lathe dropped into the bin. Mike, clad in an oil-spotted apron, slapped the red "stop" button and slid the door aside to retrieve the parts. He'd come in early that morning to machine the shafts, more to calm his jitters than finish the small job. The smell of cutting fluid and the hiss of the carbide cutter were like a balm on his frayed nerves. He set the gleaming items in a partitioned plastic bin and trundled them to the deburring station. He took a deep breath and looked at the wall clock. Eight-fifteen. He had forty-five minutes to kill before the inspectors from the FAA and DCMA showed their faces.

He walked to his office and lit a cigarette. *If the pressurization is to ship in four weeks, the fuckers have to certify us today—there's no time left. Fat chance after I dumped on them.* It had been over a month since he'd lost his temper at the bar, daring them to shut down his company. They hadn't the guts to call his bluff, so Mike, lacking any other option, continued to run his company

He waved a cloud of smoke from his eyes. Art, he knew, had questioned both government organizations, but the devious bureaucratic shits dodged around every issue. Art, realizing he was being sandbagged, teamed with a couple of colleagues who were experts with fraud cases. They were able to kick their arguments further up the bureaucratic maze, but so far there hadn't been any concrete results.

Mike figured by the end of the day, the returning inspectors would kill Optimal Systems, slaying them with a thousand cuts. He lit another cigarette and paced. Because the industrial job-shop market was on its ass, particularly in California, his thoughts searched for proprietary products—something Wyatt could invent. He considered pressure regulators or big filters for factories under the thumb of the EPA. But worries of the imminent confrontation with Karl and Jason commandeered his mind. So he paced and smoked, paced and smoked and watched the hands of the clock creep toward his destruction.

Karl Leechmann sat across from Mike and fiddled with the latches on his brief case. "DCMA has asked me to double check the findings from our visit last Month. My superiors have reviewed certain parts of the new regulations and have reinterpreted a few of the directives. I'm thinking you'll be happy with the changes."

Mike was astonished. And suspicious. He wondered what the nitpicking, pumped-up bodybuilding asshole had up his sleeve. Mike had already wasted hours and hours, more like centuries, on rewriting his quality manual and partitioning the stockroom in response to Leechmann's orders. *Has a steroid overload scrambled his brain as well as bulked up his biceps? Or is he serious?*

"We can get started if you want," Mike said. "Or, we can wait for Jason Meil. He's due any time."

Leechmann opened his brief case, removed a laptop and set a folder of papers on the desk. "I think we should wait for the FAA. I'm told they've altered their rulings too."

"Really? For the better or worse?"

"Better? Worse? I wouldn't know about that."

As they waited, Leechmann squirmed in his chair and picked at a hangnail, looking ill at ease. Mike was mystified. The conceited, brash, obnoxious inspector had morphed into a Teddy Bear. Had his boss teed off on him? Had big departmental policy changes stirred his soup? It was possible Art managed to rattle a few things. No matter, something had come down.

Sam, the last remaining shipping clerk at the new Optimal, stepped into the office escorting a tiny man, about five-foot four, 120 pounds with a pock-marked complexion. "This guy's here to see you, Mike."

"I'm Hamilton Greaves," the man said in a feminine voice. "FAA."

"Pleased to meet you," Mike said, shaking a limp

hand. "This is Karl Leechmann of DCMA. Have a seat. We haven't started yet—waiting for you."

"Sorry," Hamilton squeaked. "I had trouble finding the place."

Who in the hell is this guy? Mike wondered, sitting in his chair. Curiosity poked at his mind. "I was expecting Jason Meil. Do you know what happened to him?"

With a twitchy look, Hamilton peered through his thick eyeglasses. "Very unfortunate. He's been accused of some sort of corruption and management put him on administrative leave. Rumors say he's in big trouble— possible jail time. Terrible."

"Jail?" Leechmann gasped. "Jason's a good friend of mine. He's done nothing wrong. Well, maybe he stretched the rules a tad; but shit—jail?"

Hamilton pulled the glasses from his nose and wiped them on his tie. He held them to the light and squinted. "The investigation is just starting so nothing is certain, but somebody must have made some serous accusations."

Mike's head was reeling. The government was "reconsidering" their regulations and Jason might take up residence in the slammer—all at once, his world looked rosy indeed.

"Any idea who's squeezing Jason?" Leechmann asked.

Fussing with his glasses, Hamilton said, "I shouldn't be saying anything, but it came from way up the organization. I got to talkin' with the Director's secretary and she said somebody from that A.I.M. outfit met with management. A couple of their lawyers dumped a bunch of papers on the Director's desk—evidence I guess. She said things got blazing hot; went at it for over two hours. Guess the bastards lit a big fire."

"Bellington?" Mike gasped.

"Naw. Somebody from his team, though. They're makin' a bunch of trouble. The whole department is nervous. As I said, terrible."

"I don't know if Bellington is behind it, but DCMA is the same," Leechmann mumbled. "Management is in hysterics. Everyone is looking over their shoulders. They told me to back off the small stuff. How in the hell do I know what's small or big?"

What the fuck is going on? Wondered Mike. *Both DCMA and the FAA crumbling? Jason looking at jail?* Then he remembered the phone records and emails he and Wyatt had given Art. *That hell-bent lawyer must have shoved all that evidence right up their ass. Hot damn!*

Both inspectors left an hour later, looking meek and subdued. Conversely, Mike was ecstatic as he watched them go. In his hand he clutched paperwork that certified Optimal Systems to manufacture and ship aircraft hardware. Was it Art and his team who jammed the change through? Maybe it was Bellington. *What the fuck does it matter. I'm rollin'.*

The next morning was a gloomy Saturday at Optimal's machine shop and Mike gathered up another handful of parts and eased them into a tote. The silence in the building haunted him— just two years ago, when he had dozens of orders, the place screeched, growled and hissed as grinders snapped back and forth, lathes whirled chips into the air and mills chattered merrily. He stacked four trays and lugged them to the shipping area where the dim light was almost as dreary as the quiet. *Fuck the electric bill*, he said to himself as he flipped on the lights and yanked a piece of butcher paper from a spool. As if handling robin's eggs, Mike tossed aside his apron, wrapped a complex new casting and slipped it into a cardboard carton. He was about to reach for the second one when the jangle of the doorbell startled him. *Must be Wyatt.*

He stepped to the man-door next to the large roll-up by the loading dock.

Mike twisted the lock and smiled as Wyatt bustled in saying, "Morning. Why are Saturdays always cloudy and cold and workdays sunny and warm?" He peered around Mike. "Where is everyone?"

"Shit, man. We're not working weekends anymore—no business."

"Yeah, I shoulda known. Those new parts ready to go?"

"Workin' on it. Want to lend a hand?"

Wyatt spit on both hands and posed like a lumberjack ready to swing an axe. "Let me at it."

They went to the table and stood side-by-side, wrapped protective paper around each aluminum housing and slipped them into a large big box.

"The parts sure look nice, Mike," Wyatt said. "These are the castings from Metalcast, right?"

"Yeah. The owner, Donnie, is a fucking champion. I gave him the order just a week back, and he delivered the castings four days later. I assigned three of my guys to machine them—didn't take long."

"Huh," Wyatt grunted. "You gotta be out of your gourd to defy Jason. He could make big trouble for you."

"The FAA and DCMA were here yesterday to redo the quality inspection, remember? Your good friend, Karl Leechmann was here. They went line-by-line over Karl's earlier findings, and guess what? They decided a few minor glitches remained, but all I had to do was promise I'd fix things. Bang! I'm blessed! I'll bet one of Art's buddy-lawyers thumped DCMA on the head. Bellington's organization was involved, too.

"But the big news concerns that fucker Jason"," Mike went on. "They've shoved him aside! Administrative leave they called it. There was a spooky-looking replacement who reviewed Jason's inspection records. He piddled around for twenty minutes, threw up his hands and gave me production approval. So, both the FAA and DCMA caved. They'll be over to see you on Monday to audit the design, software and quality aspects."

"Yes. I got a call. I'm sweating buckets."

"Don't. They were pussies. I'm guessing the higher-ups must have a goddamned headlock on these ding-a-lings."

Wyatt smiled, sat on a stool and swiveled to Mike. "Hope you're right. High-five, my friend, we're at T-minus-five and counting."

Thirty minutes later, Mike and Wyatt finished the task and were walking toward the door when the phone rang. Mike answered, listened a moment and then said, "Lauren."

Wyatt set the phone to his ear. "Hi, Dear. What's up?"

With a hysterical pitch in her voice, she said, "I just heard from Lee. Emile told him the Dali is authentic! All the special chemical tests and x-rays were perfect! It goes to auction in two weeks!"

Wyatt gasped. "My God. A miracle! Did they say anything about its value?"

"You won't believe, Honey...Emile said it appraised for between $600,000 and $800,000!"

Wyatt felt lightheaded and collapsed against a bench, his mind spinning.

"Honey?" Lauren said. "Are you there?"

"Yeah. I'm fine."

"With an official appraisal," Lauren continued, "Lee authorized a swing loan against the Dali. He understands that it's only two weeks until auction, but paying commissions and processing the currency exchange takes time. He figured we'd want the funds as soon as possible. It was funny. He tittered just like a girl when he told me he'd anticipated this and made the arrangements weeks ago,"

Wyatt nearly tittered himself. "I'm coming home; we'll celebrate big-time!"

He slapped the phone into its cradle and jumped up. "Mike! Hear that? The Dali is worth a bundle! We've pulverized one more blockade."

Mike's fist bump was followed by an exuberant high-five and finally a hug.

As Wyatt dashed through the door headed for home, Mike called after him, ""I'll call Bernie and the others with the news."

*   *   *

Now that they had cash, Lauren helped Mike clean up his financial clutter. Feverishly, she paid delinquent invoices, wrote checks, fielded phone calls from surly accounts-receivable clerks and organized the combined company's books in general.

Wyatt mentioned she looked haggard having endured long hours: days at her own workplace and nights and weekends at Optimal. Yet, she was cheerful, saying, "We're well on the way to integrating the two companies. It's one thing to sign an LLC, but another to integrate two accounting systems. Once you, Mike and Bernie sort out manufacturing paperwork, quality procedures and sales, we can go after the big production order. Exciting times."

Chapter 33

Two weeks had passed since the government officials blessed Optimal Systems authorizing them to ship hardware. Thrilled, Lauren settled into a methodical routine of tidying up the books and monitoring cash flow. Although the swing loan solved the immediate liquidity problems, Lauren shared her husband's fear that the FAA's ruling would finish Optimal. There was just three months before it was due to become law. In spite of A.I.M.'s posturing and threats, Lauren was concerned their demise was a distinct possibility. Still, perhaps they could survive if the merger with Mike...

But today, Lauren's peaceful workday was blown apart by Lee Wong's late afternoon phone call. She could hardly contain a simmering burst of 'the giggles' as she slipped out the back door at work scurried to the bank. "$1,080,000 net," Lee had said. "You'll have to sign papers."

Lauren took a seat across from the prim banker and brushed a wisp of hair back from her cheek. "Wow, Lee, incredible news! I've called everyone, of course; they're astounded. Wyatt was so excited he said he knocked over a bin of screws scattering hundreds across the floor. Me? I feel like a young girl in a field of daisies. I don't need to tell you that the money puts Optimal on a sound footing. We're going to deliver the test hardware within two weeks, you know." A wistful thought came to her. "I hope that new law doesn't get implemented—the one that would force us out of the aviation business. So far Washington isn't budging."

Lee smiled and with a tilt of his head, said, "Remember what I said about the year of the Dragon? Things will work out, I know.

"Back to business. I was surprised the Dali brought such a high price; appraisal people don't often miss the mark. Then again, I'll never understand buyer sentiment in the fine-art market."

Lauren pressed her fist to her lips to suppress a titter. "Well, I'm sure they lean toward the conservative side."

"I'm sure." Lee handed his pen to Lauren. "The funds arrived as a wire transfer, converted to American dollars. I'll need your signature here and here," he said, pointing to "X's" on the deposit paperwork. "Unlike the loan that required both your and Wyatt's signature, a deposit needs just yours. You'll note that I've already paid off the swing loan."

"Lee, you're the best. I don't know what I would have done without you." Lauren dashed off her signature and slapped the pen on the desktop. "That's that." She drew in a deep breath and shook her head. A huge sense of relief flooded her mind and again, a giggle bubbled across her lips. "Sorry, Lee. I'm beside myself. You don't know the thrill I feel about my mother's inheritance and the security it brought."

"I'm extremely happy for you and pleased that I have been of assistance." Lee opened a desk drawer and removed a small, velvet covered box. With a nearly imperceptible bow and a hint of a wink, he gave the box to Lauren. "For you, with my affection."

Curious, she took the box and opened it. Inside was a pretty diamond tennis bracelet, glittering in the light. Stunned, Lauren murmured, "Lee, what..."

Lee laced his fingers and leaned toward Lauren, looking anxious. "I'm sure you've noticed I'm often awkward in social matters and, as a result, have become a rather lonely man. Over these months, I've enjoyed our relationship but never could express myself. The bracelet is my way of saying thanks. I sincerely wish the future will see our relationship grow."

Lauren eased the lid closed. "I can't accept this. It's lovely, but..." Suddenly, she realized what had been happening. There had been subtle hints at the Fourth of July party when Wong seemed so nervous. He'd hovered near her elbow the entire day and insisted on running little errands, like filling the punch bowl or setting out fresh napkins. She hadn't noticed then, but now she remembered Lee touched her hand when she handed him the peanut dish and patted her arm, breathless after running with the sparkler. When he left that night, Lee hugged her, a delicate, but lingering hug. Had he fallen for her?

Since then, there were occasional phone calls, "Just checking to see if you need anything," and a thank-you card bearing the bank's logo, but harboring a personal note. A curious thought came to her. Over the past few weeks, Lee seemed very cool toward Wyatt. *Now that I think back…*

True, her affection for Lee may have been misleading, leading him to hope she had romantic feelings. Perhaps the stress in her marriage this past year was more overt than she suspected. Did Lee see the friction with Wyatt and become encouraged? Did Lee suspect her husband was going to jump ship? Or was her natural outgoing nature and friendliness a lure for Lee's yearnings? Lauren trembled, thinking she'd unknowingly led him on.

Or was it unknowing? Wyatt's tryst still augured into her late night attempts to sleep, even though cognitively she'd set the issue aside. There were times she felt inadequate because her husband sought comfort with another woman.

With a snide edge in her voice, Madison had bragged that Wyatt shared her passion of science and thus accused, Lauren found herself with a foreboding sense of illiteracy, not the inability to read, but ignorance of calculus.

Little wonder Lauren needed Lee, his respect and adoration. He gave her a sense of worth and validated her values and skills. *Madison and Wyatt linked in the world of science, Lee and I in finance.* Lauren sighed.

No! This cannot be!

She looked into Lee's eyes that glittered in apparent anticipation. Lauren thrust aside an aching feeling of pity mixed with guilt and said, "Lee, this is a very thoughtful gift, but you understand I can't accept it. It's obviously expensive and far too intimate. We have a friendly, professional relationship and I'm sure you know I'm fond of you. I value your help and knowledge of finance and

I'm enthused you've become a partner in Optimal. I look forward to an exciting future working with you.

"But, I must be clear. I'm a married woman very much in love with my husband. Please respect that. I hope I've done nothing to deceive you because I value your friendship and would be extremely sad if we couldn't keep working together."

Lee scowled, took his fountain pen and slid it on his polished mahogany desktop. Rigid as a statue, he stared at it, avoiding Lauren's eyes. He pushed the pen a few inches, his shoulders sagging. Finally, he looked up. "I didn't mean to be presumptuous. My time with you has been delightful. As I said, I'm lonely and I've always looked forward to spending time with you. Your laughter, your smile…" Lee paused and then looked Lauren in the eye. "Wyatt's a very lucky man. As for me, I shall be extremely pleased to continue my work with Optimal."

Lauren nodded and stood. "Thanks for understanding." As she walked away, Lauren glanced back over her shoulder and saw Lee, looking forlorn, gather the deposit papers and slip them into a folder. He seemed small and defeated. Lauren shivered.

Chapter 34

Earlier that Saturday afternoon Lauren had thrown a big party for Timmie's eleventh birthday. The celebration had been in the planning stage for several weeks, but the sale of the Dali magnified everything.

To Wyatt, it seemed that every time he found time to focus on Optimal, Lauren planned another extravaganza. He decided to seek refuge in engineering logic and weighed the trade-offs using a formal cost-benefit analysis. The cost of her gatherings was distraction. The benefit was Lauren's vivaciousness and cheer. He decided vivaciousness and cheer won. Besides, he was a millionaire.

Of course, the roster abruptly expanded to include the Optimal gang: Art, Mike, Bernie and Lee. The house had been awash with a joyful throng.

Yielding to a rare romantic impulse, Wyatt had dashed to a small bookstore early in the morning, purchased a first edition Steinbeck and presented it to Lauren before the festivities began. She'd squealed with joy, making Wyatt blush.

Now, the din of the raucous party still echoed in Wyatt's ears as he leaned back in his seat, immersed in the camaraderie of his family and the tranquil atmosphere of the Plaid Bear restaurant. In addition to his friends, there had been over a dozen kids: school friends, neighbors and soccer-mates, everyone possessing 120 decibel lungs and the frantic energy rivaling a destroyer at general quarters.

He took a sip of wine and rubbed his sore knee. The "hopping around in a burlap bag race" was a bad idea, but the kids roared with laughter as he staggered twice, twisted his knee and fell on his face. Bernie, shouting with glee, sprinted over to help. Wyatt was embarrassed as the sixty-something wisp of a man hoisted his bulk to his feet. Even so, Wyatt shed his bag and joined in the cheers for the winner. But now, the throbbing in his leg reminded him he was pushing forty and competing with eleven and twelve-year-olds was foolish.

Timmie huddled alongside Lauren, squinting in the dim light, trying to decipher the menu.

"Chicken cord-on blue? What's that?" Timmie asked.

"It's a French dish," Lauren replied. "It has ham and cheese along with chicken."

"Do they have hamburgers?"

Wyatt held the menu close to the faux kerosene lantern centerpiece and scanned the entrées. "They do, Timmie. The regular kind and fancy ones."

"Regular kind."

Flush with money, Wyatt smiled like a sailor with the wind at his back. "I'm going to pop for the porterhouse—I have a man-sized hunger. Lauren?"

"I'm in an extravagant mood tonight, so I'll have the Chilean sea bass; I don't care if it *is* $43."

"Even though you've been queasy this past week?" Wyatt asked. "I see you're still avoiding wine. You should try this one—it's really good."

With an odd grin, Lauren said, "Another time, when I'm feeling better."

The waiter, apparently clairvoyant, emerged from the shadows to take their order. On learning it was Timmie's birthday, he promised a treat for dessert.

"I want chocolate," she proclaimed.

The waiter winked and said, "All women prefer chocolate. I'll check with the kitchen." Then he stole away.

Timmie puffed out her chest. "See? He thinks I'm a woman."

"Well, nearly," Lauren said. "In two more years you'll be a teenager."

"God help us," Wyatt quipped.

Soon, the meal was served and, between mouthfuls, they chuckled about the antics at the party.

Wyatt had been surprised to discover he actually enjoyed the melee. He'd looked with pride as Timmie played the role of honoree with confidence, helping direct the games and dishing out slices of her birthday cake. She was growing up.

He'd seen glimpses of his daughter's blossoming maturity before and was intrigued by the vision. He didn't connect easily with little kids, he knew, but found comfort in being able to engage Timmie as a semi-adult. *Yes, she is growing up.*

"Is this the restaurant where you brought those two inspectors?" Lauren said, breaking into Wyatt's reverie.

"Karl and Jason? Yeah; a complete waste of good food. Waste of time, too."

Lauren nodded. "Now that the certification business is behind us, you'll be able to ship the qualification test systems, right?"

"Yup. They'll go in a couple of weeks. The source inspector from AirEnvironment has to buy them off first. It looks like we'll make the deadline providing they sign off on everything."

"I get to help," Timmie boasted. "You promised."

"I need every hand I can get," Wyatt said. "You're on the team."

"Speaking of two weeks," Lauren interjected, "A.I.M.'s deadline is also the end of the month. What will happen if they strike?"

"We'll ship anyway," Wyatt replied. "No other choice. Future production would be up for grabs, though. I'm not going to think about it."

"There was an editorial in yesterday's newspaper that hinted Washington might be wavering. That's a good sign."

Wyatt dismissed the news with a wave of his hand. "Washington can't get out of its own way much less make a quick policy change." *If Bellington and A.I.M. fail to stop the new regulations, we'll have mayhem. Optimal would...* He didn't want to worry about it.

Gorged from the porterhouse and mellow with wine, Wyatt unlocked the front door and settled into his recliner with a contented sigh, enjoying his newfound fortune and the memories of the party. Lauren disappeared into the kitchen while Timmie sat on the floor and explored her new birthday gifts. Wyatt rejected any thought of politics and savored the moment with his family. A tiny grin molded his lips as he recalled Timmie's poise at the restaurant. More and more, she looked like Lauren: pretty, fresh and freckled. Soon he'd be herding vast throngs of pimply boys queuing up to date his daughter. Somehow, the idea was pleasant.

"I thought you'd enjoy a touch of port to cap the evening," Lauren said, setting a small cordial on the table between their chairs. "I'll stick with apple juice." With a curious looking grin, she hummed a bar from Savage Garden's *I Knew I Loved You* and lit the candles.

"Well now," she said, easing into her chair. "I'm guessing you two might be interested in a bit of news."

Wyatt raised his eyebrows, wondering if something was amiss, like the kitchen trash had overflowed or his bathroom light repair didn't last.

Timmie hardly looked up from her excavations in the wrapping paper.

"Timmie?" Lauren beckoned her daughter.

As Timmie squirmed over and sat at her feet, Lauren turned to Wyatt and paused. Holding his eyes but addressing her daughter, she said, "Timmie, you are going to have a baby brother or sister."

Wyatt wasn't sure he heard right. "Huh?"

"A baby, Hon. We're going to have a baby."

Timmie's eyebrows climbed high on her forehead. "Yeah!" she yelled.

Stunned, Wyatt gasped. His fragmented thoughts thrashed around, chaotic and blurred. "What? How..."

Lauren grinned, her blue eyes sparkling in the candlelight. "I'd think by now you'd know how."

Her joke never penetrated Wyatt's mind. He wiped his mouth and stammered, "You're sure?"

"Ninety-nine percent sure. I did one of those home tests. I'm guessing I'm seven or eight weeks along. That's why I haven't been feeling so hot lately."

"When, Mommy? When?" chanted Timmie.

"Probably in seven months or so. I have an appointment with the doctor next Monday to confirm things."

"I want a brother!"

"We'll find out soon enough," Lauren laughed.

Wyatt coughed, trying to clear his throat. Tears welled in his eyes and slithered down his cheeks. "Lauren..." He wrung his hands. "Wow. I never figured we'd..."

"Here, my Love. Take a sip of port. We can't have you falling apart in front of your daughter."

Wyatt drained the glass in a gulp and coughed again. He blotted his cheeks with the back of his hand and snorted. "Damn, you got my heart racing like a Ferrari on a straightaway." He bent over and patted Timmie's shoulder. "Some kinda news, huh? You want to help with the little one?"

A look of confidence covered Timmie's face. "Of course. Besides, now you'll have to stop calling me 'Little One.' We'll have a *real* little one soon."

Wyatt nodded and soft sobs choked him once more. He drew his daughter onto his lap and squeezed her. He reached for Lauren's hand saying, "Boy or girl, it'll be an engineer for sure."

With a solemn tone, Timmie said, "I've been thinking, Daddy. I'd like to be a nurse, but an engineer is better. That would make three of us."

"That's a *fine* idea," Wyatt said.

His mind flashed back to when he was six or seven. To the day his father trundled him to the park with a big box from the hobby store under his arm. He remembered he was jittery with excitement as his father opened the carton and removed a sleek toy rocket. Not a toy, exactly, but a flying model just like those he'd seen the previous week when the older kids flew theirs, hissing on a column of smoke into the sky. He remembered crouching to help assemble the launching platform, threading the rocket onto the guide rod and connecting the battery. He remembered his father's smile as he said, "Why don't you do it? Take out the safety key and push the red button."

Wyatt hugged Timmie a little tighter and closed his eyes. He remembered the whoosh as the rocket leapt into the air, saw the white puffy plume and saw the billowing parachute. He remembered the wonder, the magic and the exhilaration. He remembered that was the moment he decided to become an engineer.

"Tell you what, Timmie. Tomorrow, let's go to the hobby store. There is something I want to show you."

"What, Daddy?"

"It will be a surprise."

Lauren gave him a quizzical look. "What are you up to?"

"It's a memorial to something that happened a long time ago, when I had an epifff…"

"An epiphany?"

"Yeah, that's it," Wyatt grinned. "Come with us, if you want."

"Tomorrow is Sunday, and the weather is supposed to be nice," Lauren said. "Guess I'll tag along—just to see what your mystery is."

"Oooff," Wyatt grunted. "You're too big to be sitting on me, Timmie. It's time to go to bed, so why don't you get ready?"

She slid from his lap and put her hands on her hips. "I'm eleven now. I should get to stay up later. Besides, sometimes Mommy sits on your lap and she's bigger than me."

"Well, that's different," Wyatt chuckled.

"How?"

"Timmie, off to bed," Lauren commanded, a snicker hiding behind her sternness.

With a profound pout, Timmie meandered down the hall and disappeared into her room.

Lauren shook her head. "She's growing up faster than gossip at my old Scrabble club. I see an awkward moment looming right around the corner; a situation every mother dreads."

"What's that?"

"My pregnancy is going to raise a few questions with our daughter. She's eleven and it's time to do 'the-birds-and-bees' thing."

Wyatt smiled. "Go for it. Just leave me out, okay?"

With a pensive look, Lauren lifted her glass of juice, stared at it a moment and then set it down without tasting.

"Things are happening so fast. The new baby will create a whirlwind in our life at the same time Optimal is exploding."

"Or struggling," Wyatt said. "We have our patent, Rav and Bernie are shots of adrenalin, the merger is finalized and we're certified to ship. The only obstacle is A.I.M. and the Washington mess. I'm holding my breath."

"Yes, things may work out for our company, but stressful times are ahead. I feel that Timmie has drifted away and the baby will become a further wedge between us. She'll resent all the hours consumed by diapers, feedings and trips to the pediatrician."

Wyatt considered his wife's concern. "Timmie is at a turning point in her life—puberty, a new sibling, a father buried in a crazy business venture. Seems I'm at a turning point, too. You and Timmie are becoming more and more important to me. I'm not so preoccupied with my engineering. Feels strange."

Lauren nodded.

They sat in silence, the candlelight flickering on their cheeks. Wyatt grappled with the idea of an infant bursting into his life. He smelled baby powder, felt the grip of tiny fingers around his thumb and heard soft cooing at bath time. He rehearsed mental scenes where the new child sought his help with school, when he opened the door into the realm of physics by launching another rocket in the park. The words "legacy" and "eternity" flashed in his mind.

Finally, Wyatt stirred in his chair and said, "I'm convinced it's time you quit your job. I want you to pamper yourself and become a full-time mom as you've always wished."

"I think so, too." Lauren breathed. "I could reconnect with Timmie and help more with Optimal. Besides, Mother would be pleased."

"Good. It's decided," Wyatt said. "Go easy on the Optimal part. I want you to take care of yourself first, Timmie and the new one next and Optimal should run dead last. Okay?"

"Yes, my Lord," she joked.

Wyatt leaned over and took Lauren's hand. "About your mother. I often grumped around with her, not really fighting, but we never saw eye-to-eye. She wanted me to give you the lifestyle that your dad did—wealthy, privileged and secure. All she saw in me was an oddball tradesman, destined to labor over obscure projects for simple wages. She never understood my passion for engineering. It's bizarre that her estate might galvanize our venture into a strong business. I think she'd be happy seeing us now."

"I know she would, Hon. You're an incredible man and I love you." Holding her glass of apple juice aloft, Lauren said, "I've already given up alcohol anticipating the doctor will tell me to stop drinking. Without Zinfandel, our Sunset Ritual will suffer like a Scrabble game without letters."

"Sand in the gears," Wyatt laughed. "We'll have to skate through on plain old grape juice. But it's only for seven months."

With an incredulous look, Lauren exclaimed, "You'd give up wine, too?"

"Of course. Think of it as sympathy labor pains, my Love."

Chapter 35

It was the morning when the A.I.M. deadline expired and Optimal was scheduled to make their first shipment. Frenzied, Wyatt started a pot of coffee, took a scalding shower, dressed and in the morning chill, dashed to the driveway for the newspaper. He settled in his chair with a mug of brew, his electric razor and the paper. Typical of every morning, Garfield sprang on his lap, turned around and lay down between his knees.

As Wyatt scrubbed his cheek with the razor, he flipped open the paper. The headline blared:

Washington Capitulates
Stocks Soar

Still buzzing, the razor dropped to the floor. Wyatt grasped the paper with both hands and brought it closer. His breath caught in his throat, blood pounded in his temples and his eyes devoured the front page. Unable to contain himself, he leapt from the chair, knocking the cat aside, and raced to the bedroom where Lauren still slumbered.

Wyatt shook her awake and thrust the newspaper under her groggy eyes. "Check this out! Bellington's won!" Jabbing the front page, Wyatt said, "The Department of Commerce and the White House officially recognize Bellington as the head of A.I.M. They're going to begin a series of negotiations next week. First topic: corporate taxes. It's a friggin' miracle!"

Lauren propped herself on the pillow and scanned the article. "Look at this. The President has agreed to place on hold all "emergency" legislation and rulemaking. Future negotiations include pending rules of the EPA, FAA and bank regulations that limit investments. Trade agreements, deficit spending and even entitlements are on the agenda. This is amazing."

Wyatt laughed. "They have four months to put a permanent stop to that idiotic FAA rule. First thing, I'm going to contact my friend from the Bellington field office and push to get that stupid regulation canceled. Top priority!"

"Says here, Honey, that the delay in passing the new rules and laws will be in effect as long as it takes to resolve the issues to the satisfaction of A.I.M."

Laughing, Wyatt exclaimed, "It seems our newly elected president hasn't much to say except 'punt.' See here? Several oddball congressmen are bouncing off the walls, trying to appear like they're in charge. Says they plan to ram a bill through Congress that would make A.I.M. illegal claiming it will gut every critical social program. Look at Bellington's reply. 'Fine. Ban the Alliance and run the country without our member firms.'" Wyatt pointed to the paper, "Says here that yesterday over fifty more companies signed up with A.I.M. Let's see how Washington muddles along when industry stops being their sacrificial cow. What will the hangers-on do then. Hah!"

Lauren got up, slipped into her bathrobe and walked to the kitchen, still reading the article. Preoccupied, she spilled a splash of coffee on the counter. She reached for the dishcloth and, looking up, saw Wyatt staring wide-eyed at her.

"Well? What do you think?" he asked. "Hot shit, right?"

"I think I'd prefer the word 'astounding.' It might be too much to ask, but perhaps the president will recognize his government is carried on the backs of hard-working people."

"Like us engineers," Wyatt snickered.

"Them too," she grinned. "Say, weren't you going to meet Rav and Mike at the office early this morning? You were going to get the systems ready to ship."

Wyatt looked at his watch. "Dang. I'm already late. I'm outta here."

Wyatt snatched the newspaper and bolted to the door. "I'll see you later at Optimal, right? It's a big day for us!"

With that, he fled; squealing tires confirmed his haste.

*   *   *

Amused by her husband's frantic exit, Lauren shook her head. She snapped on the television and tuned to a newscast. The anchor seemed unraveled as he babbled about the impending economic disaster and vilified Bellington. "A bad sport who can't accept defeat at the polls."

Disgusted, she turned off the TV with a grunt.

Lauren heard a slight hum and wondering what it might be, looked around. There, on the floor by Wyatt's chair, she saw his electric razor, buzzing forlornly. *My nutty husband.* She reached over and turned it off. When Lauren set it on the table between their two chairs, she noticed Wyatt's coffee mug, abandoned and growing cold. She chuckled and remembered his panicked exit. Half-shaven, he'd barged through the front door while his shirttail dangled from the back and an untied shoelace flapped underfoot. *More like an eight-year-old urchin than a high-powered engineer.*

Garfield wandered over and rubbed her ankle. "The head of our household was a bit scattered this morning," she said to the cat. With a sigh, Lauren rubbed the fine fur on Garfield's shoulders and reached for her novel.

Today was her first day as a full-time mom. Lauren had given notice at work two weeks ago and planned to sleep in a few minutes this morning—a celebration of sorts, but Wyatt ruined that. Regardless, Lauren had thirty minutes before she had to wake Timmie for school. Thirty minutes of indulgence. Why not? They'd dodged the specter of financial oblivion, Optimal suddenly had working capital and a flabbergasting political upheaval cast a liberating light on her spirits. She felt as if she'd been freed from a dungeon. The best news, however, was Wyatt Jr. was happy "in the jig," as Big Wyatt liked to say.

She crossed her ankles and began to read.

*   *   *

"I've *seen* the fucking news, Wyatt," Mike growled. "Read about it, heard it on the radio and TV, even three of my machinists buttonholed me. Chuck the goddamned paper and lend a hand. We've hardware to ship."

Wyatt blushed like a chastised school kid, tossed the newspaper on his desk and joined Mike and Rav at the workbench. "Sorry I'm late. The news blew me away like a naval broadside."

"Not a problem," Rav said, his head bobbing in time to a soft thumping that was wired to his ears via the perennial iPod. "We're on top of it."

"Shee-it," Mike grumbled. "Rav's been smokin' weed again. The inspector from AirEnvironment is due in an hour and there's a thousand loose ends."

"I don't do pot, man," Rav laughed. "Although a bong or two might help me put up with grumpy old machinists."

Wyatt laughed while Mike scowled.

"Who's coming from AirEnvironment? Wendy somebody?" Rav asked.

"Yeah. Wendy Agajanian," Wyatt replied. "She does source inspections all over Southern California. She works directly for AirEnvironment, not the government jerks."

"I hope she's better than those fuckers Jason and Karl," Mike snarled.

"There's nowhere to go but up," Wyatt chuckled. He picked up an inflow control valve. "I'll go ahead and attach the nameplates. Three inflows, three outflows, three heat exchangers and six isolation valves. Fifteen total."

"I'll install the protective plugs and caps for the ports and connectors," Mike said. He rose and walked to a storage shelf where Timmie had labeled the bins of small parts. Mike scanned several bills of material and began collecting handfuls of hardware.

"Rav," Wyatt said, "Make sure the ATP data sheets are complete and have our Q.A. stamp. Run copies for our files."

Without further words, they went to work.

Wyatt was exhilarated. Not only was the baby doing fine and Lauren's nausea had subsided, but Bellington had slain the fearsome Washington juggernaut. He knew the government would have to yield to A.I.M.'s demands and permanently stop the rule where his design would be thrown out and his competitors grandfathered in. Wyatt reflected on his conversation with Lauren that morning and realized his work at Bellington's field office had earned him respect, and he began mentally drafting a letter to his political connection there. He'd demand that A.I.M. keep the FAA's ruling on the front burner. *Slam dunk*, he thought. I'll write it tonight.

There was one last worrisome thing. Optimal had to pass the source inspection from AirEnvironment. If Wyatt's experience with the FAA and DCMA inspectors was an indication, big trouble would walk through the door within an hour.

He tried to set his worries aside. Yesterday's final system tests had been flawless—the only thing left was paperwork. Today culminated three years' work. Now at last, it was done—just tie the cord. Spread before him were assemblies of hundreds of bits and pieces, each crafted to help move executives and warriors to their rendezvous—to their fulfillment. Although inanimate, the gleaming metal mechanisms embodied Wyatt's mind, his passions and his destiny.

As he watched Mike and Rav, immersed in their tasks, he realized there was a bond between them. Not just a bond, he thought, but an interlocking purpose in life that transcended casual friendship. This was not the shallow ribald conversation between buddies on poker night or shared interest in short blocks among hotrod builders. It was not the bravado of fishermen or statistics-gibberish of baseball fans.

Their link was more. It was profound. Three minds had reached into the realm of innovation, of excellence, of vision. Three minds had melded into a dynamo of creativity, each with different skills, but with common purpose. They were a team, but "team" was a woefully inadequate word. A Super Bowl team shared the intensity and focus that Wyatt had with Mike and Rav, but the product of a football game is just that: a game. Wyatt's team had advanced the art and pushed back scientific frontiers. And that mattered.

Of course there were others, those he labeled facilitators. If Mike, Rav and he were the creators, Lauren, Bernie, Lee and Art were the doers. A lump rose in Wyatt's throat as he came to understand how lucky he'd been to marry Lauren and be supported by his colleagues and friends. He knew his skills were too narrow and had to be augmented. Wyatt felt the pressurization system was a noble thing, worthy of being held aloft, high above the heads of onlookers. Such a task requires bearers, and the Optimal crew carried their burden proudly.

"I'm looking for a Mr. Morgan. Wendy Agajanian from AirEnvironment."

Wyatt, jerked from his reverie, stood. "Hi. I'm Wyatt Morgan. Come sit." He quickly introduced Mike and Rav.

The officious looking middle-aged women shook hands all around, plopped her attaché case on the conference table and extracted a laptop. Peering through her trifocals, she said, "You're trying to ship three complete cabin pressurization systems, right? Let's have a look."

The take-charge pugnaciousness of the new inspector made Wyatt wary and he saw the strained expression on Mike's and Rav's faces. Once more, a stranger unfamiliar with Optimal and the technology, had a foot on the throat of their future.

Their fear was brief. With crisp requests and fluid business-like motions, Agajanian surveyed the test equipment, spot-checked traceability records, sampled a few interface dimensions and studied the ATP data. After an hour and a half, she said, "Looks good. All I need are the Certifications of Conformity, then I'm out of here."

Wyatt and Mike looked at one another with raised eyebrows. "That's it?" Wyatt asked, handing her the paperwork.

"Everything's fine." She stamped the data sheets and shipper then tucked her computer back into her case. She stood and extended her hand. "Nice job."

"It's almost lunchtime. Our treat," Wyatt offered.

"No thanks. I have to rush to another appointment. I have a sandwich in the car. Appreciate the offer, though."

For Wyatt, all the tension in the room followed

Agajanian out the door. He tried to squelch a giggle as Rav offered a fist-bump.

"That woman is a fuckin' dream," Mike chortled. "I'll put the arm on AirEnvironment to make sure she does all our source inspections."

"She turned down lunch," Wyatt laughed. "Imagine."

They sat around the table, numb with relief. They could ship the hardware. On time.

"Well, kiddies," Mike said, "if we're to kick this shit out the door, we'd better get everything boxed."

Happy to be done, Wyatt pasted the last shipping label on a box when Lauren burst into the room flashing an immense smile. She set a large tote bag on the desk and asked, "Everything great?"

"Great? No," Wyatt said, giving her an enthusiastic hug. "*Way* beyond great! We got the green light to ship. UPS will be here this afternoon."

"I guessed everything would work out," Lauren said. "So I did a little shopping after dropping Timmie off at school." She reached into the canvas bag and extracted several Styrofoam boxes of savory smelling Chinese food and a chilled bottle of carbonated apple cider. "I even brought along crystal flutes from home."

Laughing, Wyatt said, "For apple cider? Our life has sunk to this—no alcohol until Little Wyatt presents himself?" Wyatt snatched the bottle, peeled away the foil and twisted off the stopper with a loud pop. With a flourish, Wyatt filled the glasses allowing festive frothing bubbles to cascade down their sides. "To Optimal," he toasted, raising his flute.

The odd taste of the liquid on his tongue brought back dark memories of the last time he'd drunk actual champagne. Madison. It was that afternoon a year and a half ago when he drank too much...when she'd swept him into bed...when he violated his vow to Lauren. Guilt washed over him. Could he ever shake the agony of that day?

No! Today is a fresh beginning. A glorious future is unfolding, and it's time to throw Madison away forever. Time to chuck the blame. Time to embrace my family without reservation.

"Yes, to Optimal," he repeated.

"And to Chinese," Rav added. "I'm ravenous."

"Cute," Lauren said. "Rav is *rav*-enous."

Within twenty minutes, the food was annihilated, Mike and Rav making sure there were no leftovers.

Content, everyone lounged in their chairs and the conversation turned to the future of Optimal.

"No stopping us now."

"Now's the time to hammer AirEnvironment for the big production order."

"The market will explode if India decides to open their market."

"I hear that Eric Magana had a breakdown. His company is in Chapter eleven. Sold his jet."

"Yeah. Art's crackin' heads. Settlement money is headed our way. That'll help cover the production tooling."

"Wait until Bellington kicks the fucking politicians in the ass. That'll streamline the goddamn regulations."

"Lee thinks we'll turn a profit by the end of next year."

The banter was interrupted when the UPS driver

tugged his dolly through the front door. "You have a pickup?"

"Not just a pickup, Jimmy," Wyatt crowed, "but a breakthrough!"

Everyone helped carry the packaged pressurization systems to Jimmy, who piled them on the dolly. He secured the boxes, waved and retreated to his truck.

Wyatt eased the door shut and turned, beaming. Mike and Rav walked over and the three shook hands and hugged. Rav pounded Wyatt on the back, chanting, "You da man. You da man."

With a surge of joy and affection, Lauren joined them. The men gathered her up in their arms and they swayed like stalks of wheat in a gentle Kansas breeze. Lauren wasn't the only one with misty eyes.

Wyatt, embarrassed with the spontaneous display of emotion, slipped their clutches, poured another cup of coffee and collapsed in his chair. The hairs on his arm bristled as he realized there was nothing to do. He was adrift, a sailor lost in a vast sea of idleness. Wyatt was so acclimated to the frantic pace of the past year, that the sudden lack of work made him feel like a junkie in rehab. Fidgeting, he drew a deep breath to steady himself. "What a trial we've been through," he said. "Money problems, patent litigation, battles over government certification, manufacturing troubles, test glitches, you name it."

"That fucking shit is behind us," Mike said, jabbing his finger in the air. "We're in gear. We're in control. It's all downhill from now on out. There will be plenty of work to do on the pressurization when we land the big production order, but I'm not going to sit around until then. I'm going to dig up a shit-pot of new jobs. Every Chinese and Indian airplane has flap actuators, landing gear mechanisms, door snubbers, hydraulic pumps, and shit-piles of special components. Companies around the world will need a top-drawer shop to machine the parts. Optimal Systems will snare a bunch of that work. Mark my words."

Wyatt had to laugh. Mike, he knew, might do it, but he missed a key point. Job shopping was too competitive. The key was to develop a line of proprietary products. Wyatt closed his eyes and laced his hands behind his head. His mind wandered aimlessly and poked into the realm of aircraft engine performance, ricocheted off ideas about adiabatic compression and wiggled around equations defining airfoil boundary layers. Wyatt hummed an unintelligible tune and sank lower in his chair.

Mike and Rav were discussing how they might bring some new work in-house, but their droning voices faded. Wyatt eased into a netherworld of snapping synapses. He heard nothing but his own thoughts and time vanished.

Then suddenly, Wyatt shattered the silence.

"That's it!" he yelled. "Mike, Rav, listen to this! Our inflow valves regulate bleed air from the engines, right? It's the same hot air they use to de-ice the wings and engine cowls. The problem is present designs squander power and increase fuel costs. What we need are sensors to tell the computer in our valves when to divert precise quantities of hot air. We can integrate pressurization and de-icing!"

Lauren blanched and slapped her forehead with the palm of her hand. "My God, here we go again!"

# # #

Glossary

Aneroid: A small disk-shaped vacuum-filled capsule used to sense altitude of the aircraft

ATP: Acceptance Test Procedure. A formal document that stipulates all tests to be performed on a piece of equipment to verify its conformance to the design specification.

DCMA: Defense Contract Management Agency. A government agency that oversees federal acquisition programs by monitoring delivery schedules, costs and conformance to design specifications.

DMV: Department of Motor Vehicles.

Double E: Electrical Engineer.

EMI: Electromagnetic Interference. Essentially spurious radio waves that interfere with the operation of electronics.

EMP: Electromagnetic Pulse. A short burst of electromagnetic energy. In warfare, such pulses are very intense and could disable electronic equipment.

EPA: Environmental Protection Agency. An agency of the U.S. federal government created to protect human health and the environment by writing and enforcing regulations.

FAA: Federal Aviation Administration. A federal regulatory organization that oversees all aspects of aviation, including design of aircraft parts and airframes, flight operations and pilot licensing.

Gerber file: A standard electronics industry computer file format used to communicate design information for manufacturing of many types of printed circuit boards.

H.R.:   Human Resources: A department within a company that oversees screening of applicants and administers health insurance, retirement funds and labor laws.

ISO: International Organization for Standardization. Develops and publishes international quality standards to harmonize activities that are international in nature; aircraft design and operation being typical.

Jet-A   Jet fuel, a kerosene derivative.

Kanban: A scheduling system for lean and just-in-time (JIT) production that controls the logistical chain from a production point of view. Derived from the Toyota Manufacturing System.

MIDO: Manufacturing Inspection District Office. A division of the FAA that approves manufacturing facilities and issues production approval certifications.

NASCAR: National Association for Stock Car Auto Racing.

NTSB: National Transportation Safety Board. An independent Federal agency charged by Congress with investigating every civil aviation accident in the United States.

OSHA: Occupational Safety and Health Act. An agency of the United States Department of Labor. OSHA sets and enforces standards for safe and healthful conditions in the workplace.

PCB: Printed Circuit Board. A non-conductive card clad with copper foil that has been chemically etched to form electrical paths and electronic component mounting pads.

P.O.: Purchase Order.

PERT diagram: Program Evaluation and Review Technique. The diagram is a graphic representation of a project's schedule, showing the sequence of tasks to be performed and task interdependency.

PTO: Patent and Trademark Office.

Q.A.: Quality Assurance.

R.F.P.: Request For Proposal.

SBA: Small Business Administration.

Solid Works: A computer program that generates graphical solid models and engineering drawings.